MW01680982

THE ALNOS CHRONICLES

VOLUME ONE

THE CHRONICLER'S ARRIVAL *and* WINTER SCHISMS

GILAINE FIEZMONT

POETRY AMBASSADORS
—Press—

THE CHRONICLER'S ARRIVAL and WINTER SCHISMS
The Alnos Chronicles: Volume One

Printed in the United States of America

Poetry Ambassadors Press
173 N Highland Ave
Los Angeles, CA 90036
213-484-0475

ISBN: 978-1-963261-04-2

THE CHRONICLER'S ARRIVAL

and

WINTER SCHISMS

To my grandmother Jeanne and my aunt Evelyn,
who fostered my love of reading, and to Tim,
who introduced me to Dune all these many years ago.

Contents

Index of Characters

The story takes place on Alnos, a planet that is undergoing climate change from a deep to a more moderate ice age. Most of *The Chronicler's Arrival* and *Winter Schisms* takes place in Alnos' capital, Zyss, and an area called 'The Lake Region', where the Pallas Clan maintains a summer vacation compound on Lake Limnos. A few episodes take place in an archipelago called 'the Islands' that stretches from the southern arctic border to the southern edge of the planet's more temperate tropical region.

Visitors from other worlds:

Azetmir Dragon Ashewe, an O'bonne planetologist studying Alnese legal systems

Raymond Diaz Ruiz, a Chicano musician brought to Alnos from Earth

The House of Pallas

Every Alnese has four clan names, two from each parent, but the custom is to use one or two primary clan names, typically the home 'House'. The Alnese custom is to put the clan names first.

Pallas Xhania Leila, Raymond's Alnese lover and the mother of his child.

Pallas Thor Eden, Leila's Alnese husband and a leader or 'Justiciar' in Alnos' main police and public security force, called Arthmis.

Pallas Thor Goal, Leila's daughter with her husband Pallas Thor Eden.

Pallas Thor Soccorro, Leila's daughter with Raymond.

Pallas Xhania Kyet, an Alnese musician and dancer who woos and wins Dragon. He is the son of Pallas Xhania Alexander and his wife Pallas Vaideh. Pallas Alexander is Leila's first cousin.

Pallas Nambo Vaideh, mother of Kyet, an astrophysicist who spends most of her time in the Lake Region's Pallas Summer Compound to avoid the light pollution created by Zyss.

Pallas Xhania Alexander, father of Kyet, a leader or 'Legate' of a more militarized security force called Mythras.

Pallas Odysseus and Pallas Illias, nicknamed Odd and Ill by Pallas Goal, twin first cousins who form part of her playgroup posse.

More Characters You Meet Along the Way:

Lady Alnos Ciani, the 32nd Ruler of Alnos; she assumed her position after a lengthy apprenticeship and is in her fifteenth year of a 64-year term when Raymond arrives.

Doctor Tzalque Peg, a physician who is a close friend of Pallas Vaideh and is the primary care doctor for Pallas House. She is also a skilled surgeon.

Kobran Ambassador Periasamy, the chief negotiator of the Kobran Commonwealth, a federation that Alnos is trying to join.

Minguard Lauran, Eden's first lieutenant, an Islander who chaperones Raymond in *The Chronicler's Arrival.*

Ixchel Aria, Pallas Alexander's first lieutenant throughout *The Alnos Chronicles.*

Kuan Kim, a young Islander who plans and executes a missile attack on an immigrant community in the Islands to assassinate immigrant leaders and intimidate them into leaving.

Maskar Enku and Nyemba Ndinzi, two mediators recruited from O'bonne to help negotiate an end to the conflict between natives and newcomers on Alnos.

Akhmin Julia, a 'Prodyn' or leader of the Order of Tomrys, the keepers of Alnos. She challenges Justiciar Pallas Eden's authority when he tries to pacify a larger conflict that grows out of Kuan Kemir's assassination attempt.

Sin'Odras Daniel, one of Prodyn Akhmin's soldiers.

Leila's father Vrezh, who has turned into an 'Ice Mentor' and adopted a spiritual path after a long career with Mythras. By becoming an Alnese monk, he has given up all clan and professional affiliations and obligations.

ONE

THE CHRONICLER'S ARRIVAL

◆ EPISODE 1 ◆

Dragon's Favorite Retreat

What can I say about Eden's wedding present to Leila? I'll just take the role of griot once more, appropriate given the Earth ties, and tell a story about my favorite residence on Alnos.

On Earth, in an old Swiss city named Zurich, once stood a beautiful fin-de-siècle villa in a garden a stone's throw from the lake. At one end an old carriage house hid a new garage; in the back a greenhouse stood near an artificial pond and brook designed to look natural; paths to the house snaked through an odd selection of trees, through carefully overgrown shrubs, across a perfect lawn to a terrace; flowering vines and rose bushes crept up the sides of the glass terrace doors, turned the walls white, pink and yellow at the height of summer.

Perhaps Eden saw an old photograph when he visited Earth, and the vision of fin-de-siècle leisure appealed to him. He returned for a second visit right after he joined the House of Pallas, taking his young bride with him, and he and Leila spent several months in Europe. Upon their return home, to Alnos, he studied our reports about Alnos' climate shift and the ways it was remaking the planet. He already knew his home planet was emerging from its latest deep ice age into a more clement climate, still an ice age by our standards, but milder. He wanted to know how the milder climate would reshape the tropical highlands of his childhood, particularly the eight lakes carved by vanishing glaciers at the foothills of Nyheim's northern mountain range where he was born.

Next, Eden negotiated for some lakeshore land on the western shore of the growing Lake Limnos, where he'd sailed since birth from his clan's estates at the northern end to the marshy southern tip to visit neighbors and friends. The land overlooked Lake Limnos, with a view towards the mountains towering into the northern sky above Thor House. Across the lake on the eastern shore, his father's clan was busy building another settlement using traditional Alnese architecture, but Eden adopted the Earth villa's design, complete with carriage house. Only the new estate's greenhouses winding up the shore from the lake followed Alnese specs. The villa compound was completed just in time for Eden and Leila to celebrate the birth of their daughter and the successful consummation of their alliance there, amidst hundreds of guests from all the Houses in question: Eden's native Thor House, Nambo House across the lake, and on Leila's side, Pallas and Xhania. Griots from each House proclaimed the day blessed and predicted that all would live happily ever after.

Leila asked her new husband if he intended to name the new compound Zurich, and in his usual tone, bland yet slightly sarcastic, he asked her in return, "Why not name it after its founder, my dear?" And so it came to pass that the Pallas clan's new summer compound in the Alnese tropics came to be called Eden Hamlet. This is one pronouncement Eden regrets occasionally.

◆ EPISODE 2 ◆

Raymond Revives on a New World

I arrived on Alnos in a coma after killing myself back on Earth. Grief and guilt pushed me to self-destruction. I'd have succeeded, too, but for my Alnese lover Leila's interference. She had me put on inter-galactic ice to slow the damage and shipped me to her world.

Alnos.

Home of the former Space Gypsies.

My name is Raymond Díaz, or Raymond Díaz Ruiz, or Díaz Ruiz Raymond, depending on the local convention. Last name first is the Alnese version. Except on Alnos it's not a last name, it's a clan name, or it would be if I were Alnese. I'm not. I'm human. An Earthling. My hosts are not convinced that's all there is to it. They suspect an Alnese connection, an Alnese great-great-great-grandmother perhaps. I haven't lived down to their expectations for humans. But I am a visitor on Alnos, one more traveler hanging with the Space Gypsies for a while.

1676 years before my arrival, a group still known as the Space Gypsies decided to make a half-frozen world their new home, or their bigger, more roomy new star ship, as Lady Ciani likes to put it. Actually, Alnos is more than half-frozen. Everyone assures me the place has become downright cozy in the past hundred years, and I believe them, but I don't have their basis for comparison. To me, the place is still a cross between Alaska and Siberia before Earth's climate shift.

Alnese legends tell of an almost two-thousand year odyssey before their prophet Pallas saw their promised land. She had a vision about the fourth planet of the next star system on their itinerary. It had a breathable atmosphere and a narrow equatorial strip of livable ocean, islands, and one continent between vast expanses of northern and southern arctic ice. Four and eight are perfect numbers for the Alnese—they have managed to hang on to some funny little superstitions through all their space travel and technological advances. The Space Gypsies followed their prophet to her fourth planet, and landed between the ice. And they stayed. That's the part nobody else understands.

My arrival didn't make the same splash.

Not that I remember it.

Going through some papers, though, I found a log of communications from the captain of our star ship to the doctor that took me on after I arrived. Here's one message with an assessment of my post-suicide state:

> From Captain Druhv, Kobran Transport Q'ron to Tzalque Peg, Chief Physician of Pallas House:
>
> I feel it incumbent upon me to inform you that Pallas Leila has requested we take on a second medical transport. Your first patient remains Pallas Socorro. We have stabilized her condition and are confident no further deterioration will occur. Your second patient is a human male, still relatively young, suffering from kidney and liver failure due to severe multi-agent poisoning, and already in a deep coma by the time we got to him. The only course of action left was to put him in stasis for the transport. Our physician recommends you maintain stasis to clean out his system and prepare replacement organs. He thinks it unlikely that the original organs can be saved, but was able to reverse some of the other damage.

I awoke on Alnos, in their 1676th year, right at the onset of their summer. Three needles threaded into one arm. Saline solution, dialysis, feeding line. I didn't feel any of them, though. I felt as if I were resting on a cloud. I stirred, and I could feel the cloud moving with me, adjusting. The lights brightened a little.

"I threw in extra, well, let's call them vitamins, to rebuild what little brains you've got left, dear boy."

I looked towards the voice. A woman reminding me of my grandmother la India was checking me out. I could have sworn her skin had a bluish undertone, but with her cinnamon skin and black hair framing lively black eyes, she evoked my grandmother so much that I briefly wondered whether I'd died after all. I hadn't expected that. I thought they would all look like my Alnese lover Leila.

Much to my surprise, I found that I still had a voice, though not a very substantial one, "Some people never gave me even that much credit."

"Humans are often perceptive." The English-Alnese translation was so well choreographed and the doctor's translated reply so fast that I didn't even realize it was a translation. A little unsure, she touched her hand against mine. "I'm Tzalque Peg. The Pallases have this bad habit of calling on me when they get sick."

"I'm sorry."

"Oh it's all right. You break my routine."

Doctor Tzalque looked fascinated, and didn't try to hide it. Over the next few days, as my waking and sleeping started to approximate a normal cycle, the good doctor got to indulge herself. She stuck another of her mysterious little probes into me every chance she got—blood, brain fluid, more blood—and returned beaming over her results.

"You can do whatever you want. You can rip all these out of your arms, go to the nearest cabinet and down another set of pills, I won't stop you."

She thought she had me psyched out.

Sounds distinguished my new medical experiences even more than the cloudy comfort of my not-exactly-hospital-bed. The time I odeed in Berlin, voices and moans mixed with shrill whistles and beeps. More than anything, the aural stew of misery had turned that experience into a nightmare. On Alnos, I was drying out mostly in silence, with occasional quiet blips breezing over my consciousness.

One more contrast lay in the leisurely pace kept by the good doctor. She even had time for conversations.

"Do you like our stuff?"

"What is it? Methadone?"

"I heard you used that. No, ours is just a different poppy. People grow it in their greenhouses. I think it's originally from Kobra, but of course the Kobran climate is totally different, so ours is a hybrid. A cross between an indigenous opiate, as incredible as that may seem, and the Kobran plant."

"Kobra?"

"One of the twin jewels, Kobra and Ko. God's cradle. Or so they say. I have yet to visit a planet where the residents don't claim godly qualities, but Kobrans may have a point. Almost all of us visit Kobra. I stayed two years to learn from their physicians. It was lovely." A little sigh emphasized her point.

"Have you gone to Earth?"

"No."

"What do people call Earth? The sewer?"

She chuckled, "The survivor."

"I have landed among optimists."

She threw her head back for a full-throated laugh, then commented, "Actually, humans have a knack for survival. The odds have been against you for the longest time and you're still around. Quite amazing. Well, how do you like our stuff?"

"I feel . . . good."

She nodded, "I'm weaning you off. Shouldn't take much longer, unless you prefer to-," She cut off, raised one eyebrow, asked, "Do you want to be put on maintenance?"

"You need my consent for that?"

"Yes."

"Doctor Peg, have some fun! Do what you want."

"Don't tempt me!"

She slapped my cheek lightly, then continued in a more earnest tone, "I wasn't just joking when I said you could do it again. Do you still want to die?"

I smiled at her. I noticed again that we had the same eyes, almost black, almond-shaped. "You would let me do what I want, but Leila wouldn't. She hasn't."

"Is there a debt between you two?"

"You could put it that way."

I had managed to damage myself so badly that it took several Alnese weeks for me to mend. Alnese weeks last eight days, one more than on Earth. Everything on Alnos comes in fours or eights, eight days in a week, eight months in a year, and strangely enough, four periods of six hours in a day, a close match to what I am used to. Doctor Peg kept me apprised of all the parts she was replacing, but I couldn't keep track. Didn't seem like much of the old me would be left.

Rather appropriate, really.

A new Ray for a new world.

◆ EPISODE 3 ◆

Dragon's Journey to Alnos

When I was a child, I had a dream. My holy dragon curled through the night sky, her tail sparking little suns into existence. Her breaths swept across a panoramic darkness and left behind clouds of nebula. Then she directed her gaze at me, blew a rainbow over me, and my skin turned lime green, yellow, blue, purple, magenta, red. Each wave of color felt like a precious jewel. The colors twirled together, six bracelets of pure light that I slipped on my arm, where they glistened like scales.

I told my grandmother about the dream. Later that day, while collecting some of her hand-scribbled lab-notes, she said quite nonchalantly, but addressing me by my full name, "Azetmir Dragon Ashewe, you will use your dragon-sight as a traveler." It did not make any sense to me at the time, but her use of both 'Azetmir' and 'Dragon' underscored what a serious pronouncement it was. Maybe that is why I still remember the dream, or maybe my crone got it right and it was a prescient dream, a message from my name-sake that she elucidated for me. What I can't figure out is why my new mentee Ray should remind me of that dream.

It has come to pass as my grandmother pronounced all these years ago: I have become a traveler, embodying the O'bonne saying, "Some knowledge can only be gained through reflection following experience." My home planet O'bonne is famous for its pursuit of knowledge, and measures wealth by libraries and data banks. As a community of scholars, we are sought out by just about everybody in our known circle of planets, and we often provide the requested analytical work. Yet this wealth of accumulated information is only our superficial glory, for our true strength lies in our continuous meditation on that knowledge. We push forward by asking questions that we cannot answer, and by pursuing these questions wherever they may lead. Travelers like me go the farthest, traveling into the unknown of other worlds and other people to find fresh sights and new insights, to mesh the known with the unknown.

I apprenticed early, accompanying my mentors in my adolescence to a beautiful lush tropical world we've studied for centuries, then to Earth, where I eventually completed fieldwork on my own. Earth has a tradition of sending scientists out to study unknown people, a tradition that can be likened to what I do. O'bonne travelers are really not unlike interstellar anthropologists, if one just sets aside the fact that anthropos refers to humans and we of course study many different sentient species. My third destination and first independent assignment, Alnos, is a planet colonized by a group of interstellar migrants after an odyssey of almost two millenia.

The O'bonne Institute of Cultural Studies has sponsored Alnese fieldwork since shortly after the migrants colonized their new world. I was assigned to continue our work on Alnese society's legal systems, and the Institute negotiated suitable agreements with a number of Alnese legal institutions. More recently, I had struck up a deal to shadow an Alnese judge and his staff for a year, possibly longer if I could stand to stay on. In this my second summer on Alnos, I had gratefully accepted an invitation to a vacation compound built by my hosts, the judge's Pallas Clan, on the shores of one of their newly expanded tropical lakes, a balmy region by local standards. Even after a few weeks of Alnese tropical sun, my bones still needed defrosting! Unexpectedly, Doctor Tzalque Peg came looking for me at the Pallas Clan's summer compound when I was meditating on the resplendent summer night sky in its 'Eden Tower'.

'Eden Tower' is the local nickname for a one-room office that rises above the compound's roof line and commands a stunning view of the lake, mountains, and sky. Like the whole vacation compound, it is named after Pallas Thor Eden, the Alnese judge I was shadowing. Pallas Eden had conceived of the idea of replicating an Earthly lakeside villa on Alnos' expanding lakeshores after an extended visit on Earth about a decade ago. The tower office can only be reached by climbing up a narrow medieval spiral from the compound's fourth floor. Once up the spire, I always readied myself against the weight of the imported O'bonne oak door, anchored in the wall with brass and iron, but then it would slide open with an unexpected hush that echoed down the stairwell.

Doctor Tzalque Peg's steps also echoed ahead of her long before she stuck her dark head into my observation chamber and coughed quite unnecessarily to announce herself. She gave me the time to emerge from my contemplations, and only started speaking after I breathed in deeply and turned to face her.

"I've come to ask you a favor."

I nodded and came to full attention. If I had learned one thing in my two Alnese years, it was the importance of the little Alnese phrase, "Could you do me a favor?"

"You have heard of my new patient?"

I nodded again.

"He needs," she hesitated, "guidance."

I breathed out slowly a second time, repeated, "Guidance."

The doctor fussed with the pillows until she had reached a satisfactory arrangement and could seat herself with her back against the wall, lifting her eyes and taking in the stars herself. I followed her gaze, tracing the outline of my sky namesake the Dragon Constellation.

Finally comfortable, Peg continued, "I'm sorry about the rotten timing. And her Grace Lady Ciani wanted you to know how much she regrets the imposition."

I dismissed her concern with a little wave, "Oh, so the request comes from her Grace? It is hardly the case that Lady Ciani plans other people's suicides, is it? What makes me fit the bill?"

Peg shrugged, "Your experience. You're an outsider and you know the clan."

"Well, I am an outsider."

"And isn't it true you've been to Earth?"

"That is the case."

We fell silent as I considered the request. It occurred to me that I had never met, let alone gotten to know Pallas Leila, and that therefore I did not know at least one of the principals in what I suspected to be an unfolding family drama. At the same time, I realized that Lady Ciani was well aware of the limits of my acquaintances, yet she obviously did not consider it an impediment. "I wonder what else her Grace knows," I murmured to myself. I could sense the increased alertness in my companion and finally turned back to Tzalque Peg, "Are we to meet soon?"

The doctor smiled, "You know how to make me happy, Ashewe Dragon!"

I returned the smile, "That is hardly the point, Doctor."

"On the contrary!" An indignant look clashed with the sparkle in her eyes, "I care very much about what makes me happy, and so should the rest of the universe!"

"Mm-hmm," I acknowledged without hiding my doubts.

We both turned back to contemplate the universe from the vantage point of Eden Tower. The sky was changing colors almost imperceptibly, entering that period right before dawn when shapes begin to take form. "Tell me about this Earthling," I prompted.

"What can I tell you? Raymond's human, a little younger than you, addicted to some strange Earthly cocktail that appears seriously damaging, and apparently tired of living with himself."

"You're guessing the last part."

"Oh, if Pallas Leila had left him behind, he would have died. And there isn't too much of him left, come to think of it. Not of the original him."

I pressed on, "All right. What do you know about his relationship with Pallas Leila?"

"Pallas Leila met him after her separation from Eden, when she returned to Earth. What was it, seven, eight years ago now? She met Raymond in an Earth city called Berlin, though he's from somewhere else. Don't ask me what he did in that city. I only know that somehow, they got together. Then, when she decided to cast about for a good environment for her daughter Goal, they moved to a nearby land, Switzerland. Apparently, Berlin is not a good place to raise children."

"You said he's from somewhere else?"

Peg continued quite obligingly with, "Well I've heard humans are quite cliquish, and apparently it matters very much whether you are from one place or another. Though really, come to think of it, you could say the same about us, what with our lineages and all … "

"Where," I emphasized gently.

She lifted both shoulders in a helpless gesture.

I tried another tack, "What does he look like?"

"You mean you can tell where they're from by how they look?" The incredulous expression on her face softened my irritation with what I took as willful ignorance, as Peg knew perfectly well that many worlds did not present as diverse a mix of people as Alnos with its tradition of inter-stellar travels and inter-species mixing. Still, I evened out my voice, "Not with absolute certainty, but looks suggest origins for humans.

For a long time, humans lived in relatively stable, relatively separate, and relatively sedentary populations, so there is a correlation."

"He could be my grandson. He has the same eyes, the same cheekbones, his hair is very black, straight. He is more angular, and taller, and he has darker skin." The look of expectation on her face after she finished was both funny and immensely irritating, but I controlled myself.

I sighed and shook my head, "He belongs to the one group that could easily come from any Earth-continent!"

"Oh."

"Well, except Europe, so he wasn't from Berlin."

After a brief pause Peg concluded with a wink, "I guess you'll just have to ask him."

"Switzerland." I murmured to myself.

"You know it?"

"Not really. My mentors thought I should go to areas where I would blend in, so I ended up criss-crossing another continent. Earth is ... Well, you've been to Ko, haven't you? It's a bit like Ko, where you also can tell most people's communities of origin, and I would never pass as a European on Earth! Berlin is in a continent called Europe. What language does he speak? I mean, most comfortably."

"He has been using something called English."

"He and Leila use it?"

"And a few other languages. The child uses . . . Français?"

"That's probably what they were using in Switzerland. The English, that's the closest humans have come to a planetary language, and you'd expect two strangers to use it."

Another quiet "Oh" followed.

"Seven or eight years," I repeated more for myself than for anyone else's benefit, "That's longer than the alliance with Eden, if I remember my Pallas trivia correctly."

Peg lifted both eyebrows as encouragement to continue. The first arc of the sun cracked through the horizon, and a beam of light crept into one corner of the room announcing my favorite hour. I reflected Peg's encouragement back to her, saying suggestively, "And she's had a child with this Raymond. Sounds like a serious relationship. But wasn't Pallas Leila serious about Eden, at the time?"

Peg did not disappoint me, "I do remember when the Pallas-Thor contract was negotiated. Everyone thought it would be a good match despite her youth. I mean, she was sixteen when she made up her mind to pursue him, and her elders really should have known better, but Pallas and Thor, old and new, the mingling of blood and all that, it was irresistible! Of course it didn't last. The same passion that started it spoiled it, and quickly, too."

That brief account gave me the chance to ask one of the many questions I had accumulated in my most recent year on Alnos shadowing Pallas Eden. I must confess my delight at this unanticipated opportunity. "What I don't understand is why Leila and Eden didn't just do what all do here, go off and each live their own life. I mean, without a public separation."

"Why indeed?" came the disappointing reply, "Most of the House of Pallas would love to know. And Thor House, too, of course."

"And why return to Earth, of all places?"

She looked at me as if that was the silliest question she had ever heard, "Well that's where they're from!"

I shot back an incredulous look, "Who is from Earth?"

"Thor. Eden's clan!"

I started to clarify what I had meant, "No, not Eden," when I interrupted myself and pursued this fascinating little tidbit of information, "They're human?"

That made Peg back-pedal, "Well no, just, the clan-mother was human, a refugee, she and some relatives, about a dozen people. Nambo Taliz was spending some time on Earth when some huge war broke out. At first she wanted to ride it out, but then things got crazy, so she came back and brought some friends. Eventually, we had to figure out what to do with them."

"And they were allowed to stay together?"

"That was what was negotiated at the time. You see, they'd lost all their relatives, so everybody agreed that the circumstances were unusual, and when Nambo House volunteered for the integration, a group split off and joined with the refugees and started the House of Thor. Not too far from here, now that I think of it."

"And they lived happily ever after."

"I thought they taught you not to make fun of your subjects!"

Peg's mock-indignant tone softened the reprimand, but I still felt compelled to defend myself, "Ah, but it is Arthmis that I'm studying, not Thor House!"

She shook her index finger at me, "An insult to one is an insult to all!" At which point I raised both hands and bowed my head, conceding defeat.

The light in the sky had strengthened. The forest below us was coming alive with sounds and the new day looked as promising as dawn on the shores of my home world, filling me with confidence and energy. I couldn't tell if it had the same effect on Peg, but her face had settled into a relaxed calm, and she sighed slowly to herself before continuing, "Now Leila, I don't know why she would choose to return to Earth. Maybe she wanted to recapture something by returning to a place where she lived her first great passion. After all, she spent nearly a year on Earth with Eden and Goal. They must have been happy there, she and Eden, don't you think?"

"That seems likely."

Shortly after this last exchange about Pallas Thor Eden and his wife Leila, we went down to the villa's dining room for some breakfast, after which I needed to sort through my belongings for my premature return to Alnos' capital city. I didn't particularly relish giving up the rest of my summer stay in the relative warmth of Eden Hamlet, but at least my conversation with the good doctor had been instructive.

◆ EPISODE 4 ◆

Raymond Scores a New Job

I knew that it was a relapse. Maybe the Alnese poppy didn't agree with me, who knows. I thought I was flying. I thought I saw the land the way it had been at the dawn of my hosts' arrival, white, cold, hostile. Alnos looked like an unending glacier when the Space Gypsies got here after hitch-hiking around the universe close to two thousand years. The wind howled right through me, then gave way to a flute arrowing a sudden silence.

Afterwards Peg said earnestly, "You've had a vision. An Earthling! Barely here a few weeks, and he has a vision. That's grace, Raymond, God's grace. I wonder what it means, seeing our current planetary space ship at the dawn of our arrival."

She decided to call their high priestess Lady Ciani and tell her about my vision.

In the dark I first mistook Lady Ciani's amber eyes for Leila's. Then I caught a glimpse of thick bronze hair falling to her shoulders, and more of her came into focus. I knew she had the "original" color from Oryn, the planet of the first Space Gypsies, but I still caught my breath and felt for the first time that I was looking at an Alien. She knew, joked, "I thought Earth lore tells of little green men." I just kept staring.

Lady Ciani continued, "It is our custom to welcome guests no matter what the circumstances. But when God visits grace upon a man, we must honor him. Peg tells me you've seen our planet as it first appeared to Pallas when she was looking out over the lay of our land and giving thanks for it."

I started to stammer something and decided to just shut up.

"Will you accept to become my chronicler?"

"Your what?"

Kick this uncouth asshole!

She smiled graciously and added matter-of-factly, "My chronicler, a historian of sorts. My old one decided to travel."

"I . . . I'm an outsider."

"A new perspective is probably what God wants us to have right now."

How do you tell a lady from outer space that you're all fucked up? I lost all inhibition and stared frankly at her gray-blue skin. She lifted her hand and offered it to me. It was warm. I turned it over and stared at her palm. Many fine lines criss-crossed it. Before I knew it, I mumbled, "You've had many lives." She looked across me to Peg, then back at me, "Do you accept?" Since I still couldn't say anything coherent, she withdrew her hand and decided for me, "Pallas Leila knows enough to get you started. If you wish to separate, though, I'll provide you with another teacher."

The name snapped me to my senses, "Leila? Where is she?"
"In Eden Hamlet."
"Can I go there?"
She shook her head, "Not yet."

◆ EPISODE 5 ◆

Leila Reflects on Her Return

Right before she left for the trip from which she never returned, my mother told me, "God has put our people's dreams into your eyes." I wondered which people she meant. On Danyx, Grandmother Dey's planet, people say that a storyteller is like a vine. It spans the space between the trees like a gigantic spider's web. The vines travel through the forest from one end of Danyx to the other, to every nook and cranny, and there is nothing that the vine does not know about life on Danyx. That is the fate of the storyteller. Then my mother added in a whisper, brushing her cheek against mine, "Your Grandmother Dey's heritage has blended with something that came from me, something that goes all the way back to Pallas. Through people's secrets you'll see right into their souls."

When I met Eden, through our whole first year of calm, I could see through his secrets, but I had not yet learned to see his soul. I bribed him with Goal. I knew how far we would slip, even then. From the first day, I loved the violence in him. I thought it matched my passion. I anticipated our collisions, foresaw each escalation, even the end.

First I thought it was all my fault.

I left.

It wasn't.

Then I inverted that first thought: The monster was Eden!

On Earth, in Berlin, I met Ray.

He wasn't.

Ray struck me as the most gentle being I had ever met. Passive-aggressive was not part of my vocabulary then.

What is it about memory that comes back and eats your soul? I sing memory and I can hear it burrow into me.

I understand them both now.

It doesn't help.

◆ EPISODE 6 ◆

Dragon and Leila Confer

Accepting my new assignment to provide human newcomer Ray with guidance did not mean I relished the prospect of leaving my Alnese summer haven. I knew how unlikely it was that I would return before Alnos' one summer month and briefest autumn faded back into the planet's damnable longest season, winter. I can't imagine what this place must have been like before its climate shift! My poor predecessors must have suffered abominably!

With this perfectly useless sympathy for past O'bonne scholars on my mind, I made my way to Zyss, the closest thing the Alnese have to a capital. Originally, their traditions prescribed that central government functions were hosted by the place of origin of each lady or lord of the planet, and since each regent had to be selected from a different clan, Alnos House, along with all high dignitaries, officials, and the Council of Eight, moved every sixty-four years. But despite various near-fanatical efforts to diffuse and decentralize power, my hosts found that some administrative needs just naturally gravitate towards a permanent center. It is certainly not every new regent's ardent desire to bother with daily administrative trivia like running the sanitation system so everyone's trash gets picked up! Faced with the necessity for some stability, all the clans had voted on one permanent administrative center a few centuries back, and they had chosen Zyss, the "City of Learning" founded by their great scientist Lann, a move I cannot but find inspired.

At the time, the City of Learning must have been a barely tolerable collection of igloos, sitting as it does in the foothills of a mountain range crossing the planet's only reasonably ice-free continent, Nyheim. The only livable area on the planet for the first fifteen hundred years of Alnese residence, Nyheim sits squarely in the middle of the planet's tropical ocean, but don't let that 'tropical' deceive you. Ice-storms sweep over Nyheim's high plain and mountains with great regularity, and Zyss's altitude only reinforces their deleterious effects. I can only surmise Lann must have been serious about Zyss being a place for study, as there is little else to do there for more than half the year.

Now that the planet is reaching the apex of its new, warmer climate, Nyheim's high plain is turning into a lovely spot from late spring to early autumn. The cold weeks dwindle steadily in both duration and intensity, and like the lower-lying tropical region around Eden Hamlet, the mountains surrounding Zyss are becoming resplendent in a more temperate mix of conifers, larches, and aspen. Everyone anticipates Nyheim will soon be covered by new forests.

After striking up my agreement with Judge Pallas Thor Eden last year, I had spent the better part of the past winter and spring conducting field work with his "Order," as the Alnese called their guild-like professional associations. By observing both routine activities and less frequent investigations and negotiations of various conflicts, I had made much progress in my studies. However, in all this time, I had learned relatively little about the man's personal history and background despite the fact that I lived with his primary clan. My practically unlimited access to the Pallas clan's family records hadn't helped much. All I had been able to make out was that the former Thor Nambo Eden had agreed to an alliance with Pallas House that had been formalized with the birth of his daughter Pallas Thor Goal, and that his Pallas wife, Leila, had then thrown him over.

Her leaving had been rather dramatic—she had gone all the way to Earth and taken their daughter with her, and he had barely seen the child for eight years. Since Alnese alliances fundamentally aren't personal relationships, there was nothing unusual about an Alnese husband and wife going their separate way once their alliance child was born. The separation of a father and child, on the other hand, was very unusual, and Eden's personal circumstances had sparked my curiosity even though they were not the main focus of my studies.

I landed in Zyss just as the sun was setting, always a splendid sight in the mountainous landscape surrounding Alnos' City of Learning. I had reluctantly agreed to use a glider, an infernal contraption that can be likened to a low-flying box with thrusters—unfortunately the only reasonable means of longer-rage transport. Having succumbed to violent motion sickness the first time I had been treated to a little fly-around, I avoided the damn things as much as possible. Everyone, including my present pilot, assured me it was the flying itself and not the glider that provoked my unpleasant first experience. And the trip to Zyss could serve as further proof that the piloting did matter, since it went extremely well. I hardly had the time to contemplate the matter, for as soon as we landed on the roof of the Pallas clan compound, my host Pallas Eden stepped out to greet me.

"You are kind to respond to our request so soon," he told me, bowing a little stiffly in my direction.

A little out of breath, still not quite sure of my footing, I replied, "I am only happy to be of service to my hosts."

Eden made a small gesture and two of the compound's younger members jumped to my rescue. With me out of the infernal glider, they lunged in and took care of my luggage, a small courtesy for which I was most grateful. I nodded to my waiting host and we both walked towards the stairs.

Eden led me straight to my own quarters, a suite of two rooms with a kitchen wall and a bathroom in the warmest and most sunlit southwestern corner of the compound. The kitchen wall had been well stocked in anticipation of my arrival, and a meal had been readied for me. I noticed that someone had gone to great pains to cook some O'bonne dishes.

"How delightful!" I exclaimed, turning back to my host with some surprise, "But why all the fuss? What's wrong with this Earthling?"

"Many things!" answered a woman's voice.

Eden warned quietly, "Leila!"

I turned to face the famous traveler and was quite taken aback by her youth. She had to be under thirty, with short-cropped sepia hair framing very white skin and huge yellow eyes. She didn't carry the store of winter fat protecting most Alnese, looking quite anorexic in comparison, probably the result of her recent residency on Earth. The androgyny of her straight, shapeless night cloak clashed with her soft voice, and with make-up and tinkling silver bracelets clearly designed to accentuate the feminine.

"So I meet you at last," I said with a nod in her direction, and I put on my warmest smile. "Did you prepare this feast?"

Leila smiled back and nodded, then threw a sideway glance in her husband's direction. He turned from her to me, "Now that introductions have been made, I best be off. I would like to have a word with you, Ashewe Dragon, but it can and will wait." He bowed again and left.

"I can imagine the buzzing voices raised by my name," Leila said almost absent-mindedly, motioning me to help myself to some of the fare, "So I'll clarify a few points now." Then she picked up a small silver pot and poured a dark-brown liquid I recognized with pleasure, "Earth coffee!"

"How do you take it?"

"In a bowl with too much sugar, like a good East African!"

That made her smile, "So you too picked up Earth habits! How long were you there?"

"The usual five years. For an O'bonne scholar, that is." I accepted the cup she offered me and took a first tentative sip. The coffee tasted like an exotic candy to my tongue, and I savored it, bracing myself for the buzz I expected after such a long period of abstinence. Then I turned to my hostess and encouraged, "Tell me about your guest."

"I met him almost eight years ago, right after I landed in Berlin." She paused. "It was like a meeting of two lost souls, in a city of lost souls. He was in a band—a musical group—based in Germany, without a place to stay. I took him home."

"Why Berlin?"

She didn't answer that immediately, looking past me blindly for a minute. Her eventual reply surprised me, "I wanted . . . the opposite."

"The opposite?"

"Of Alnos. Chaos, urbanity, and especially anonymity. I wanted anonymity above all. And of all the places Eden had taken me to, Berlin was the most anonymous, and it offered the most extreme sense of the abyss."

"And Ray did, too?" I offered.

"I suppose so." Another pause followed, and she served herself some coffee. "Of course first impressions are always wrong. They have this totality about them. There is a part of him that's the abyss, but there's another that's extremely grounded. I would never have thought ..." she struggled on silently and then gave up.

I distracted her with, "Is he European?"

"No," came the immediate answer. She followed that with, "Well, one of his great-grandmothers was German, but he never knew her. You know about their World Wars, don't you? One great-grandfather was an Allied soldier and I don't know if it was an affair or a marriage but he had a child. The German woman stayed behind when the man returned home, but he took the child."

"That's unusual for Earth. Home was?"

"Texas."

"Is that where Ray is from, then?"

"His family is from there. His father was also a soldier, so they kept moving and Ray doesn't really feel that he is from anywhere."

Another gypsy, flashed through my mind. It might explain the relationship better than anything else. "What did you want to tell me before I hear it from others?" I continued.

"He thought . . . well," she broke off, took an audible breath, and started over, "I let him think that our daughter Socorro had died when I left Earth. That's why. . ." she trailed off again, shrugged. "He surprised me. I never thought he'd actually do anything like that."

I decided to learn more about my Alnese assignment, and asked, "Did Ray know about you? That you were not from Earth?"

"Some things he knew." Her next shrug radiated the bafflement she must have felt about what to say and how to say it. I understood, even though I had stuck to my resolve not to get involved with the natives on Earth and had never been in her shoes—not there, anyhow.

"You know what's really funny?" Her lips smiled, but her face flashed unmistakable anger, "He started to use heavily after I conceived Socorro, and he really dove into his drugs when she got sick. There hasn't been much passion for a damn long time, not much of anything, really. Why would he suddenly come back to life when he thought she was dead?"

I didn't have an answer for her question, and got the impression that she didn't really expect any. After letting her regain her calm, I observed in my most neutral voice, "Doctor Tzalque led me to understand that your kinspeople are very interested in the child."

"Of course they are." If anything, her face flashed even more anger.

Maintaining the most neutral expression I could muster, I continued with, "They wonder whether the child belongs to Thor or whether she will have another lineage." It went without saying that the baby belonged to her mother's Pallas clan.

Leila practically snapped, "That hasn't been negotiated yet."

"I see." My gaze turned probing despite my best efforts, "But she was not an alliance child, was she?"

She shook her head, and I sensed just a trace of amusement in her when she reflected, "No, not an alliance child, but a child of passion. That's your point, isn't it?"

I assumed an apologetic expression and continued, "I truly don't mean to intrude, Pallas Leila. It is just that now that I have been asked to help your human friend, I prefer to know as much as I can about him, and, well, your relationship." As I spoke my observations I realized that Pallas House wasn't about to let an opportunity to mend its alliance with Thor House slip through their fingers, and I had an almost prescient insight as to what that meant for the three involved parents. No wonder everybody had agreed to Ray's rescue! As the clan's actions fell into place, I felt an inner tremor about the implications of the case for me, and promptly set it aside. I couldn't think about my problems just now. Instead, I turned back to Leila and changed the topic, "I am glad Socorro made it. I know Earth medicine. It must have been torture."

"You know, when she was born, I had readied myself for anything because I knew about the potential incompatibility, and I knew our meditations didn't always work. Then she was born healthy and . . ." She clasped her hand over her mouth for a second and I could hear her regulate her breath once more before she concluded with a throaty voice, "I let my guard down."

I made an unconscious sympathetic gesture: *Don't we all in this business!* But of course she isn't in the planetologist business, just an Alnese traveler keeping up the gypsy tradition of her ancestors.

"So what's next?" I asked after she had regained an outward calm.

"Peg tells me that Ray has resigned himself to living. Those are her exact words."

"She suggested not telling him the truth," I inferred from that rather opaque statement. I was disappointed in Peg. "That is not right."

"You see, you are the perfect person."

"For what?"

She didn't answer. Instead, she looked at me, got up, moved to the window and looked outside. When she turned around her face had set into a determined expression, "I have come to a decision about where I want to be, where I want my children to grow up. Eden is part of the package, but so is Ray. Help me with Ray, please."

I sensed that I would have the easier part of her project. I rose and put a hand on her arm. “All right.”

The determined look on her face softened somewhat, and with a formal timbre she intoned, “I am in your debt.”

I nodded, then told her as I was turning back to our evening meal, “You do not know it yet, but we will help each other.”

◆ EPISODE 7 ◆

Raymond Meets the In-Laws

The day they put Socorro back in my arms I cried harder than she did. Goal had brought her sister. She took the baby back and started to walk around the bed to calm her even as she occasionally patted my hand reassuringly. Finally, after succeeding in putting her little sister to sleep, she laid her down next to me. It felt like heaven. I moved to caress Socorro's hair with one hand and gathered one sheet up to my face with the other in a shaky attempt to clean up my face. Goal took the sheet and helped me, then climbed next to me on the other side and like a little angel laid her head on my shoulder.

When I could breathe more normally, she lifted her head and stared at me gravely, but I didn't dare turn away.

"You won't do it again, right?"

I shook my head, echoed back, "I won't do it again."

She didn't ask me to promise. She sensed that I was serious. I felt another great wave of emotion wash over me. I choked out, "I didn't think about you. I'm sorry."

She put her head back on my shoulder and let it go at that. I leaned over and kissed the top of her head, repeating, "I'm sorry."

A little while later Doctor Peg appeared at my bedside. She surveyed us for a moment, then announced, "Ray is about to see his physical therapist now, Goali. Take your little sister back home."

Goal lifted her head and stared the old doctor down in one second flat. "He wants her here."

I stirred and whispered, "Obey the doctor. I'll be okay now." She hugged me then, long and as hard as she could, kissed me goodbye, walked around the bed, and picked up Socorro. Goal shot a haughty glance at the doctor on her way out.

"You've done a good job with the girl, you know," Peg remarked while glancing at her machinery over my head. I suppressed an absurd need to thank her for the compliment, and could feel my emotions pressing around my throat again. Peg added, "She even gets on brilliantly with her father. You don't know it, but that bodes very well for you."

"Bodes well for me?"

"I'm assuming you want to maintain contact with both girls."

"What do you mean?"

"Oh it's too complicated to explain. It involves our family customs. Now that you are here, you will have to adapt."

Leila had tried to communicate something like that during an early lucid period, and I had thought she meant Goal. Socorro's survival was still too new for me to start making plans. The day of reckoning between Leila and I was coming closer, but any thought that it would involve the children was unbearable. I repeated to myself silently, *These people are not monsters.* And yet a new suspicion burrowed into my mind: Did they bring me here for some kind of sick experiment, to see what stresses a human can take before he chucks it all? But no, I had it the wrong way around. I had chucked it all and they had saved my life.

The irony of that last thought sank in, and I started to laugh quietly. They saved my life, my life! They hadn't left it at that either. The balancing act to which I had devoted well over half of that life, my love affair with heroin, had ended. The Alnese opium had served as a way-station to sobriety. Doctor Peg cast a quick glance my way, intuited that I wasn't about to say anything, and left me alone.

For the next ten days a succession of people brought Socorro to me every day. They didn't expect me to react to anything but the baby. I secretly observed every single one of them. They all looked human to me, even the bluer ones. They all had two legs and two arms and a human face with the same play of emotions. I had the same feeling about the two therapists who started working with me, getting me up and moving every morning until I was ready to leave my sick room.

I was taken to a bright, cheerful suite that I took to be my new prison. The huge compound, a labyrinth of rooms and hallways, echoed with the activity of dozens of people. The first day, I stayed put in hopeful anticipation that my daily visits with my girl would go on. When one of the many people I had seen in my sick room showed up with her, I could have thanked him on my knees. Controlling myself, I took the baby from him and cherished my hour with her.

On my second day in the new suite I met Dragon Ashewe. She came with Goal, who leapt up at me and clung around my neck until Dragon felt compelled to warn her, "Ray is still weak, girl; don't go throwing him off balance!" She held out her hand to me and said, "Hello, I am Azetmir Dragon Ashewe. I am called Dragon. I want to give you a tour of this place."

At first glance, I had assumed her to be another Alnese, but she spoke English. After taking a second look I wondered aloud, "Is that an African accent I hear?"

"It is. I learned your language in Ghana and Kenya. I spent about three years wandering about the Sahel to round out my Earth education."

"You're not human?"

"I am from O'bonne. Has anybody mentioned O'bonne to you? No, I can see they have not."

"They mentioned Kobra."

"That they would, yes. You could say Kobra is the center of our interstellar universe."

We examined each other. Health and strength emanated from every pore of her, especially from her smooth dark skin and onyx eyes. Her face looked regal, a quality also mirrored in her bearing, and her long limbs and movement seemed the embodiment of grace and style. Next to her, I must have looked pitiful.

She gestured toward the door and asked, "How about the tour?"

"Yeah. Let's."

She led me to a big hall in the middle of the labyrinth before she began, "This is the center of the compound, the clan room. It is used for clan meetings, for alliance celebrations, something akin to weddings, for other big celebrations. Tradition dictates that it always remain at the center, so if a clan adds on rooms or apartments, someone always needs to be mindful of the proportions. Compounds traditionally have at least three more dedicated areas: the area of the keepers, something like a temple, usually in the southwest wing; a study area, a cross between a school and a multi-media library; and a garden or greenhouses of some kind. The Pallas compound has the typical roof greenhouses of Zyss in addition to four courtyard gardens. Traditional compounds usually house thirty-two apartments throughout the building. The largest ones have more than double that, smaller ones typically house eight. Everything on Alnos is done in eights or fours, you know, though thankfully, they adopted the Kobran decimal system for practical applications about three centuries ago. Ideally, the apartments are planned and added in fours, but that is one area where sticking to the holy numbers gets a little tricky. The Pallas compound in Zyss houses sixty-four apartments of various sizes. It is quite large. The clan is an old one."

Just like my suite, the hall had a heated floor. Several skylights angled towards a central circle around which disorderly collections of seats and pillows clustered. Tapestries on one side displayed a number of people in an icy environment, while adopting more varied themes on the other. I moved to one of the central portraits on the ice-wall and contemplated a middle-aged gray-blue woman enveloped in layers of indigo fabric whipped by a fierce wind. She was standing on a cliff over a menacing glacier, pointing the way towards the rising sun.

"Pallas, the clan mother," my tour guide informed me. "The one who first saw Alnos."

Goal, who had been running about us like a puppy, piped up at this point, "She saw this was God's world for us in a dream, and then she led us here."

"And I am with her clan now?"

Dragon nodded.

"Goal's father is a Pallas?"

"He is now. In Earth terms, he married into the clan."

"Leila is a Pallas?"

"Yes, though of course as an Alnese, she has three other primary lineages, a second one from her mother, and two from her father. If I remember it correctly, it's Pallas Xhania Nambo Tsenyx."

"Sounds like a lot of relatives."

"Enough to fill sixty-four apartments here, and several other compounds around the planet. Although … well, Tsenyx wasn't Alnese, so that would reduce the number a bit."

Dragon made a move towards one of the doors, and we followed her as a more complete tour of the Pallas labyrinth followed. The compound felt like a cross between a Club Med resort and a New York neighborhood. It was obvious to me that many days would pass before I could make head or tail of the place. At the end of the tour, we ended up in a small living-dining area that Dragon identified as her own, where she prepared some coffee for us all. I sat down on what she called a settee, a low couch-like contraption that seemed to mold itself to my body and felt warm and incredibly comfortable. Goal joined me.

"In case you have not already guessed it, I am to be your guide in other areas besides the compound," Dragon informed me as she handed me my cup. For Goal she had prepared a bowl of milky, sugary coffee designed to lessen the ill effects of the brew.

"I haven't thought about it," I confessed almost absent-mindedly.

"You don't have any questions about what you are doing here?"

I stole a glance at Goal and lowered my voice, "I am obviously here because of Leila. She could have let me go. When she wants me to know why she did what she did, she will tell me."

Dragon sipped her coffee and pondered my reply before she said, "I don't think that she knew what she would put you through, Ray."

"How could she not know!" I snapped back.

"I suppose she only thought about her child."

I didn't answer.

She continued, "You don't protest? But you must have questions."

After I didn't take her up on the offer, she added, "Remember, I am from O'bonne."

That prompted me to examine her again. I shrugged and asked, "What's it like?"

"Warm," she sighed with great longing.

I couldn't help but smile. She smiled back and said slowly, "I have more insight into your situation than you could possibly know, Ray. I would consider it a great honor to gain your trust."

Goal meandered around the room. We watched her find her way to the windows. Something akin to cushioned seats were built into the bigger window frames, and Goal settled down in one of these nooks to stare out the tempered panes.

I turned back to Dragon, "How long have you been here?"

"It is the middle of my second year."

"And what do you do here?"

"The simplest answer to that is, I study. O'bonne people are scholars. I've been studying Alnese legal systems, shadowing various people involved with it."

I leaned back, "Hm. I'm supposed to become a chronicler."

Dragon nodded slowly, "Yes, there is a similarity."

Goal started to move back towards us, crawled onto a second, much shorter Alnese couch where Dragon rested, and looked royally bored.

"Honey," I said, "you should find something to do. Or go out and play."

She giggled, "Out? Not here! When we're back in Eden Hamlet, maybe."

Dragon pushed Goal playfully and admonished her with, "Girl, your uncle has never been here, and he has just come out of intensive care. What he does not need is a smart mouth."

As usual, the reprimand washed off Goal like water off a duck. She slid off of Dragon's settee and moved back towards mine, sat down next to me and wrapped her arms around me as if to show her who was queen here. I put one arm around her shoulders and asked softly, "Where can you go?"

Her nonchalant reply was, "To see Odd and Ill."

Dragon protested, "I do not want you to use those names."

"Okay, okay!" She wrinkled her nose rebelliously, but complied, "To see Odysseus and Illias."

"Go to it, then."

"What's the big deal?" Goal felt compelled to protest, "They don't understand it anyway."

Whereupon Dragon concluded, "Thank Goddess for that! Off you go."

After Goal had left, Dragon turned to me and said, "I know it has only been ten days since they have restored your daughter to you, and so you are still reeling from her loss. You may think she could be gone again by a snap of someone's fingers. The Pallases do have that power. Some have been tempted simply to leave well enough alone now that you have recovered, perhaps ship you back to Earth quietly and keep you out of all further negotiations. Leila put an end to such ideas. I believe Leila deeply regrets that she let you think your daughter had died. And she didn't do it because it was convenient, whatever you may hear in the future."

"Yes, of course," I interrupted, "She did what she thought was best." At the same time, I wondered, *Negotiations? About what?*

Dragon shook her head, replied quite oblivious to my sarcasm, "I don't think that she thought at all. She just acted."

More than anything, her tone of clinical detachment made me back off. "I don't blame her for my part, Dragon."

That caught her off guard. She examined me with renewed curiosity, then said slowly, "Could it be that this emotional firestorm burned you that clear?"

I tried to egg her on wordlessly, but she only fluttered her fingers, "All right. Leila made her decision: You are, as she says, a part of the package now."

Part of the package?

I rose and stepped to the same window Goal had sat by. Outside, I could see a ring of mountains. "I guess you better tell me about the package, then."

"The package, yes. Where do I start? Well, you know that Leila has a husband, Eden."

I shrugged, "Leila's ex? Goal's father?"

"Well, he is not exactly her ex. Leila and Eden entered into an Alnese alliance twelve years ago, an alliance consummated with Goal's birth."

"Leila's still married to Goal's father?"

"Well, not exactly married, no. Leila and Eden have entered into a contractual relationship establishing a tie between their Houses, or their clans, with Goal as a concrete representation of that tie. That's what an alliance is, what an alliance does. Two clans quite literally create a blood tie through the conception and birth of a child, an alliance child. Other societies have, well, arranged marriages, so the concept is hardly new, but the Alnese have managed to come up with some unique twists. On Alnos, an alliance child forms a living link between clans. Of course a contract involves all kinds of clan politics, about who will move into which residence, how the clan that loses its member will be compensated, whether the two most directly affected parties are well matched, but in Alnese terms, the clan that gets the child wins, and that is what it all comes down to in the end.

The Alnese count lineages as one of their four wealths. They are also quite convinced that an abundance of lineages leads to an abundance of the other three, knowledge, trust, and hospitality. Concretely, that means children."

I mapped the explanation onto the people I cared about, "Sooo, the Pallas clan won with Goal."

"Precisely. Now an alliance is not like a marriage in that it really does not concern the couple. A good relationship is desirable, and of course, they do need to get on well enough to create the new life between them, but it is of no great importance how long their relationship lasts once the alliance has been established through the birth of the alliance child. After that, as long as they fulfill their clan obligations, the relationship between an Alnese husband and wife is what the Alnese consider "personal," something that concerns only them and that they can arrange as they see fit. The new relationship between the two clans is what does matter. In fact, it is paramount, and an entire cycle of favors and mutual support begins between linked clans."

I let the wheels turn a bit, then prompted, "And Socorro?"

"If she stays here, she could become a second link between Pallas and Thor, Eden's primary clan."

"But she's not his!"

"No matter. According to Alnese custom, any child of Leila's cements the alliance between Thor and Pallas, even if she acknowledges an additional lineage. Leila would have to disavow Eden specifically, as a matter of fact. Pallas Eden is an important person now, and Leila obviously feels differently than she did when she left him."

Then I have lost her! A stab of anger swept through me, followed by the same bitter taste that welled up when I contemplated my recovery. I had started using almost every week after Leila got pregnant, and after Socorro got sick, I just couldn't function without my daily dose. Well, function was hardly the right term. I ran to my drug, started using so heavily I hovered just this side of an overdose. And yet I could stand here and feel robbed? Yeah, right.

Dragon, who had let my emotions play themselves out, rose from her Alnese settee and joined me at the window.

"Is that why they never divorced?" I asked.

"You cannot divorce two clans."

There was logic to that statement.

"But of course, Leila did not conceive your daughter as an alliance child. Alnese women control conception, you know. They learned how somewhere on their odyssey through space, and ever since, Alnese children are born when Alnese women choose. And they choose to conceive a child for one of two reasons: To establish an alliance between clans, or out of love."

Something in Dragon's added explanation didn't sit well. I hadn't exactly thought that Socorro was an accident, but what other explanation could there be? Who would plan to have a child with me? I wasn't husband material, not someone you take home to your parents. Except … well, here I was, in Pallas House.

"I will take you back now. You're supposed to have a job, and I want to get you started. The job was a lucky break, you know. It gives you a connection, and what a connection! You are working for her Grace Lady Ciani of Alnos, the ruler of the planet!"

It was a bit abrupt, and I wasn't quite ready to go back to my suite. I followed her there anyway. A short while later, my time with Socorro had arrived. I wondered who besides the O'bonne scholar would ever call her mine again.

◆ EPISODE 8 ◆

Dragon Is Asked for Another Favor

The day Eden and I finally got down to our next meeting, my first surprise lay in his initial announcement as I was led into the office kept by the Alnese equivalent of a Chief of Police in Lady Ciani's residence, Alnos House. "Contrary to what you may believe," he said, "what I am about to ask you has nothing to do with my wife and our problems."

Thunderstruck that he had surmised my thoughts, I momentarily shrank from him. His deduction, combined with my own complete lack of foresight, added up to an almost unforgivable intellectual lapse for an O'bonne scholar. The domestic intrigues of the Pallases had obviously lulled my brain into near-idiocy, and Eden's announcements felt like a wake-up call.

I took another look at him. He looked haggard, and his official finery showed traces of ill use that I had completely missed in my initial survey. As I fumed silently at the mounting failures of my vaunted powers of scholarly observation, Eden told me the reason for our interview, starting with, "You've heard of our Island Troubles?"

I nodded, now frantically trying to recall a host of half-ignored hints and dropped comments that had come my way for the past two months. Some murders in a wilder Alnese area, a rare enough event that had nevertheless not roused much spirit because the victims were immigrants. Pallas Eden had been charged with the investigation at the end of spring, just as I was about to leave for my summer vacation, and I had found myself unable to give up my few weeks of warmth.

"Nine heshtis were found dead on the first day of Holdin, frozen quite solid. They had been ritually murdered and then left to freeze so they could be staked into view on what most likely was the appropriate day, though I cannot tell you what that day represented. Both the manner of their deaths and their display left no doubt as to the crime having been committed by one—or several—of us. In spite of the gravity of this situation, the Island clanspeople did not send for Arthmis, and when word did get around to us, they tried to pass off a ludicrous story of fratricidal fighting and suicide. Even now they're still hindering me at every step."

Nine murders! I stopped kicking myself mentally and re-focused my faculties on the present in an effort to make up for lost time, "Good heavens, what a regular massacre!"

Eden nodded agreement.

"Which Island clan is involved?"

"The fog-brained Chanticos," Eden hissed through clenched teeth. Then he added more calmly, "You know I don't approve of heshti ways any more than the next person, but these wild Islanders aren't much better. I have been knocking myself out flying back and forth between Zyss and the Islands to resolve this matter, and the situation has only worsened. The heshtis have begun to arm themselves. A group of them is willing to be moved, but a hard core is talking some nonsense about taking over an island of their own. Of course we can't have that, but in a way I understand them. I just wish they weren't so difficult about integration."

Integration. For their entire residency on Alnos, the former Space Gypsies had devised a simple and ingenious strategy to deal with any and all newcomers: Find a clan willing to add a few new members and make sure all children were fully enculturated into the clan-structure. In the unlikely event that a few lost souls wished to stay together, as some of Eden's ancestors had stipulated upon arrival, a new clan could be created. This rare and dispreferred option was soon remedied through inter-clan alliances, which spawned the connections between new and old that the Alnese equated with stability.

The changing climate had changed everything: No longer did a few dozen stragglers err onto an icy world only a hallucinating space witch could love; newcomers now numbered into the thousands! They had started building their own communities, and a strange grouping of non-Alnese Alnese was beginning to take form in the cracks of the old society.

The Alnese called immigrants heshti, a Kobran loan word meaning "alien" or "outsider," a word replete with all the negative connotations it had on many other worlds. They were beginning to talk of a "heshti problem" in terms that could be very disturbing. 'Heshti' was increasingly reserved for an un-assimilating core of "alien separatists" that refused to enter into most relations with their hosts, presenting the clearest challenge to the old clan-order.

I knew the incipient conflict between natives and immigrants had grown worse as I had been sifting through Arthmis records and indulged little side trips into recent Alnese history, but I had not paid any more attention to it than the vast majority of Alnese. Most of them still couldn't fathom that a few thousand immigrants could be anything other than a temporary if annoying nuisance. They still thought good old-fashioned, if slower-paced integration would eventually resolve the issue. The Chantico murders signaled something different: at least one group of Alnese were no longer complacent.

Eden broke into my musings, "Now that you have returned from our summer compound, I assume you'll be joining me again as I continue this investigation. What I wanted to ask you was . . . would you consider helping? I could use some help."

"I don't understand. Help with what?"

"I'm sorry, I haven't explained properly: I'm moving all the heshtis back to Nyheim. They cannot stay in the Islands, and I have found an appropriate resettlement area. Now, half of them are begging for safe passage, and the other half adamantly oppose moving. I was hoping that you could help me persuade them."

From the way I looked at him, he knew what I thought.

"You disapprove, of course. But Dragon, I'm not asking you to coerce them. I'm quite capable of doing my job. I would just like to persuade those who can be persuaded. The fewer people I have to drag away against their will, the better."

"How long have they been there?"

"The first ones have lived there about eighty years, but most of them started their residence more recently, with the development of the new greenhouses. We'll compensate them for their material losses. They are rather obsessive about that."

After a few more seconds of hesitation, I proposed, "If you offered to give them some form of title to the new land, they might all go."

"Only clans have title. You know that as well as I do."

I thought it over. Entering into an Alnese mediation process with their newcomers would put me in the midst of a delicate situation. The many restrictions and harassments the Alnese had contrived for their more standoffish immigrants were deeply offensive, and I wanted no part of it. At the same time, my blissful ignorance of the brewing crisis between Alnese and immigrants seemed quite unconscionable in its own right.

"How would you like it if someone asked you to evacuate Eden Hamlet?" I needled him.

He replied with his even voice, "That would depend on who did the asking."

I should remember never to underestimate Pallas Thor Eden.

As I pondered his request, it occurred to me that changing from merely shadowing his work to the more involved role of a participant-observer could deepen my long-term O'bonne research study, a bribe he surely had anticipated. Still, I resisted, "I'm sorry, Eden. I am a researcher, not a mediator."

He inclined his head slowly, accepting my decision, "I'll inform my lieutenants that you'll be along again, in your usual observer role." He paused, then proposed, "How about consultations?"

"Consultations?"

"I would be in your debt if I could consult with you about our negotiations. We've often discussed cases, but you usually ask the questions."

I smiled, but tried to stay non-committal, "As I have said, I am not a mediator, but if you want to hear the observations of a scientist … You have certainly waited patiently for your turn."

He smiled back briefly, and informed me, "We'll return to the Islands tomorrow."

Without actually saying so, he'd concluded this particular interview. I rose, then recalled, "Oh, but what of the new chronicler I am supposed to be training?"

He shrugged, "Take him with you."

◆ EPISODE 9 ◆

Raymond's Islands Adventure

I wonder if Leila knew what world she was taking me to when she decided to save my life. Her stay on Earth probably prepared her, sharpened her perception. Still, people tend to remember the world of their childhood with childhood eyes.

Her world was in the midst of a transformation, a transformation for the better in most visitors' opinion. The Alnese, though, considered this warmer, greener, more desirable world a mixed blessing. They were used to their igloo; they were not used to visitors beating down their doors and staying through more than two winters.

From what I gathered after my Islands adventure, visitors started to turn into settlers about sixty years before I showed up. Frictions between hosts and settlers soon followed, and more recently, the frictions had flared into conflicts. As it happened, Goal's father Pallas Eden turned out a high-ranking law officer right in the thick of it all. Here's an informative sample of the communiques flowing between my new boss Lady Alnos Ciani and Justiciar Pallas Eden:

> From Pallas Thor Eden, Twelfth Justiciar of the Order of Arthmis in Zyss to Lady Alnos Ciani, 32nd Regent of Alnos:
>
> Report on the Status of the Island Heshti Murders, 1 Koreh 1676
>
> The situation in the Islands is rapidly becoming critical, so much so, in fact, that I now hesitate to press for my own earlier recommendation. I know I asked for your Grace's assistance when we spoke last. Yet now, two months after the murders, I am no closer to solving this case than I was last Holdin. Moreover, now one terrified group of refugees is begging me to help them move back to the mainland while another is forming a heshti militia ready to take matters into their own hands. Your Grace may still be the only one who can persuade the Island clans of the need for justice, but I cannot guarantee your personal safety and must caution against a personal visit.
>
> The manner in which these murders have been carried out indicates that the murderers think themselves justified. Unfortunately, the clans are saying nothing about the events that led them to take nine lives and shield the responsible parties. We have learned that three Chanticos and some clan allies carried out these nine pre-arranged executions, but no one will explain why. No one will tell me how these nine migrants

supposedly brought their misfortune on themselves. I am used to the wildest rumors, with migrants usually accused of everything from rape to child stealing, but in this case, nothing.

For now I can only arrange safe passage for the Heshtis that wish to leave. In the long run, there is no question of any migrants remaining in the islands: they must go! In the meantime, I have deployed my four companies and requested several more companies from other Justiciar units to keep everyone on opposite shores. I am regularly taking people into custody for loitering about in the wrong place at the wrong time. As a matter of fact, I could use still more reinforcements, but Arthmis cannot focus all its resources on one case.

Outside mediation might inspire the heshtis with a bit more confidence in our investigation. Perhaps you could discuss the situation with Ashewe Dragon or Ambassador Periasamy? They may be gracious enough to help. Considering the fact that heshtis hate everybody equally, I have my doubts about the idea, but it's worth a try.

Pallas Eden sounded more reasonable than I expected from a law officer, particularly one with a high rank. I was more than a little curious about him, and not just because my first assignment turned out to be chronicling the beginnings of Alnos's Islands Troubles.

◆ ◆ ◆

Dragon and I barely had time to settle into a study schedule when Alnese history intervened. Unannounced, she rushed into my quarters early one morning dragging a long, multi-layered garment that looked like a stuffed jumpsuit. "Ray, we have been called into action. I know we have not had a chance to do much more than talk about Alnese customs, but sometimes this kind of crash course turns out for the best. I have brought you something to wear."

Not yet awake, nor up to regular information processing, I stared at her like an uncomprehending idiot.

"Try it on." She encouraged. When she realized I was uncomfortable with her presence, she stepped back into my living area until I had slipped the garment on, whereupon she stuck her head back into my room for a split-second before proclaiming, "Perfect! I've got a whole suit of work and snow clothes picked out in the same size, so you don't need to pack. Let's go."

We swept out onto the Pallas Compound roof and Dragon had me bundled into the box-like Alnese glider. Before I could gather my full wits, we were already taking off. A collection of compounds littered a mountain basin beneath us. Then a ring of mountains formed around the city. Finally, the Alnese pilot turned the glider westward and we took off in a burst of speed. We crossed the first mountain crest only to find a second, then a third range blocking our progress. Each time, the pilot boosted both speed and height. I was beginning to feel like Icarus.

Dragon looked sick during our entire time in transit, despite the fact that our pilot coaxed a reasonably smooth ride out of his boxy vehicle. We flew southwest, leaving behind the planet's dark green belt of growing forests, crossed an ocean beyond it and ended up over a forbidding white landscape. Just like on Earth, the shortest distance to the other side of the planet was over one of the poles. I wondered if the Alnese, like the Eskimo, had come up with over twenty terms for ice and snow. The ice soon broke up into icebergs and I realized we were flying over another ocean, and in the distance, hundreds of islands alternated between light and dark green.

After we landed, Dragon first recovered in a plane pitbar with a collection of hostile-looking Alnese. She began to explain that the area where we had landed was called simply the Islands (really?), essentially a holding dock for non-conformists.

"Non-conformists? You mean they don't all go traveling when they can't stand to be around each other?" was the first question that popped into my mind.

Dragon laughed, "It is true that Island clans were started by returning travelers. Alnese always return at some point, no matter how far they go, Goddess knows why."

For a long time, only the most northern islands had even been habitable. As the planet warmed, the two dozen or so clans in this area had all quadrupled their land holdings, and they were still realizing a bonanza. This land rush had catapulted them from relative obscurity in matters Alnese to a position of some note. They'd gotten so influential, in fact, that the next Lord of the planet would be an Islander.

Dragon took advantage of this wrinkle in the story to explain the complications of Alnese rule and its succession.

Future regents were selected at birth by what Dragon called a "spiritual" order founded by the great Pallas herself. A successor was usually chosen when the current one turned 64, mid-way through a term of 8 times 8 years. Once successors turned sixteen, they had eight years' training, and another eight years of apprenticeship as a leader of the planet's Council of Eight to ponder whether they wanted the title, and the job. Accepting meant forfeiting all clan-ties, as well as agreeing never to have children. Dragon concluded with, "You see, a lady or lord of Alnos can only have loyalty to Alnos."

"And have some actually declined the job?"

"A few." She gave me a benevolent smile, as if to signal she understood my skepticism.

"So the new successor's an Islander?"

She nodded, "Of the House of Kuan. Lady Ciani has only been regent for sixteen years, so it is still too soon to choose a successor. She came from one of the border clans, the ones that like to live in the arctic parts of the planet."

After Dragon's recovery, we were ushered into something that looked like a modest lodge ringed with miniature cottages. The cottages lacked the ubiquitous floor-heating of Zyss-compounds, but made up for it with a roaring fireplace large enough for people to sit inside. Dragon and I wasted no time starting a fire after nightfall, when the fall chill began to seep in. And there, soaking up the warmth with me, Dragon continued her orientation.

"Actually, Ray, this doesn't concern you at all," she said, and then proceeded to tell me how not all was well and peaceful on Alnos. Thousands of people were arriving from other planets, and they were staying. The Alnese hadn't even noticed at first, or they'd figured the immigrants would freeze to death in their first winter. But some of the crazy settlers hadn't frozen to death, and were now making demands that didn't gel with the natives.

"You must understand," Dragon added almost apologetically, "the Alnese have no experience with this kind of group-migration. In the past, newcomers were always promptly allied or adopted into a clan. And since the Alnese are used to integrating new individuals without any problems, they simply don't know what to do. They've never had to deal with a whole group that didn't want to be like them."

She fell silent, and we both stared into the flames. I wondered how on Earth—so to speak—anybody could possibly fail to assimilate in this interstellar melting pot where ethnic identity didn't figure. As far as I could tell, everybody looked different from everybody else on this planet, and not just racially. It was almost a matter of pride with them to distinguish themselves somehow. I finally asked, "So tell me about your case. What brought you out here?"

She revealed in bits and starts, "About four months ago, nine immigrants were murdered here." Pause. "They were involved in a dispute over some recently transformed islands." Pause. She got up from our walk-in fireplace. "Pallas Eden," pause, "feels that there is no other solution than to move the immigrants out of harm's way." She began to pace back and forth in short loops.

"Pallas Eden, as in Goal's father?"

Dragon nodded absentmindedly.

"He's some kind of governor?"

"He is a Justiciar, the head of a martial order traditionally in charge of keeping the peace, the Order of Arthmis." She misunderstood the expression on my face and started to explain: "An Order is something like a professional group. When your training is complete, you can join the Order of Chroniclers."

"He's a cop?" I broke in.

She pondered that for a moment, turned around again, then rocked her head and one hand simultaneously as if to say "sort of," adding, "I suppose one could put it that way, but he has a lot more power."

I commented dryly, "I've never thought of a cop as powerless."

"Eden is also," she continued, "quite good at what he does. He is very young to be a Justiciar, and he spent some time in ice, too. He has managed to avert or solve quite a few problems since he was offered the title, so the Order's confidence in him appears justified. But anyhow, he has decided to move the immigrants, and he hopes to persuade some of the more recalcitrant ones on this trip."

I could tell she wasn't entirely happy with the idea, but didn't press her.

The next morning we were summoned by the man himself. He was housed in a suite in the main lodge, a short walk from our cottage. After we'd been announced and seated, he served us each a very hot cup of coffee. Dragon showed obvious delight in hers. They launched into an Alnese conversation that obviously didn't involve me, and outside of Zyss, my simultaneous translation was sketchy at best. I spent my time sipping my coffee, a rather close match to my particular preferences, and examined the man at my leisure. His chestnut hair and short-cropped beard were speckled with gray, a color scheme reversed by freckles on very white skin. He was a tall man, and even under the customary layers of warm Alnese finery, I could trace the outline of a powerful torso. The man was so obviously healthy, strong, and handsome next to me that I really couldn't fathom Leila's preference.

After a good twenty minutes Eden and Dragon reached some kind of agreement. Apparently feeling obligated to acknowledge my presence, he asked me in English, "Did I get the coffee right?" Seeing me nod, he added, "I know you would have preferred to stay close to the children for a while longer." He hesitated, then concluded with, "I do hope this matter is resolved quickly." I noticed his eyes were dark gray, like a cloudy sky. There didn't seem to be a trace of Alnese in him (and what would that be?), and not a trace of him in his daughter, come to think of it (wishful thinking). Not really sure how to reply, I mumbled, "I suppose this is how I get to see the planet."

This completed our first interview.

The next few days, we flew further south to another island every morning and landed in what looked like a fort next to a natural harbor. Eden had apparently agreed to meet the immigrant leaders on what could be called their turf. The immigrants had no legal claim to the island, which was noticeably chillier and more arctic than ours, but it was theirs nonetheless. Dragon was always immediately whisked into a large, crowded hall where the Alnese were meeting with a group of men and conducting long and sometimes agitated talks.

At first, I couldn't figure out why the immigrant group looked strange to me. Then it struck me, and I began to understand how the immigrant settlers managed to stick out in this world: They were all men, and the men all looked the same! They all had dark brownish hair, olive skin, and light eyes, and most of them had beards. Except for their darker hair, they reminded me of some overly bronzed Vikings I found in Goal's European comic books.

Since I had nothing to do during these sessions, Eden soon sent one or another of his lieutenants around to whisk me about. We weren't exactly welcome, but people generally stayed out of our way, and we had free reign of the island. We exhausted the possibilities of the fort the first day, then looked into the surroundings. On the third day, my guide found two tough-looking ponies that turned out surprisingly gentle, and we started on a wider circle. The ever-present island wind blew right through us as we rode about in a monotony of gray skies, gray rock, and gray sea broken only by green bogs and fields. A few gnarled trees fought against the wind in one or two protected hollows. I couldn't imagine what kind of living the settlers scraped out of this landscape.

On the fifth day of my meanderings, the peace shattered. While I was out exploring the coast south of a natural harbor sheltering several fishing vessels, someone blew the meeting hall sky-high.

◆ EPISODE 10 ◆

Raymond's Chronicling Turns Official

Even though the blast of the explosion had alerted my companion and we had started back immediately, two hours passed before we actually made it back. Gaping holes in the buildings surrounding the pulverized meeting hall bore witness to the force of the explosion. The fort itself appeared subdued. Control reigned anew.

Dragon told me later that Eden—who had been called out of the hall just moments before the shell hit—had immediately taken over, performing a personal triage and shipping the wounded off to a regional medical center in record time. Her salvation had been her positive addiction to sunlight. She sought it out every chance she got. The sun had broken through the gray that morning, and she had taken advantage of Eden's brief absence to go on a short walk and catch some rays. The blast had blown her off her footpath and several feet further, but her injuries were more painful than serious. Several of the fort residents, particularly the leaders inside the hall, were not so lucky.

My chaperone rejoined her boss, who looked ready to level a building of his own with his bare hands. Dragon, who looked worn despite her luck, kept shaking her head, and murmuring to herself in a language I'd never heard before, one my translator didn't turn into English for me. Eventually, we were both led without further ado to a waiting aircraft and taken back to our accommodations. Once there, Dragon burst out in English, "I have been a fool! Anyone with eyes could have seen it coming, and instead, I have let my brains rot in the lovely summer sun of Eden Hamlet! Goddess almighty, do you have any idea what this means?"

Agitated, she swayed before our unlit fireplace, her hands pressing together. I stepped in her way to make her stop, and wrapped an arm around her shoulders, "Look, if someone had just tried to blow me into Kingdom Come, I'd be upset too, but what's with this self-blaming? What are you talking about?"

She sighed deeply.

"What is it?"

She leaned her head against my shoulder. Her tight curls felt like little sponges, soft yet sprightly. She confessed finally, "We may have been used to set them up."

"Really?" After a moment of reflection, I asked, "Eden is that kind of cop?"

She lifted her head, considered my reaction.

She thought about it for a while, then shook her head, "No. He is not. And that means," she paused again, then completed slowly, articulating every word, "He was set up."

The expression on Eden's face flashed back, "Didn't like it much, I'd say." And to myself: I'd say the man looked ready to kick some ass.

That brought a bitter little smile to Dragon's lips. "Not at all," she echoed. And as if she guessed my unspoken thought, she continued, "It won't take him long to find them, and he is not known for hesitation."

◆ ◆ ◆

WE WERE AWAKENED IN THE EARLIEST HOUR OF DAWN FOUR days later by an insistent knocking. When Dragon opened the door, my chaperone with the ponies stepped in and announced, "The Justiciar has made ready." Dragon invited her in and the lieutenant nodded in my direction, obviously weighing her words.

"Well?" Dragon encouraged

"The presence of a chronicler is customary in such matters. Perhaps Lady Ciani's new man is up to the task?"

Dragon's lips came together in a tight line as a somber mood set in. She fairly radiated disapproval. Picking up on it immediately, Eden's lieutenant proposed, "I can guide him in this matter. You need not inconvenience yourself."

Dragon snapped back, "And so it has come to this: Justiciar Pallas tries to tell me I am not involved!"

"Both of you will come, then?" The young woman replied evenly.

She retired outside while we pulled ourselves together and Dragon explained, "I am trained to approach cultures without prejudice, to seek understanding, and to stay as objective and detached as I can. But in spite of my training, Ray, I am troubled by the escalation I am witnessing here. I wonder how much further it will go. I am finding it hard to maintain detachment." After that confession, she retreated into silence.

Turned out the entire operation was over in less than an hour. Eden's troupe used about a half dozen gliders to surprise their quarry in what looked like an Alnese summer cabin on one of the more lush northern islands. A loose circle of mostly sleeping people in front of the cabin were guarded by four woefully inadequate sentries. Eden's foot-soldiers took out the sentries with barely a sound, then moved in on the sleepers with the same silent skill. One by one they were overpowered. Finally, three troopers slipped into the cabin itself, and only then did something like a scuffle ensue. Our lieutenant-chaperone leapt into it, abandoning us briefly to sock it to some rebels who sought to make a run for it.

I had to admire the Arthmin fighters. Stripped down to an elastic, body-hugging jump-suit, they moved with a fluid grace I associate with Asian martial arts back on Earth, with little wasted motion and almost no sound, barely a hint of increased breathing. Every move anticipated the reactions of a foe, as if designed to draw from that opponent energy. The fighting style funneled both offense and defense into a paralyzing defeat.

Soon, two dozen rebels crouched in a subdued circle before the cabin. Most hid their faces from us and from each other, but I could tell they were Alnese. Our chaperone came back and waited at our side as two commandos dragged a woman out of the cabin. Two others pulled something heavy and metallic out behind them, and the rest of Eden's soldiers assembled a collection of bags and cases next to the prisoners.

A hush fell when the man himself, Justiciar Pallas Eden, emerged from the cabin and stepped over to his prisoners. Another lieutenant jumped up and offered him a coat, a formal affair with wide sleeves and a stylized white hunting bird swooping down one side. A crest of some kind, a hawk or maybe an eagle. He made a small hand signal and surveyed his quarry silently as two troopers scrambled back to one of the gliders. They came back with two men from the settler fort and a third man I didn't recognize. He also looked to be a prisoner. My chaperone signaled me to step forward, and soon the settlers, the unknown prisoner, their escorts, and the two of us formed a loose semi-circle around Eden. He stood before one woman from the cabin. The immigrant-settlers and their companions were to my left, while the captive and her escort stood to my right. My chaperone got the translator working and I slipped an ear piece in.

Eden examined the woman. She made every effort to ignore him in return. With her black hair and bluish-white skin, she reminded me of Leila, but more heavy-set, with darker eyes. Eden picked up the metal object brought from the cabin and held it up. It looked like a rocket-launcher. He threw it to the unknown man with one powerful thrust and spoke to the captive. My ear piece seemed specifically tuned into his communications, capturing, "You have much to learn about guerilla warfare, Kuan Kim. Perhaps you should stick to murder in the dead of night."

The unknown man looked down to the launcher at his feet and sighed, then murmured something to one of his guards, who relayed the information with a look and yet another hand signal.

"What should I do with your weapons-supplier, now that he has betrayed you?" Eden asked the woman-prisoner.

She glowered at both Eden and the man, then shrugged, "Would you kill him if I asked you to?"

"You can take him on if you wish it." From his sleeve he took out a long, thin blade and offered it to her.

"Arthmin I am not, Pallas-Justiciar," she shot back.

"That is obvious."

She hesitated, then held out her hand. Eden gave her the knife. She turned to face her former ally, hesitated again, then stepped up to him and stared at him without moving. He was doing his best to control himself, but I caught a sharp intake of breath. She wrapped both of her hands around the handle of the knife and struggled with herself, then we all heard a suppressed sob. Eden, who had stood still as the woman was making her approach, turned around and walked up to them. He placed both of his hands over hers and, with the kind of fluid, economical movement I'd been admiring all through the assault, buried the knife deep inside the man's chest. The man and the woman crumpled to the ground. I heard Dragon cry out behind us and turned to find her staring in shocked surprise.

I turned back to the knot of people to my left. With one hand, Eden jerked the captive back up to her feet as he pulled out his knife with the other. "Do you think war is a game to be played long-distance, without contact, without flesh nor blood? Think again, Kuan Kim. Bury your hands in this blood to feel the blood you spilled from a distance, with clean hands."

The woman choked back a second, louder sob. Eden forced her to kneel, and she stretched out her free hand as if to stem the blood oozing from the man's wound. When he let go of her, she stood back up. Her breathing ragged, she had to lean against one of her guards with one hand to steady herself.

Eden stepped up to her and placed the knife at her throat, said quietly, "You I will give a choice."

She whispered something back which neither I nor my chaperone heard.

Eden stepped back and intoned loudly, for all to hear, "Face me."

The woman did as he asked.

Once again he placed the knife at her throat, and proclaimed in the same loud voice, "Kuan Kim, you have killed six people and two children. They did not injure you. Your actions are an abomination. Now you choose: The justiciar or the ice."

The woman looked over to her companions and back to Eden. With a more steady voice, she announced, "I choose the ice."

Eden removed his knife and continued in the same voice, "You can choose four of your co-conspirators to go with you."

A wave of emotion washed over Kuan Kim's face and she whispered something to her judge that my translater did not catch.

He replied more quietly, "They all knew the risks, did they not?"

She did not respond. A look of horror spread over her features as she covered her mouth with her free hand.

Eden shook his head, "What kind of fool do you take me for? I cannot allow a rebel militia on Alnos, not even in ice. For now, I have offered your militia's work as reparation. It has been accepted. If any of your co-conspirators try to evade us, I'll send Mythras after them and they won't have a choice." After watching her sigh with relief, he added, "I offered two Kuan children, too. The only reason your clan keeps them is because they were not wanted."

He turned to the circle of prisoners to his right and sized them up one by one. Like their leader, they looked young and thoroughly chastened. Eden advised over his left shoulder, "Choose wisely, Kuan Kim. They are your life and you are theirs." Then he turned back to face her one last time, motioned for his deputies to carry out instructions, and started to move away. Passing the spot where I stood with my chaperone, he said curtly, "Answer all his questions." He said it in English.

He walked to where Dragon stood and he extended an arm for her, making it clear that she was to accompany him. She agreed wordlessly, and from my left, I saw the two 'heshti' observers led in the same direction. I looked back at Kuan Kim just as someone motioned for her to come over. She had a forlorn look about her. Sympathy tugged against my memory of the carnage wrought by her actions.

I followed my chaperone back to our assigned seats in the glider. She turned to me and managed to signal acquiescence while making it clear that her attention was still focused on the field in front of us. In the distance, I could see two deputies dragging the collection of rebel arms and materials they had gathered back towards the cabin.

"What am I supposed to do? As a chronicler, I mean."

"A chronicler bears witness."

Not the most helpful answer.

I persisted, "How?"

She shrugged, "That's up to you."

My irritation must have shown, because she continued unprompted, "If you wish to talk to any of the involved parties for your records, now may be the best time. Kim's militia members will be taken to ice or to their construction site soon, and the Justiciar has concluded his business here. We'll be leaving the Islands shortly."

"The construction site?"

"They'll help build a heshti settlement on the Eastern shore of Nyheim."

"That's their sentence?"

"For now. The Justiciar will decide what to do with them once they complete that task. As the leader, Kuan Kim must go into ice, but the others may be salvageable. They'll probably have to serve some time in ice, but they won't be banished there. Justiciar Pallas has started negotiations with our rehabilitation units, to see where they could be sent."

I followed her watchful eye to the circle of rebels. Their heads were together in quiet discussion. The body of the slain arms-dealer had already been taken away, and I could see one deputy set fire to the cabin.

"What is Mythras?"

"The second wave. If Arthmis judgements are not followed, the matter goes to Mythras."

Another unhelpful answer, so I asked, "So … something like special forces?"

I could tell that 'special forces' did not resonate the same way it did for an Earthling, but she tried another explanation, "If Kuan Kim tries to return, Mythras will meet her."

So there were other police corps on this little planet. Considering the skill I had just observed, I doubted that defiance was a good bet.

"Do you people generally … survive in … what was it? Ice?"

"An Arthmin survives. These . . .," she waved a hand as if to say: So-so, about a fifty-fifty chance. I saw some of them embracing now. It looked as if their leader had made her choices.

"I will need names."

"I'll make a list for you. Mostly Kuan and Chantico, and one Minguard."

"And you?"

Her lips quivered up for the briefest moment, "Minguard Lauran."

"You're an Islander?"

She nodded.

Curious now, I tried to keep my examination discreet. She reminded me of some highland Mexicans I had met while cruising through Zacatecas and Jalisco with my cousins once. Same unsettling combination of light and dark. In her case, cinnamon skin and chestnut hair with the most unsettling moss-green eyes. She averted them when my gaze became too obvious.

"What about the dead man?"

"The arms dealer? He was a traveler."

Outsider. Didn't count. I cast another sidelong glance at her, "Did he know?"

"If he didn't, he was a fool."

I wondered how Eden had got him to talk. He hadn't looked worked over, but I couldn't fathom the man just volunteering information about where to find his customers. Maybe he'd thought to save himself with that information, not knowing that his death was pre-ordained. That would make him the fool my chaperone pronounced him to be.

"So I can ask the Justiciar questions if I want?"

A hint of nervousness punctured her studied cool. "I hope to answer to your satisfaction, so the imposition will not be required," she offered.

Whose imposition?

Quite the diplomat, weren't we? I decided not to push that button, "Mostly, you have. Please prepare the list. Later, I'd like you to tell me more about the founding of the order of Arthmis."

It was an unspoken agreement between us. I would steer clear of her boss in return for help learning my new trade.

◆ EPISODE 11 ◆

Dragon Faces the Music

When we arrived at the lodge I was in for another shock: I was led straight into Eden's temporary Islands office to find Lady Ciani.

"Hello, old friend," she greeted me, "the Justiciar has asked me to help resolve the troubles with our young rebels, and with you."

"And what trouble have I given him?" I snapped before I came to my senses. After a deep breath, I bowed and offered an apology, which was countered with a dismissive gesture and one of Lady Ciani's melodic laughs. A second gesture towards a chair followed with, "Please have a seat, Dragon. I will let him explain that."

When he appeared, he had changed clothes and quite obviously washed. He apologized for keeping us waiting, pulled up another chair and sat down in front of us as if for judgment, something lost on neither of us. He collected his thoughts while one of his underlings served us choctea. When the server had gone out again, Eden looked straight at me, but addressed her Grace, "I'm afraid one of my acts has deeply offended our guest today. And since I need her, I cannot let it be a personal matter."

I turned to him, "What would have happened if Kuan Kim had chosen not to go into ice?"

"She would be dead."

"Why didn't the arms dealer have the same choice?"

"It was not convenient."

"You deceived him, didn't you? You made him think he'd get a sentence similar to Kuan Kim's young fighters."

He paused, considered his answer first, then admitted, "Maybe."

"The choice you gave her was . . . understandable. What you did with him was heinous, and I cannot countenance it."

He did not argue with me. We both sat in silence, examining each other across the short distance between our chairs. How could I have spent months observing this man without even suspecting that he was a cold-blooded killer? Just a little logical reflection would have sufficed in alerting me to the possibility, but Justiciar Eden's necessary job qualifications had never even crossed my mind, as if they were irrelevant!

It was Lady Ciani who spoke next, "In our eyes, the arms dealer shares equal responsibility in the crime. The debt weighs equally on him as on Kuan Kemir and her followers."

"I understand, your Grace, and accordingly, he should have had the same choice of judgments."

Eden stayed put.

Finally, I let out a frustrated sigh and asked him point-blank, "How many people have you killed?"

"I have held my title for three years, as you know."

"That is not an answer."

After a short silence, he angled his body slightly towards the regent. "Your Grace," he asked quietly, "Ashewe Dragon may be looking for new hosts now, and it would be a great favor indeed if you were to harbor her until she finds a clan to her liking."

Lady Ciani looked from him to me and back again, then she spoke the traditional formula, "Friends brighten one's house. You are welcome, Dragon," making me sigh again.

She turned to him and asked, "How bad is it?"

He reported in his usual, calm, inflectionless voice, "The situation is much more serious than any of us imagined. I still haven't found the original murderers, and I sense a more experienced hand behind this last group of young fools. I think the heshtis will be satisfied with one death and the banishment for now. Those who've agreed to leave are moving to the Eastern seaboard according to schedule." He paused, shrugged, continued, "But others have armed. The next incident will lead to violence, guaranteed."

"Tomorrow I will ask Kuan House to give up the murderers. The Kuans know how important their conduct has become since my successor will be chosen from among them. They will tell me."

"The heshtis will demand more blood for the original crime."

"If they want a duel, that is their right."

"I see." After a short pause he continued pensively, "Ashewe Dragon may have judged correctly: convenience only counts with strangers." Then he turned back to me, "Four, all with Arthmis. This was my second as Justiciar. So far."

"What is it you want of me?" The anger in my voice betrayed me, and even as I spoke I knew he could tell.

"Help me avert a disaster. First, when we continue to negotiate, tell me where the agitators are."

"You cannot be serious!"

That got through. "I did not come through three years of my office by killing indiscriminately!" he flared.

I had to recognize that, "And second?"

"We need O'bonne mediation, the sooner, the better."

Wise thinking, I had to admit, however grudgingly. I leaned back into my chair and lifted my cup to my lips, contemplated wordings and communication methods. I would have to be prepared for some fancy talk on my own behalf, confess my own lack of discipline. Oh Goddess, another cultural planetologist gone native!

Lady Ciani husked melodiously, "And if she agrees to help us, what have you to offer her in return?"

He said quietly, "I cannot give up the means to avert further bloodshed."

Ignoring him, I proposed, "How about clan status for the newcomers?"

"Clan status?" He shook his head, "These heshtis reject our ties!"

Lady Ciani broke in and cut him off, "Clan status may be possible for their children, eventually. It certainly would be a good starting point for negotiations with our recalcitrant newcomers, if our O'bonne friends would be willing to help us start such a process."

He bowed to her, then said to me, "I can find you a new Arthmis company so our dissociation can proceed. I'll arrange for Pallas Vai to broker introductions with her cousin. She won't be pleased at my interruption of her work, but she'll do me the favor."

I came to a decision then, and informed my interlocutors of it presently, "I am happy to be of service to Alnos and request O'bonne mediation if that is indeed what your Grace and the Council of Eight decide. As for dissociating from you, Pallas Eden, that would make me a poor planetologist, would it not? I would appreciate widening my Arthmis circle, of course, but I will continue my studies, finish what I have started."

Even as I spoke my decision, I wondered how far I was letting personal convenience get in the way of my judgment and dictate my choices, an uncomfortably close parallel to the very behavior I was objecting to. After all, if I really had severed my ties with Pallas Eden and moved to another clan, I would have given up months of my work, and I would have had to decide what to do about Kyet.

◆ EPISODE 12 ◆

Off to Eden Hamlet

Dragon and I were reunited the evening of our eventful day with Justiciar Eden, and she looked only a little less agitated. "I have extended my pact with that devil!" she announced unbidden. I felt like pulling her into a hug, but at the same time, I couldn't really understand her reaction. She must have guessed some of these unspoken thoughts, for she murmured close enough so I could hear, "I suppose I did not stay on Earth long enough to understand . . . convenience."

When I asked her what she was talking about, she only waved me off with "Oh, nothing, nothing," and rubbed her eyes. I finally did pull her into a hug. After some deep sighs, she looked up, black eyes huge and deep, "I can see the sweetness Leila so appreciates."

I smiled a quiet thank you, "Tell me something. Where am I supposed to write up this encounter I bore witness to?"

"When we get back to Pallas House, I will show you. In the meantime," she whipped out a palm-sized little black box and tried to press it into my hand, "You can talk it through on this."

"Talk?" I returned the object. "I don't think so."

"You cannot talk through writing? How interesting."

The exchange had provided the moment of levity she needed.

We returned to Zyss the same day, but we didn't stay. "Time for you to join Leila, and for me," Dragon shot me an oddly shy glance and slipped out before finishing her sentence. Everything was ready for a second journey even as we stepped through the roof-door of the House of Pallas. When we stepped back out to the roof, Goal and Socorro were waiting inside the glider. I embraced the elder and took the baby from her waiting Pallas kinsman.

I did not give her up that night.

We arrived late in Eden Hamlet. The house was different. It looked like a real house, a big villa close to a lake, something that could have come from Earth. I was taken up two flights of stairs to a room also strangely reminiscent of Earth, and my guide did not insist on taking the children elsewhere. I told him to let Leila know I was grateful, then prepared to get as much rest as possible with Socorro and Goal alternately demanding my attention.

The next morning, Goal and I woke up early and slipped away as quietly as possible. She took me down to a large kitchen and dining room facing the eastern sun, a bright and lovely morning sanctuary that beckoned with some promising scents. We found our evening guide there, and this time he introduced himself, and just like in Zyss, the translation to

English was seamless, "Hello again, I'm Pallas Kyet. And you are Raymond, Leila's friend." He looked like a toasted version of Lady Ciani, with a distinct indigo undertone, wavy hair auburn and long, his eyes the same coffee black as Dragon's. I experienced the sensation of coming face to face with an Alien again, and did my very best to suppress it. But once I got over the alien part, I noticed how handsome our young host was. Come to think of it, he reminded me of a young Robert Plant with that wild curly hair flying about his head. "I hear you and Dragon have been over to the Islands."

"Yeah. Is this Leila's place?" was the first casual thing I could think to reply.

He nodded, then added, "I mean, it's a clan house. I think Leila plans to move here. She wants to see you."

I accepted a proffered hot drink and he said with an Alnese timbre, "Choctea." When I sipped it, I knew I would have to get used to it, and couldn't come up with a single thing to say or do. My young host rescued me with a suggestive, "I hear you're a musician?"

"I . . . was one." Before the junk started to outweigh the band.

"My mother belongs to Lann, but as she says, there is a relationship between music and math, so is it any wonder I turned out the way I did?"

I looked at him blankly.

"Lann is what you would call physics, or astrophysics. I was supposed to follow in her footsteps."

"But you're turning into a musician?"

He nodded.

"What do you play?"

"Keystrings. And I dance. You?"

"Bass. Guitars. But in the band it was bass."

Goal piped up behind us, "You're not gonna talk shop, that's just too boring!"

"Ai, little cousin!" Kyet turned around, swooped her into his arms and started to turn round and round. Goal's giggles told me that she was used to his horseplay. When he stopped, she squirmed a bit and cried, "Oh, let me down!"

"Not until you let us be boring," he struggled, trying to maintain his grip on her as she moved all over him like a feisty kitten. She went still, "You can be boring now." She said it in her most regal tone, making clear that she was granting us the good favor. He grinned back and put her down, and she started to hunt around the kitchen.

"Here," he pointed to a pancake-like confection on a stove. "I've been preparing it especially for you."

"As a bribe for him, you mean." But she snapped the plate to her and looked quite pleased.

"I thought I'd give you the grand tour," Kyet directed at me.

The house had four stories. The ground floor held several large rooms that looked like a cross between Alnese clan-halls and the earthly living and sitting rooms more in keeping with the villa's design. The second and third stories were replete with the living quarters I had encountered in Zyss—two or three connected rooms clustered around a walk-in closet and bathroom. Kyet didn't show me the fourth floor. "Uncle Eden works there, and my mother," was all he casually dropped as we passed a narrow, spiraling staircase. He was much more interested in showing me his collection of music paraphernalia, among which I found a Fender guitar just like the one I had left behind on Earth. I wondered if that was truly a coincidence.

"Is this like a Pallas summer villa?" I mused while examining the bass.

"You could say that. Uncle Eden had it built about ten years ago, a year after Goal was born. He worked out the arrangement with Thor house, about the land, and several Thors even came over and helped build it. My mother uses it most. She practically lives here, 'to get away from distractions,' she says. Dragon and Uncle Eden use it frequently, too."

With her sixth sense, Goal had known immediately when the baby had woken up, and had slipped out to go get her. When she rejoined us, she had already prepared a morning bottle. Before I could, Kyet swooped both baby and bottle from her and sat down cooing at Socorro. After he had coaxed her into accepting what was offered, he commented, "This kid has your eyes. Coffee-colored, like mine." He cooed some more and then resumed, "I've always wanted to go to Earth for the music, but with the skin it's a hassle. The only reasonable dye would be as dark as Dragon, and then I'd still look weird. I suppose I'd fit into Brazil. Not a bad place to start."

I tried to picture him with Dragon's skin. He was right about the overall effect.

"Do Alnese often go out and build houses like this?"

He thought about it.

"Started when it got warmer. All that land just sitting there, all these changes just waiting to be explored . . . ," he looked quite dreamy.

"I have to write something up soon."

"Ah yes, and why don't you start by telling me what got under Dragon's skin?"

He started to rock Socorro gently, and I could tell she was going to sleep again. After a few minutes he realized my silence was deliberate.

"I know she went to the Islands to observe Uncle Eden working as a Justiciar. I know what that means, sometimes," he said encouragingly.

I threw him a long look, "Maybe she didn't."

"He . . . took care of somebody else?"

Else?

He broke eye contact, "I see." It was a low murmur, almost a whisper. I scanned the room for Goal. She wasn't paying us any particular attention. Kyet's face resumed the dreamy quality of deep thought. When he came back out of it, he motioned towards his suite's door and said, "I'll show you where you can work for now."

We climbed up the spiral staircase to the top floor and turned down a long, narrow hall with Goal tagging along behind us. The staircase continued up, and an undercurrent of curiosity tugged at me as we stepped out into the hall. Mostly empty rooms jutted to our right and left. Kyet stopped at the third, where a long, flat desk on slender, gently curved legs greeted us. "One of Leila's," he informed me with a proud little smile. I recognized her style. Behind it a counter ran the length of the wall, rounded the corner to a sky-light window that could be propped open. The machinery on the wall didn't look too strange, though I couldn't read any of the lettering.

Kyet waved me to what looked like an ordinary office chair and bade me sit in it, "It'll read your body and adjust itself, and from now on it'll be ready for you." Even as he spoke, I could feel subtle, comfortable changes. He put the sleeping baby down on a loveseat in one corner, disappeared, and came back with what looked like a little laptop computer. When he snapped it open, that's exactly what it turned out to be, a laptop with an English-based keyboard. He fumbled to place it on a corner of the desk and adjusted a little socket in the wall until a thin laser-light briefly made contact, "You can chronicle in your language for now. The CPU will translate. When you're ready to switch, you can use this one." He brushed over a corner of the elegant, slim desk, and a second, built-in screen and keyboard with the funny Alnese characters emerged.

"Do these things do music, too?"

"Yeah. Leila told me about your newer computers. I'll rig yours for the programs you're used to."

We were so immersed in our joint exploration that we didn't notice the woman who came into the room until Goal squeaked, "Auntie!"

"Ah," Kyet sat up, "Ray, meet my mother, Vaideh of Pallas, or Pallas Vaideh, as we say here."

His mother nodded a greeting and readied herself just in time for Goal's enthusiastic embrace. "Actually, in this house, it's Vai. So you've come. Have you seen Cousin Leila yet?" I could see the family resemblance with both her son and Leila. Long, curly black hair cascaded wildly about her dark face and dark eyes. Unlike Kyet and even Leila, though, she was a little on the pudgy side. She extricated herself from Goal and moved closer to the loveseat, "May I see the little one?"

I'm not sure she saw me nod, as her eyes were already fixated on Socorro. After a brief examination, she said with a satisfied grunt, "Finally, a kid that takes after me! I've been waiting a long time for one like her!"

I could see Kyet roll his eyes, "What a heartbreak I turned out!"

"Indeed!" She sounded dead serious. "So, has my son at least extended proper hospitality?"

I nodded.

"And this jotun-witted fool thought she would have peace and quiet in Eden Hamlet." She still sounded serious.

"I'm a quiet man."

"So gossip tells it, but I will make my own determination. You," she shook a finger at her son, "What did you do to Dragon? The woman looks like she's half out of her mind."

"It wasn't him," I pre-empted.

Her eye-brows arched up, then down again. "Islanders!" This time the grunt sounded decidedly dissatisfied.

I felt obliged to add, "Eden, actually."

"An Arthmin matter," clarified Kyet.

"Is that why he wants me to escort her about and introduce her to cousin Medece? I don't have time for this nonsense!" She shook her head, "You'd think an O'bonne planetologist studying our legal system would pick up a thing or two, wouldn't you. She's been shadowing him since winter, and she's surprised when he has to kill someone? And she has Dragon eyes!"

Kyet observed behind us, "I don't think Ray has the faintest idea of what you are talking about."

I ignored him, "Her reaction does seem . . . intense."

"O'bonne moralists! Who needs them!"

"Will you stop insulting a Pallas guest!"

We all fell silent. Presently, she raised both shoulders in an emphatic shrug and asked me, "Were you working right now?"

I shook my head.

"Well then, now that you've interrupted me, I'll get some breakfast. Why don't you all accompany me?"

It seemed a good idea, so we did.

◆ ◆ ◆

After breakfast, my O'bonne guide made a whole selection of O'bonne information available to me in English. A lot of the material took the form of transcribed talks given at one time or another by Dragon's O'bonne predecessors on Alnos. Some I found particularly instructive. Here's one that caught my eye because it described the very people I had just been introduced to:

> Alnese Martial Orders: Some Reflections on their Regulating Functions in their Society. Talk presented by cultural planetologist Ndinzi Nyemba at the 280th biannual meeting of the Cultural Planetology Society, Anno 4093, at the First O'bonne University.
>
> In recent years, Mutaka (4013), Makalanyone (4028) and Tebe (4055) have all attempted functional analyses of Alnese quasi-religious orders. Mutaka ascribed only a religious function to them and has written extensively about their regulation of religious ritual on Alnos.

But as Makalanyone and Tebe have since pointed out, orders like the Order of Tchen, to which all of Alnos' medical personnel belongs, or the Alnese Astrophysical Society, the Order of Lann, hardly fit Mutaka's analysis. And even the Order of Pallas-Métis, deeply involved in the Alnese pantheistic religion though it may be, does not fit the model proposed in that first analysis. I propose that Alnese orders help organize Alnese society and codify behavior through their activities, activities to which, significantly, adolescents have initial access.

As far as we know, Alnese orders are fairly loosely constituted, quite in contrast to Alnese clan structure. Most orders have a specific founder and have woven an elaborate mythology around this figure. Membership is open to anyone for any order; aspiring members simply need to show an interest in the occupational activity of the order in question. However, maintaining membership is by no means easy. Only worthy followers of the exemplary founders deserve to remain, and the pressure to equal or outshine saintly founders is even more acute for positions of leadership and control. Of course, the more prestigious and established the order, the greater the need to excel.

In the interest of saving time, I shall limit my comments here to one particular group of Alnese orders, the half-dozen or so martial orders I have investigated for the last two years. Alnese martial orders evince an almost militaristic social organization. They are much more hierarchical than most other organizations on the planet, though of course they still have a few of the famous features of Alnese anarchism. The Order of Arthmis is the planet's major martial body, and members (called "Arthmin") are consistently called into action when foul play overwhelms clan elders, who typically resolve disputes. The lowest ranked Arthmin are its cadets and new recruits, followed by journeymen, full members, temporary 'lieutenants' whose tenure ranges from four weeks to four years, and finally, the titled "Justiciar" or permanent leader of a particular troop ranging from 32 to 64 members.

A Justiciar commands complete obedience, whereas everybody else can expect what could be termed "reasonable" obedience from lower-ranked individuals. A Justiciar's title is earned over several years, and inscribed with permanent tattoos over the course of four to eight months on the title-holder's body. In a manner typical of all things Alnese, lieutenant positions are constantly rotated as specific needs or missions come up. A first lieutenant usually holds that position for four years, while second lieutenants typically assume leadership roles over eight of their fellow Arthmin for four or eight months. Lieutenants or deputies therefore have no permanent claim to power, and cannot lord it over their colleagues for too long.

Arthmis includes an elite corps that functions almost independently, Mythras, the so-called "second wave". Mythrans typically take over when the decisions and judgments of Arthmis have been challenged or ignored. They also frequently concern themselves with matters involving planetary security and dealing with visitors from other worlds. Mythras bestows its own permanent title, the title of 'Legate', but follows Arthmis organization in every other respect.

Martial orders have considerable executive powers in matters of public behavior. They carry out investigations of suspected crimes and mete out justice in accordance with Alnese laws and traditions. As most of you already know, Alnos has no jails. Most judgments involve making aggrieved parties whole, with most convicts agreeing to appropriate restitutions. Serious crimes only have two possible outcomes: Banishment or death.

Typically, Alnese convicted of serious crimes are sent "into ice" to fend for themselves. How much time they must remain in the arctic banishment zone and how much training and support they get to survive their time in ice depends on the severity of their offenses. In part, this "shunning" is meant to teach the consequences of anti-social behavior. Those who refuse to comply or try to return before completing their ice penance are killed. Death sentences are also carried out for very serious crimes like murder, particularly if a victim's family requests it.

Of course my detractors will immediately point out that Alnese society lacks the characteristic paranoia associated with the presence of powerful police societies. Their point is well taken. I suspect that the

> strong Alnese family and clan structure, at the core of all social relations on Alnos, circumscribe the power of the martial orders even in matters not already defined as personal rather than public. Unraveling the Byzantine complexity presented by the interplay between clans and orders on Alnos is my current challenge as I continue my analyses.
>
> Thank you very much for your patient and attentive reception of these few speculative remarks.

Eden's Lieutenant Minguard Lauran had done a pretty good job explaining what had happened in the Islands, but this O'bonne talk definitely added to my understanding of what had gone down. And as I kept exploring, I found that of all the materials available to me, O'bonne reports and O'bonne research were the most instructive, even when they were written for a more acadmic crowd than me.

◆ EPISODE 13 ◆

Leila Takes Stock

So they've brought you here.

Socorro reminds me daily how deeply you burrowed into my being.

Without sound nor fury, just those soulful black eyes.

After all the sound and fury with Eden, you suited me.

It did take almost seven years.

I learned all about comfort. You would sit close to me with your acoustic guitar, strum a few chords, and start to sing an old folk song. You would play hide and seek with Goal and her little Swiss friends for hours. You would take the sand paper out of my hand and finish the corner that had to be sanded down.

And you listened so well.

For hours.

For days.

Through my long silences.

Strung together my little stories like worry beads, as if getting ready for a rosary.

Comfort.

The old farm house in LaVaud wrapped around us like the softest Alnese cashmere blanket, a cocoon of Swiss routine punctured by the occasional excitement of your touring. Another advantage of hooking up with a musician, especially one good enough to find steady work on Earth. Goal and I grew quite spoiled.

And after seven years, I let the comfort take root and express itself, embody itself inside of me.

Comfort.

Love.

And that's when all the trouble between us started.

Isn't it?

◆ EPISODE 14 ◆

Dragon's Dilemma

Kyet caught up with me in my Alnese vacation suite, where I had sought refuge from the maelstrom of my thoughts. I looked up and saw him standing in the doorway, waiting. I had never seen any martial tattoos on his limbs, yet a moment of panic flashed through me as I realized, *Goddess, he could be one of them. He moves just like one of these killers, does he not?* I couldn't deny him any longer, but I tried, offering no welcome, hardening my voice and lambasting, "So which one are you with? Arthmis? Mythras?" And when he shook his head from the doorway, I continued in the same accusing tone, "Then why do you move like they do?"

"What?"

"Just now you came up and I didn't hear a sound! I recognize the same stealth, the same grace."

Unbidden, he stepped across the threshold towards me, "Azetmir, I'm a dancer!" Reaching the bed where I'd reclined to regain a calmer state, he crouched down, waiting to be sent off. When I didn't lash out again, he flowed to his knees and reached for my hands with his, sending further tremors into my reeling mind. He leaned forward ever so slightly, and I shrank from him. He stopped, flowed back up, seated himself on the edge of my bed, then moved one pair of joined hands slowly, gently, giving me every chance to withdraw, and touched my hand against his cheek.

"It's true that Eden trained me. With my father. They did it for their own reasons. Azetmir, what's the matter?"

"If I tried to explain to you, you would never understand."

"Because I am not O'bonne and you are not Alnese."

We had traveled down this road so many times, both refusing to hear the other. I the experienced adult, he the romantic youth, we each knew we were right. With such notions I had resisted him almost an entire winter, had refused to acknowledge the intoxicating effect of this boy-man, this native, this alien, only to fall all the harder when I finally gave in. And now my O'bonne mind told me to seize on this chance to break off what must surely be a disaster in the making, while my body was beginning to hum with the blood-fever we had unleashed together.

Perhaps sensing my lack of resolve, he grew a little bolder. He moved my hand from his cheek to his lips. When I started to withdraw it, he held on, slipped his lips over the tips of my fingers. Slight tingling gradually turned into dew drops of pleasure down my spine.

I did withdraw the hand.

"O'bonne . . . never kill?"

"Oh," I almost laughed, "even O'bonne suffer from moments of madness."

"Go on."

"This was cold-blooded murder masquerading as law enforcement."

His lowered our joined hands, rested his left one on my right knee. He leaned forward and brushed against the other knee with his mouth. He adjusted his position forward and his hair tumbled into my lap as he kissed his way down, then laid his cheek against my flesh and waited to be pushed off. I wrapped my fingers into the tangled mass of curls and tugged gently. His hands slid down my legs, slipped under my day gown, fingernails scraping. I tugged a little harder, let go with one hand and pulled him up with the other until we were face to face again, and this time, when he leaned forward, I stayed still.

"Azetmir, I'm not with Arthmis. I'm not with Mythras. I'm not with Tomrys. I'm not with Kalafo," he whispered just before brushing against my lips. "I am a Pallas, and Eden's my uncle," he continued more soberly, "I didn't think O'bonne were into guilt by association. Use your Dragon sight and tell me if I'm lying."

My hand, still tangled in his hair, turned into a fist. He quieted under it, let me ride out the wave of conflict washing through me. When he felt my body relaxing, he reached for my face and stilled it for our first lovers' kiss. The drops of pleasure mixed with a dry sob I could not suppress, and he broke it off, pulled my head to his shoulder just as Ray had. I hiccupped through another sob, my emotions dissolving into a mixture of tears and tingling. "What Dragon sight? I didn't see the attack coming. I didn't know Eden was going to sacrifice that arms dealer to convenience. I didn't know Alnos is on the verge of civil war."

"Civil war?" He stopped and sat back, "We have some problems, true, but let's not get carried away. Maybe you didn't see the attack coming in the Islands because you've been so immersed with your studies, you're out of practice. When I don't practice, my dancing unravels."

Immersed in my studies indeed. I had sought refuge in my studies from the emotions stirred up by our unexpected spring thaw after two Alnese winters by myself. Observing Pallas Eden adjudicate this and that disagreement, observing him meet with colleagues and lieutenants to coordinate his work with other Arthmis companies ... what better way to distract myself? Add to them all our subsequent friendly meetings to hash out historical questions and pursue endlessly contradictory aspects of Alnese contractual law as if great consequences would follow from our discussions. Limitless access to the inner workings of an Arthmis group—what a perfect, most seductive bribe for an Obonne scholar!

After two years immersed in Alnese history with nary a care for the present, I clung to that comfort zone once Kyet fissured my Alnese stay. But I could no longer deny the fissure, the present, Kyet's thorough disruption of my ordered, scholarly life. Trying to clear my mind by pursuing yet more information, I smoothed out my voice as much as I could and asked, "So you're not one of them, but you've trained like one of them. Why?"

"Oh my." He averted his eyes, suppressed a sigh. "It's a little embarrassing."

I stilled my heart, focused clearly on the quality of his voice.

"You know my lineages. Xhania and Nandez come from my father. He shared those lineages with one other person for twenty-two years, until she gave up all ties to serve Alnos. I was three years old at the time."

"Lady Alnos Ciani."

"My former aunt. That and," he paused, "his work ... He thought it would make me a target. He started training me from the day I took my first step."

Many O'bonne planetologists had wondered how real the disavowal of family and clan ties by Alnese rulers was. We knew it was real enough to have prevented blood relatives from succeeding each other in the seventeen centuries since their arrival on the planet, but that didn't tell us anything about other, less obvious forms of influence. After all, the Catholic Popes on Earth had been subject to similar rules, and they had found many ways to subvert them. "A target?" I repeated.

"Not everyone understands our customs, and it's not that hard to make the connection. Dad isn't paranoid about it, but he's always taken precautions."

"Precautions?" An uncomfortable realization hit me like a bucket of cold water in the depth of an Alnese winter: our secret was most likely shared by a number of faceless Alnese bodyguards. I marveled mostly to myself, "I've never noticed anything."

"If you had, my father would be very disappointed in his people." A shy caress feathered over me, then he kept one finger on each knee, "I could have alerted you to it. I didn't. I'm sorry."

And I could have used my head and figured out that in an affair with Lady Ciani's only nephew, whether disavowed or acknowledged, discretion took on a whole new dimension. I closed my eyes and asked, "So they know? Your parents? Your clan?"

"I don't think so. My bodyguards keep me safe; they don't spy on me." He inched a little closer to me and murmured against my right ear, "Azetmir, I know how important it is to you to keep our relationship private, and I've really tried. My bodyguards suspect something, sure, but that's as far as it goes. And in any case, they don't report on my activities."

He moved my hand down and let me feel him hardening to my touch. Our current sparked through me, but I held back. When I had taken leave of my good O'bonne senses to take a native lover, I had fooled myself into thinking I would be able to keep it secret. Wrong. Passion really is a form of temporary insanity, as we O'bonne well know, and in my case, it had eclipsed my rational mind fully. I forced myself to consider the likely consequences of my continued entanglement with this man-boy, tried to channel the heat rising through me out of my mind, to disconnect from my own flesh.

He let go of my hand. I withdrew it only a little, let it rest on his thigh.

He grew very still, then edged my hand back between his legs, leaned forward and closed in on my ear again to whisper, "Please don't ask me to stay away from you. I couldn't. Not now. My senses sing for you, Azetmir." My hands came alive for a long caress down his back. The tingling I had tried to disconnect trickled back, quickened into a pulse that echoed through me.

I straightened my legs out from under me, dove back into his hair and locked onto his mouth. The flame had been lit and it was dripping into my fingers, my breasts, dripping between my legs. I let the rush of desire pulse through me and accepted his body's pressure towards the pillows, accepted his bolder entanglement with me once there.

"Azetmir. Azetmir." He caught both my hands in his, tugged me closer, stretched out next to me. Our dance turned rhythmic, indolent, smooth with a few more vigorous volleys. A rush of blood coursed through me, and I thought I could hear the pumping action of my hormone-mad heart beating itself into a frenzy. We were spinning off into our senses, into breaths and moans and shudders of delight, and pleasure overwhelmed all concerns.

◆ EPISODE 15 ◆

Raymond Reunites with Leila

What do you say to someone who has saved your life? You shouldn't have? Especially after you first taste life again, really taste it, feel the sweetness of water on your tongue, feel cool air against your skin, feel sensations you thought you'd dulled out for good.

Leila was wary during that first meeting, wary and sorry. I could see it in her eyes, her caution, her silences. Like every other resident of this blasted planet, she walked in on me early in the morning, before I had even had time to braid my hair. What is it with these good people? Couldn't one of them turn out to be a night owl? After a few minutes of awkwardness, we both felt compelled to talk. We started at almost the same time.

"I hear . . . "

"So this . . . "

She nodded for me to finish first, and I mumbled, "So this is your world."

"It is." She pulled a chair up and sat down. "How do you like it?"

"It's all right."

And as much as my father, and my mother, would have hated it, I felt myself agreeing with my grandmother: It does matter how someone looks to you. This time, stealing looks at Leila's yellow eyes, I tried to make it not matter, and I couldn't. I wanted to trace her body all over again, check every bone under that white skin with its faint undertone. And I had to ask, "How much blue blood do you have in your veins?"

But they don't have blue blood; it's red.

She volunteered her hand and I turned it up and down, staring. "Lady Ciani's mother and my father were brother and sister, that's why I have the same eyes. But many of the people in my family came from traveling."

"A bunch of mutts, eh?"

"This is a planet of mutts." After a second of reflection, she added, "Except for the heshtis who refuse to breed in. I don't get them."

She withdrew her hand, sat back.

"What about Eden?" I wanted to know.

"What about him?"

"Well first, why does he look so European? And second, in view of his abilities, and his power, why hasn't he slit my throat and eliminated the competition?"

"First, he is human-European, at least half, that's why he looks it. Second, there is no competition."

"You're sure about that?"

"Are you worried?"

That was the Leila I knew all right! For a second we had succeeded in dispelling the ghosts between us.

I continued with, "Who gave him that name?"

"I don't know. I never asked him."

Raymundo was my grandfather's name, but I didn't tell her that. Instead, I decided to bite the bullet, "All right, now what?"

The ghosts came back.

"I'm sorry, Ray. I shouldn't have let you think she had died."

I accepted the apology with the tiniest nod.

I even offered her an olive branch, "Was it just one needle too many?" And I remembered our last few days on earth, Socorro hovering between delirium and coma, ravaged by the auto-immune disease triggered by our inter-species incompatibilities, and me making sure I didn't live a single conscious moment of it. I could understand Leila casting off the dead weight. In the beginning, she'd announced that she didn't consider drugs a problem, much to my delight. Then, in the face of my steady descent from the occasional dalliance to my binges, some of that Alnese tolerance wore off. Her protective interference (keeping both the smack and the needles clean) had become first more reflective, then more grudging.

"I didn't think that you cared one way or the other."

Well, I had set her straight about that.

"Now what?" I repeated.

"It's up to you."

"What does that mean?"

"You'll have to choose. Do you want to stay with the children? Go back to Earth?"

"I left Earth before you brought me here."

"You want to stay?"

"Why not?" Then I asked, "How will that sit with your relatives?"

"Can't you tell everyone here wants the baby? They'll put up with you."

My next question was not easy, "Is she . . . all right?"

She looked at me gravely, then said, "Peg worked hard. Now she predicts normal physical and mental development for Socorro."

I tried to communicate my gratitude without speaking it. I still hadn't forgiven Leila, not completely, but wondered whether I had been forgiven.

"Would you like . . . to help me with my hair?"

One of Leila's favorite morning rituals. She got up, found the brush, came back and started. Her fingers slipped into the familiar rhythm of untangling and brushing, untangling and brushing, separating the strands, weaving a secure braid that wouldn't have fly-aways after the first hour. When she was done, I put one hand on her knee to keep her next to me. I put an arm around her and tried to gather her to me, but she resisted, remained stiff. And I realized that my anger wasn't as strong as my need for something I had sacrificed to my addiction a long time ago: our comfort with each other.

I came to a decision then.

I slipped down to the floor in front of her and kneeling, I looked up, "What do you want in return?"

"I don't know. Start by not making promises you can't keep."

"One day at a time, eh?"

"One day at a time."

We stayed like until I felt her relax a little, as if she'd started exhaling.

◆ EPISODE 16 ◆

Dragon Redirects her Studies

Having been wrested from my long dalliance with Alnese history and swept into Alnese history-in-the-making, I determined to hunt down the few analyses—O'bonne or other—that might give me some insight into the unique dynamics of the present situation. I returned to Eden Tower—which Eden very thoughtfully vacated—and used his links to generate subspace access to our master files. It took a few days for request and clearance to wind their way through sub-space channels, and the inevitable space static played the usual havoc with the netted files, but in the end I had a reasonable collection of studies at my disposal. I went to work.

I made short shrift of our contributions on the subject: Even O'bonne scholarship, for all its breadth, had rarely encountered an immigrant assimilation problem stemming from a flat refusal by the immigrant group to adapt to their new world. The few documented cases, however, proved quite instructive.

One of the more troublesome attitudes I had encountered during my period of Island observations was the utter contempt of Alnese spiritual practices exhibited by the newcomers. The Alnese use of the unflattering and ominous term "alien" for the settlers was matched by the latters' almost exclusive use of the word "pagan"—a term that didn't even exist in Alnese and for which we all used a Kobran loan word—for their hosts. After several days of hearing them whining about the "cults" practiced on Alnos, and after eliciting some less guarded comments several days into Eden's attempted mediation, I realized to my horror that the settlers saw Alnese religious orders as a collection of witches' covens which they associated with their own anti-god. They had no understanding whatsoever of Alnos' spirituality. Their attitude amounted to an incompatibility I couldn't begin to unravel!

The Alnese refusal to grant their new population full Alnese citizenship was not arbitrary. It stemmed mostly from a flat-out rejection by immigrants to engage in social and religious practices considered concomitant with being Alnese. To be Alnese meant to participate fully in the never-ending inter-clan dynamics of rivalries and alliances. It meant accepting the clan as the basis of all social and familial relationships, and that included a certain mindfulness of ancestors and ancestral inheritance the newcomers equated with ancestor worship. Professional and occupational participation in Alnese society meant entering into the parallel system of Alnese orders, many of which also combined occupational fellowship with their own spiritual practices. Alnos' resistant immigrants rejected both systems with uncommon vehemence. Their rather rigid religious and social convictions clashed with Alnese beliefs in both areas.

I had suggested to Lady Ciani that the Alnese explore conferring clan status on newcomer settlements; now I realized just how impossible that would be. On the surface of it, turning settler family groups into clans was an easy transformation. In reality, it meant re-structuring immigrant family life. The settlers had fairly fixed ideas about social and family roles, and adhered to a patriarchal family system maximizing the accumulation of property. By Alnese standards, immigrant settlers were quite obsessed with amassing material wealth. That tended to discourage exogamy, and thus inhibit the formation of inter-clan alliances, the basis of the entire Alnese social order. The goal of material accumulation also created a whole other layer of conflict with the Alnese, who did not consider nearly as many "material" things alienable enough to be owned and traded. Instead, to the consternation of their newcomers, the Alnese viewed many social and familial relationships very flexibly.

How to resolve incompatibilities like these? One opening, perhaps the only opening, lay in Alnese flexibility in defining social and familial roles. Perhaps that flexibility could allow the Alnese to see some of the less male-dominated extended settler-families as transitional clans, and perhaps they could pursue some temporary relationships with them. Once nursed into being, such transitional clans and their temporary alliances with their Alnese neighbors could at least set inter-clan alliance dynamics in motion. I couldn't afford to be overly optimistic. For one thing, it was hard to imagine Alnese women agreeing to any kind of relationship with settler-families. Whichever results I extrapolated from my models, the integrative process between the two groups looked protracted, probably too slow to defuse the crisis growing between the two communities.

As I mulled over my reports and demographic models, it became clear to me that Eden understood a good deal more about the problems brewing beneath the still calm surface of things than I had given him credit. He knew that an inevitable confrontation was in the works, and that the religious elements of this show down could make it intractable. Having ruled out the possibility of a win-win type of agreement, and knowing full well what the Alnese were capable of should they feel threatened, he was trying to avert a worst-case scenario. I began to understand why he was so unyielding on the question of land tenure, and on granting any clan-rights to unassimilating settlers. It was of paramount importance to keep up the pressure on immigrants so alternatives would at least be explored. It was equally imperative to minimize contact so as to minimize provocations.

In keeping with our devil's bargain, Eden told me about a challenge he received after closing in on his suspects. The martial Order of Tomrys, a group of enforcers particularly popular in the Islands, had challenged him to a duel. If he won, he might get more information. If he lost, he'd agreed to conclude his official investigation and retreat from the Islands.

The Tomrys challenge told us who might be behind Kuan Kim's little band of would-be fighters, and that made me privately appreciate the measures taken by Eden. If Tomrys was behind the current low-intensity fighting, the next round would surely be of a different caliber, and that could precipitate a much broader conflict. We reviewed my analysis and both agreed that his initial dismissive appraisal of the motives behind the Island murders had been wrong. Though we still didn't know how immigrant settlers had incited the Islanders, we concluded that something quite outrageous must have occurred.

I shuddered at the thought of a Tomrys-led movement against immigrant-settlers. Not only would it make the Island-murders look like a picnic, but it would also set one martial order against the other. Then it would be only a matter of time before the Alnese would unite against their common foe—and we both knew who that would be.

As Eden told me in one less guarded moment, "Then what? If my people close in on them, where could the heshtis retreat to? We have no other world to give them."

◆ EPISODE 17 ◆

Raymond Has an Audience with Eden

In Eden Hamlet, Kyet took it upon himself to introduce me to Alnese music. It had a vocal emphasis, a surprising fact considering the possibilities of their technology. Picking up on my reaction, he explained, "It's the climate. Music here has always been intimate, something for the clan room at night. It's hard to host spectacles in enclosed spaces." Made sense.

He took me to a structure at the other end of Eden Hamlet's garden, a dance studio on top of a boat house with a view to the lake. We hooked up the base and his keystrings and jammed together. He surprised me. He obviously knew enough about Earth music to come up with some interesting riffs. "You know any drummers?" I joked as we were winding down over choctea, the local morning brew, "We could start a local band."

He thought I was serious, "We have some percussion, but nothing like your African rhythms."

That much talent wasn't needed. When I told him, he caught on to my tone, and we had a good time spinning our wheels, thinking up one more implausible scenario after the other. Then, when Goal popped in, we monkeyed around a bit. Goal got into the keystrings and, with Kyet's help, composed some ditties which I mercifully erased once she returned to the main house. Before taking off, she dropped casually, "Dad's back." She stayed long enough to observe the unmistakable "oh oh" cross both Kyet's and my face.

I felt comfortable enough with him to inquire, "What is it?"

"He's probably here for Az- um, Dragon. You?"

"I'm not all that sure he wants his wife's lover around."

"Oh that! Not to worry!"

"And what does he want from Dragon? She's made it clear she hates his guts."

"It's the heshti problem. I've heard there are armed bands now. Eden is trying to settle the situation, and he wants her help. O'bonne are excellent mediators. They know how to find common ground. I think he'd like her to start helping now, before the O'bonne mediators he's requested arrive, because she's got Dragon eyes."

"What's that?"

"All O'bonne are empathic to some extent, and with her it's truth sense. She knows when you're trying to hide something."

I could see the advantage in that.

"How long has this thing with the immigrants been going on?"

"You mean with the murders?"

"No, in general."

"I don't know. Before, we never had any problems with travelers. Now they want our planet, but they don't want to respect our ways. Do you think that's right?"

"I . . ." had heard statements like that before, both in San Anto and in Berlin, but he obviously hadn't. I didn't think he knew how far his attitude had been taken on Earth, so I decided to waffle, "I don't know enough about it."

He didn't press me.

◆ ◆ ◆

Kyet informed me that Eden had not come for Dragon after all, but to take a short break from his duties after the immediate crisis of the Islands shelling had been resolved. Rumor had it that he was closing in on at least one of the original Islands killers, and that he needed resting up for that next confrontation.

I don't know what I had expected. A patriarch maybe, dominating this odd familial configuration, pretending to tolerate my presence even as he was plotting my demise. Days passed and there was no sign of Eden. It was almost as if he didn't live in his own house. At first I took that to be an unspoken message to me, and I obliged by staying out of his way. Then I realized that he had a general aversion to people, and that the only ones he suffered—and then mostly at appointed times and for specific activities—were the hyperactive power-packs masquerading as children in our midst. Still, when he called me up to his monk's cell, I put off going until he sent Goal down to get me.

"Come on Ray!" It was funny seeing a child her size bundle

me up all those stairs. "I haven't been there for days." Her eyes were bright with excitement at the prospect of invading her father's forbidden domain.

When I stepped into his tower room, his eyes were already on me. "Here," he nodded towards the screen, "My intelligence officer finally cracked the code."

He leaned back just enough for me to read the intercepted missive, obligingly translated from its original Kobran into English for me:

> The Pallas Justiciar is in a secret hamlet on the southwestern shore of a glacier-lake at the foothills of the Midient Mountains, but we have been unable to penetrate their communications. Our suspicions are that the Earthling has disappeared there as well, although we still don't know why he was brought to Alnos. We have not been able to get the story behind his secret hospitalization, or what brought the leader of the medical society as well as Lady Ciani herself to him. Officially, he's a chronicler. Intelligence has been put on the alert to try to uncover the real purpose of his sudden appearance and subsequence disappearance.

"You've stirred some waves." Eden remarked.

"What is it?"

"One of the many messages we intercept daily."

"From spies?"

"Something like that. For the longest time, only O'bonne scholars would come here, but ever since the climate changed, there's been an upsurge of interest in the former Space Gypsies. Even the great Kobra is wooing us."

His voice dripped with irony, but it wasn't directed at me. Kobra—Doctor Peg's favorite planet, the inter-stellar power player in these parts. I read over the intercepted message again, concluded, "I didn't know I was important enough to get noticed by interstellar spies."

This time Eden smiled up at me, "Of course you didn't."

He turned around and the screen behind him dimmed, "Actually, while I thought it might be amusing for you to read it, I really wanted to talk to you about the implant." Goal took advantage of the opening presented by his new posture and crawled into his lap. He put an arm around her and said to her in Alnese, "You're getting too old for this, you know."

"The implant?" I echoed.

"Something we use. To learn languages, and . . . other things. Peg sent it over, and advised that you're well enough to receive it. It's something like a neurochip that sets up a feed-back loop with your neurolinguistic centers. Usually, you get fluent within weeks, and become near-native within months."

"So this would be for my Alnese?"

"Yes."

"And it needs to be implanted?"

"It's a neurosurgical device. We implant it close to the affected brain areas. It's made from material that eventu-ally dissolves and is absorbed by your body. You needn't be concerned about any immune reaction. We have tried it on humans."

Looking at him like that, next to his daughter, I could

see a physical resemblance that her coloring obscured. Her eyes had almost the exact same shape as his, only the color was green instead of steely-gray. Her nose followed the same straight line, her lips had the same fullness.

"If you have the implant," he continued, "that could facilitate your accompanying Dragon, Vai and myself when we return to the Islands. I shall need a chronicler again, and her Grace is happy to lend you to me if I may so impose on you."

I broke off my examination, "Go right ahead."

"I'll tell Eden Hamlet's physician. Thank you."

There was a note of dismissal in the last words.

"You want to stay here?" I asked Goal.

She nodded.

He tousled her hair and murmured, "I think it would be better if you join me again for practice."

"Okay." She stood up and reached for my hand. As I later observed, Goal didn't argue with her father. She didn't argue with her mother, either. Just with me.

Practice was a daily ritual of his, usually together with Kyet. That night, I decided to accompany Goal and observe them.

We reached Kyet's dance studio—which doubled for Eden's practice sessions—right after they had started. They both wore skin-tight exercise garments that looked like a cross between spandex shorts and scuba diving skins, leaving legs and arms exposed. Kyet sported the powerful, yet lean musculature of a dancer. He was well matched by the older man, who looked, if anything, even stronger and more powerful. Kyet had tied his unruly curls back and wore a bright, multicolored headband around his forehead. Eden wore a simpler headband with the same stylized raptor I had noticed on his Justiciar coat. Tatooed blue wings spanned the length of each arm, with the final, longest feather pointing to each wrist.

They circled each other. Again, I admired the economy of every move. When Kyet lunged at Eden, the latter barely moved back, yet the youth found himself flying right past the older man. He had to make an obvious effort to stay on his feet.

"You gave that one away," Eden evaluated coolly.

Kyet's next attack was more effective. The men locked into a wrestling-like pose. Kyet pushed a leg under one of Eden's and struck him off balance. Even as the older man was falling, though, he managed to land a painful blow on the younger's midriff, and Kyet doubled over just long enough to let go of his quarry.

"Better," came Eden's judgment.

He followed up on it by pulling Kyet towards him, spinning him around and almost getting him down on the floor, but the youth broke Eden's grip and twisted out from under him.

They circled each other again.

"Knives?" Kyet proposed.

Eden shrugged.

They went to a little table next to Goal and me, and each chose a weapon reminiscent of the one I had seen Eden use the day of Kuan Kim's judgment. The next few thrusts and parries held an extra note of excitement. Each man was more careful, yet at the same time Kyet showed a grim determination to score points. He gradually grew bolder, slicing ever closer to Eden in his attacks. Sweat and heavy breathing permeated the studio. During a moment taken to adjust headbands, I heard Eden mutter, "Keep it that serious." Kyet nodded.

The next time the two locked onto each other Kyet successfully used his leg trick to tumble Eden, who rolled off barely in time to miss the blade directed at his chest. He got back to his feet slowly, watching every move. Several near-misses followed, with either one or the other man managing to command an advantageous angle for a fraction of a second. The two knives even met once, and Kyet's quicker twist drew blood from the older man's hand.

After one more successful stratagem tumbling Eden to the floor, Kyet pounced again, but this time Eden was way ahead of him, so that Kyet found himself knifing empty space. The older man twisted into position behind the younger, shot one side-kick at the back of Kyet's left knee, and grabbed his hair as he went down. I heard a muffled oath. Eden snapped Kyet's head up and placed his knife at the exposed throat. Kyet went rigid, then, as if to signal surrender, slowly relaxed under Eden's knife. The victor removed the knife from the young man's throat, "The hair really gives me an advantage, you know." He said it as if to apologize.

"Never seems to give you one with my father," came the cocky reply.

"True." Eden held out a hand and I thought I could see Kyet weighing one last trick in his mind, then casting the thought aside. Eden looked amused, helped him up.

"You know, if you are really serious about being matched for the duel, you ought to call dad back," Kyet proposed, stretching himself back into shape.

Eden rolled his own shoulders, "Not possible just now. He's in deep ice."

Goal grabbed two towels and walked out to them. "Time for my lesson!" she reminded Eden. The men took the offered towels and sponged off the sweat on their faces. Kyet twirled around to the other end of the studio and came back with a small, hand-held apparatus and a bandage for Eden. The little machine hummed briefly, the blood disappeared from Eden's hand, and Kyet pressed the bandage on. "Ask your uncle if he's interested," Eden told Goal in English with one look in my direction.

I was, but it could wait for a lesson with Kyet, who came over and took Goal's place next to me. I shook my head slightly.

Seeing Eden with Goal on that dance floor revealed more about their relationship. I could tell they were in the beginning stages of her martial training. He was focusing on what he repeatedly called "body awareness," teaching the "basic eights," a Tai-Chi like routine as a centering preliminary to the faster, more precise steps of the fighting dance. Goal was her usual semi-cooperative self, and I had to admire Eden's gentleness. She was awkward, impatient, eager to skip back into her more hyperactive mode. He demonstrated some of the basic steps again and again, waiting each time until she was ready to imitate him. He finally got her to perform a few of the connected steps, "Breathing, honey, breathing," he murmured soothingly when she was about to burst into an excited shriek to celebrate her accomplishment. She held in the outburst, continued to breathe in rhythm with her father. Gradually, her focus increased. She would reach a centered state soon.

"Do you continue with her when he's not here?" I asked Kyet.

He nodded, "But with us it's irregular. She's much more disciplined with him."

It sounded as if Eden and Kyet were reprising a pattern Leila and I had established: Goal cooperated with the first, and relaxed more with the second. That thought gave rise to a deep satisfaction within me, which I did not examine too closely. And it alerted me to a jealousy I had not anticipated and was not ready to deal with.

Eden worked with Goal for an hour, and then we all sipped the customary choctea to wind down before we made our way back to the house.

◆ EPISODE 18 ◆

Lady Ciani Comes Calling

In Eden Hamlet, my O'bonne Alnese orientation progressed. There, the short Alnese summer lasted into Ostyx, the month of changes. Loxi and the onset of winter followed, a season that lasted through two long Alnese months, Holdin and Jotun. After presenting her overview, Dragon sighed long and hard, but concluded philosophically, "At least here in the tropics, Loxi almost qualifies as an autumn. No snow, usually."

More Pallases appeared one fine morning a few days later, among them young cousins Odysseus and Illias, much to Goal's delight. Just two years younger, they proved ideal play mates. Goal was used to the company of her classmates and friends on Earth. The Hamlet was practically deserted in comparison. Goal soon ruled a little playgroup that included our resident musician. I started to tag along on most afternoons, usually with Socorro in tow. Often, we'd skip out and go sailing on a catamaran anchored in the boathouse below Kyet's dance studio.

Lake Limnos held an amazing similarity to its Swiss counterpart, Lac Leman, where Leila and I had found our converted farmhouse. A narrow stretch of water between rolling green hills on one end, it broadened and then narrowed again closer to high foothills on the other, where the coastal Alnese Midient Mountains rose. At the southern end, Lake Limnos converted to a soggy swamp, and unlike the Swiss back on Earth, the Alnese had not interfered with it. A mostly coniferous forest blanketed both shores, punctuated by the occasional meadow.

Eden Hamlet had been built about halfway from either end, where Lake Limnos thickened. The Hamlet sat on a parcel of land borrowed from Thor House, Eden's clan of origin, in a complicated arrangement that sounded a little like an Alnese lease. The Nambo clan held title to most of the area, and had built a new clan house on the other shore not too long ago. Thor House had terraced a promontory of land on the mountainous end and built up a huge clan estate. The two clans were our nearest neighbors.

Kyet, Goal, the twins, and I sailed the estate catamaran over to Nambo House across the lake one bright Ostyx afternoon, met up with the locals to sip some of their choc-tea and eat a scone-like confection. My Alnese still couldn't quite keep up, but I caught the local welcomes and Kyet's introduction of me as her Grace's new Chronicler, the human with the Alnese vision.

Or hallucination, more likely.

The neighbors were suitably impressed.

Goal and the twins vanished soon after our landing. With help from a mobile Alnese translator, English presented absolutely no problem, and we spent the remainder of the afternoon switching back and forth as we alternated between local gossip and questions about Earth.

Towards the end of our visit, I went for a walk on the grounds. Nambo House looked like a cross between Pallas House in Zyss and the Island compound where I'd been put up. A big octagonal hall anchored a labyrinthine collection of connected apartments up four stories, with two circles of cottages clustering down to Lake Limnos and up the hill into the forest. Rows of traditional Alnese greenhouses snaked between the residential buildings. I could hear excited children's voices echo through the greenhouses. Slow counts to twenty would be followed by silence, then the occasional shriek and excited outbursts. I turned away and meandered down to the lakeshore. When Kyet joined me, I nodded towards the greenhouses and commented, "I hate to break up the party."

He shrugged, "I've left a message for Aunt Quantal about leaving the kids here. I could return to get them in a couple of days. I could take a solar and have a lot of fun on the way back."

Solars were the Alnese equivalent to personal transportation. The size and shape of a wind-surfboard, they hovered about one meter above any surface and were amazingly maneuverable. I was still learning how to 'sail' one, and could get by as long as we didn't exceed twenty kilometers an hour, but Kyet was an expert solar-sailsman. Since solars flowed over water as easily as over land, I could imagine the fun Goal and the twins would have horsing around on the boards and trying to push each other into the lake as they crossed back over to Eden Hamlet.

"Sounds like a great idea. Tell me, are you related?"

"Ray, everyone on Alnos is related. But in this case, my grandmother came from Nambo, and Thor House originated from Nambo and on Nambo land."

"So, what's the relationship? I know it's not Pallas Nambo Kyet."

He laughed, "Yeah, it gets complicated. Pallas Xhania Kyet, son of Pallas Nambo Vaideh and Pallas Xhania Alexander, originally Xhania Nandez Alexander."

"I'm never going to keep all these ... What do you call them? lineages? straight, you realize that."

"You'll get used to it."

"How do you keep them straight?"

He shrugged again, "Don't know." Then he smiled an absolutely dazzling smile, "Guess it's just drummed into us from birth, Díaz Ruiz Raymond, the eight lineages to whom we are in debt, up four generations. In my case, it's Pallas Xhania Nambo Nandez Pallas Nambo Medece Tzalque Xhania Nandez Tsenyx Eng."

"Good grief!"

He chuckled.

"I'm gonna make a poor chronicler, that's for sure!"

"Not to worry. Lineages aren't your concern. Storytellers get to work on that part of our collective memory."

"Storytellers?"

"Like Aunt Leila. But she's still a journeywoman."

I had always known my lover as a furniture maker, and secretly suspected some illegal enterprise on the side, given her limitless income in Switzerland. Pretty far off the mark.

I consoled myself with the thought that I had at least figured out she was doing something on the side.

Kyet jerked his chin towards the main compound, "Time for the two of us to get ready." As we climbed back towards the house, he explained, "Storytellers teach with stories. Most of them are born with a," he paused, "sensitivity." He paused again, evaluated the word for a moment, then threw me an apologetic look, "A sensitivity."

"And she's still a journeywoman?"

"Storytellers teach about debt. They cannot do that until they themselves understand debt, understand it in their bones, in their marrow. She's too young."

"Look who's talking!"

He grinned, "I dance, Ray. I don't need to wrestle with other people's secrets, with, how do you put it? with their skeletons?"

I grinned back, "Something like that."

We'd almost reached the compound, and fell silent. I made a mental note to take a closer look at one of Dragon's half-finished talks about her work on Alnos, the one entitled, "The Concept of Debt in Alnese Society."

Once inside, the Nambos informed Kyet that Pallas Quantal, the twins' mother, had responded to his earlier message and finalized arrangements about leaving the three Pallas cousins with their Nambo kin for a few days. We rounded them up only to be told we were rudely interrupting the best fun they'd had in weeks. We repeated the usual parental directives about being on their best behavior, then took our leave and sailed back to the villa with Socorro.

Much to my regret, I didn't get to accompany Kyet three days later, when he went to collect the children on one of the larger Eden Hamlet solars. I did hear that the foursome arrived back at the Hamlet dripping wet and with still enough mischief left over to flood the boathouse bathroom in a final water fight. I would have liked to chronicle that fight! Goal and Kyet each claimed victory, and the twins changed their story depending on which of the two older cousins they happened to be with. After surveying the mayhem, Eden ordered a thorough clean up of the boathouse bathroom. The twins tried to make themselves scarce, but he had one of his lieutenants round up all four cousins and they spend an afternoon detailing that bathroom until it sparkled.

I missed out on the whole adventure because none other than Lady Ciani came calling on her new Chronicler.

◆ ◆ ◆

We met in Dragon's favorite 'salon,' a sun-lit living-dining room on the lower floor. French windows opened onto a terrace lined with fragrant Alnese plants and a stunning view of Lake Limnos all the way to the Midient Mountains to the north. Her Grace was standing in the open windows and admiring the view when I joined her. Her attendant stood ready in the adjoining kitchen. I had a fleeting sense that the one visible captain by the door had some less visible help nearby.

Lady Ciani turned towards me, "Ah, Díaz, Ashewe tells me you really enjoy this Earthly concoction, coffee." She was using Alnese rather than English, a choice not lost on me. It announced her purpose before she spoke it. With a quick smile, she pointed to a pot on the table next to the French windows, "I'm not at all confident my cook knows how to prepare it, but there it is."

"Thank you."

In a moment of panic, I realized that Dragon and I had not yet covered proper Alnese protocol with the ruler of the planet. I had no idea how I was to conduct myself, and little confidence in my ability to understand, let alone respond appropriately. With a little wave, she simultaneously directed me to the table and her attendant to pour a cup of the coffee. I slid into one of the chairs and tasted the brew. Her Grace employed excellent staff.

"Tolerable?"

"Better than that."

"How gracious of you to say so." She stepped closer, and the same attendant that had poured my coffee pulled a chair out for her, then set a steaming cup of choctea on the table. She sat down, started to sip the choctea, and said, "My physician tells me you have recovered. Do you agree with her?"

"I feel much better."

"Well enough to join us back in Zyss soon?"

I took the safest course of action and nodded silently.

She continued with another smile, "I was hoping you and I could agree on a schedule. Perhaps you could return with me, spend a few days in Zyss. Kobran ambassador Periasamy has taken up residence at Alnos House. You could begin to witness some of our conversations."

I decided to try one of my emerging Alnese phrases, "If

that is how I can serve your Grace."

"Another gracious comment! I'm going to finish this day deeply in your debt."

I couldn't think of a thing to say in return, certainly not in Alnese. Dragon rescued me. Lady Ciani looked up and her smile brightened a few notches, "Ashewe! How nice of you to join us! Coffee or choctea?"

"If I may so impose on your Grace's generosity, I will have the coffee."

A slightly raised finger brought about a third steaming cup.

"My dear Dragon, I truly regret the imposition, but I would like to invite you and Díaz Raymond to Alnos House. You've told him about the Council of Eight?"

Dragon nodded.

She had. Eight Alnese leaders were chosen from among all the Alnese Orders to four-year terms as "Councilors" to the Alnese Regent. Dragon had detailed the orders involved, but I could only remember the familiar ones, Lann, Arthmis, Pallas-Métis. I remembered the structure of the Council a little better. The Regent and the Council met on the fortieth day every month to discuss important issues until consensus could be reached. According to Dragon, the Alnese were great believers in consensus. While meetings concluded on the same day most of the time, some discussions could go on for days.

"Our next meeting is on the fortieth. It would be a good time to introduce my new Chronicler. And as I was just informing Chronicler Díaz, Ambassador Periasamy and I are about to have some conversations about our joint future.

The Council would truly appreciate an O'bonne perspective."

"I am happy to repay my debts to Alnos any way I can, your Grace."

"O'bonne guests are so civilized." Lady Ciani turned to me, "It's short notice, I know, but how does, say, a week before the next council meeting suit you?"

Another moment of panic struck. I couldn't really answer her. I wanted—I needed—to find out what Leila planned first, but didn't know whether that constituted an arrogant presumption on my part. I had no idea how Lady Ciani viewed my relationship with my daughter, whether she even thought I had a daughter.

Without ever discussing it, Leila and I had slipped back into our old rhythm, the one we had established in Switzerland before Socorro was born. She spent mornings with the children, I took over in the afternoon. But we had not sat down and talked, and she had let me understand I was to keep out of her way. My anxiety about Socorro, allayed by the recent weeks of familiar routine, throttled back to life.

Once again, it was Dragon to the rescue. She cleared her throat, and once we both adjusted in her direction, she observed, "Your Grace, I am sure Chronicler Díaz will be able to work out a suitable schedule, but he needs to consult some other parties first."

"Of course. Pallas Eden told me as much. I am sorry, Díaz Raymond. Perhaps you can take the date I have proposed under advisement and let me know by the end of my visit?"

I nodded.

Another smile rewarded me.

"How long will your Grace remain with us?" Dragon sought to clarify.

"Overnight. Pallas Eden has agreed to take me sailing, after a little persuasion. The Justiciar has been overly affected by recent events in the Islands. He's getting worse than my bro-," she stopped for the tiniest break, continued, "than Pallas Alexander."

Dragon's expression dimmed, "Perhaps. Many histories teach us that Pallas Eden's concern is warranted."

Her Grace turned back to me, "A sail around the lake is not much time, only a few hours. Nevertheless, I would like to ask you to join me again for a walk around the gardens upon my return. A more private hour before dinner?"

I bowed a little, "As you wish."

"Thank you Díaz. I am in your debt. To try and ease it a little, I've had my cook prepare you both some of our morning pancakes with springberry preserves. I hope you will accept this small gesture." She rose, "The Justiciar has granted me a visit to his tower. I hear the view is well worth the climb."

This time Dragon and I replied almost simultaneously, "It is."

"Until this evening, then."

And that said, she glided by us to the door and vanished into the house, followed by her attendant and her captain.

◆ EPISODE 19 ◆

Dragon Acknowledges a Debt

Right before her afternoon sail around our expanding Lake Limnos, Lady Ciani invited me for a garden picnic in Pallas Eden's favorite greenhouse. It had been designed for herb growing and featured a dryer climate so a fragrant collection from half a dozen worlds could thrive. The greenhouse also numbered among my favorite spots in Eden Hamlet. Special clear panels had been installed on the side overlooking the lake, and the solar heating panels maintained a wonderful, almost O'bonne balminess to complement its herbal scents. These past two summers, whenever I needed to ponder a particularly vexing question, I would stroll through the herb garden until I reached a low bench installed right in front of the view panels. Such a loverly, soothing spot on my igloo-planet. Her Grace was sitting in that very spot for our meeting.

"Ashewe," Lady Ciani rose to greet me as I stepped into my little summer oasis, and I quickly bowed to her so she would slide back onto the bench, "Justiciar Pallas tells me you find a little solace in this particular patch. I am so happy to hear it. I'm about to impose dreadfully on you. How does that very wise Kobran saying go again? Offer someone a drink and they'll soon claim the whole well?"

Her words did not come as a surprise. The moment I had given in to their combined pressure and accepted to continue working with Pallas Eden in the Islands affair, I had let myself become enmeshed in a problem far bigger than I had imagined. Now the price would have to be paid. I knew the favor she was about to ask, that I postpone my O'bonne shore leave due to start the next Alnese month. Postponement at this point really meant canceling it altogether, at least for this year, and the thought of staying through a third winter on Alnos made me shiver even before she went on.

Lady Ciani signalled to her Captain and the Captain stepped out of the herb garden only to return with a field chair for me. After I sat down, she said, "Dear friend, not only am I about to ask you to remain with us and help us work towards a resolution with our newcomers, I'm about to request O'bonne mediation formally. I've discussed the proposal with the Council first, of course, and my eight advisors agree. Even the few short days I spent on the Islands made it plain that Alnos is in crisis."

Her words made me feel trapped, gasping, as if the room had suddenly emptied of air. Staying here would also mean wrestling with the genie I had let out of the bottle towards the end of last winter, when I had finally succumbed to my young Alnese suitor's warm smiles and even warmer body.

Even though I knew deep in my heart that I would not have been able just to run away and leave him, somehow, I needed that option.

I sighed, and she smiled an apology, and continued, "I understand your distress, Ashewe, even though I know that sympathy makes little difference. I still persist in my selfish desire to keep you here with us."

"It is not selfish, your Grace."

"Thank you, Dragon, it's most kind of you to say so."

"I am happy to convey your Grace's request to the O'bonne Assembly, and do not doubt that it will be granted."

"It would give me particular pleasure if my old friend Nyemba were available."

Nyemba was my predecessor on Alnos, and the sponsor of my current studies. Inclining my head, I pointed out, "My esteemed colleague will be honored by your Grace's particular attention, of course, but he is not a trained mediator."

"Well, we'll need one, of course, but I'm sure my old friend would acquit himself admirably. As would you, if you decided to step outside of your primary call as an observer. No doubt all planetologists are innate mediators."

"I only hope we prove worthy of your Grace's kind assessment."

Lady Ciani waved away the acknowledgement and continued, "Alnos is fortunate to be able to count on O'bonne assistance in this matter. We are faced with a daunting challenge, Ashewe Dragon. And since you agree to convey Alnos' request to O'bonne, dare I hope you'll also agree to stay?"

"That is a very difficult question."

With another smile, she deflected, "And of course, here I go again impatiently pressuring when I know I have made the request and need to give you time to consider it. What a poor choice of sovereign I make, so completely devoid of all the necessary qualities! But let me at least offer you this: If you agree to stay, my steward will make every effort to craft a schedule that allows you frequent visits to this little oasis, and my gardeners have already started to install an herb chamber in Alnos House's roof garden. I would be honored to have them proceed with a similar addition to Pallas House. I do think it an excellent innovation."

"It is kind of your Grace to think of my comfort."

"Dragon, if matters deteriorate here, we shall all of us have preciously little comfort."

She looked out over the lake, and I let my gaze follow hers across the water towards the northern, mountainous end. Her face turned resolute, "I will not allow my world to drown in a sea of debt for generations. That's what happens once a crisis turns into a war. And the eventual outcome scares me the most. How can any people ever recover after committing genocide?"

"Your Grace!" burst forth before I could clamp down.

Her smile turned sad and grim, "Has anyone told you how Mythras got started?"

"Mythras? Arthmis' second wave?"

"Arthmis' second wave, yes," something about that description amused Lady Ciani, but I couldn't quite put my finger on what, "Well, has anyone told you their ... what do you call it? Their origin myth?"

I shook my head, and she continued, "Mythras was created during the days of Lord Daimyo, who, like me, grew up in the Borderlands. In those days, an Island clan, Ran, insulted a border clan, Nandez, and gradually, the conflict escalated into a vendetta and then full war, until one fateful day Islander clans Ran, Kuan, Chantico and Minguard joined forces and overwhelmed Nandez House. Then Nandez called in its closest Borderlands allies, Vinyat, Xhania, and K'elle, and set out to destroy Ran House. The four border clans knew no bounds, killed every adult and divided up Ran's children among themselves."

During my studies, I had come across stories of inter-clan conflict, but I was startled by that outcome, and by the bluntness with which Lady Ciani described it. Alnese conflicts were usually buffered by accumulated blood ties, which often enabled cooler heads to prevail and put an end to fights before they spun out of control. I wondered what ties had existed between the eight clans in question, all the while keenly aware how our mountain people claimed the same shared blood could also intensify the rage of an erupting conflict.

After a brief pause, Lady Ciani continued, "Of course the children's Island and mainland relatives called in Arthmis, but every one realized that the Order could not enforce its judgments or re-establish the peace. Then Lord Daimyo went to the border personally and demanded that the border clans yield up the stolen children. He went straight to the great hall of Xhania House, his former clan, and proclaimed that their heinous actions had saddled all of Alnos with an unpayable debt. He refused to listen to any of the Border people's rationalizations and swore he would personally find every single stolen child and return her to her kin. Once he started to follow through with his threat, the four Border Houses finally realized what they had done, realized the weight of their debts to Ran, to Alnos, and to God, and they yielded. Then, Lord Daimyo made it clear that the four Border clans could repay their debts by creating a special Arthmis unit that would protect the new Ran House. He challenged the border people to send the best of the best, those Arthmin that had distinguished themselves over the years. And they did."

She paused and let the tale sink in, then added a coda, "To acknowledge their debts, the Border Arthmin also swore ice penance. And during their time in ice, they started to invent new training routines, new ways to refine and improve Arthmis techniques. And that is how Mythras came to be."

Long before she finished, I realized the story was a bribe, or perhaps something like an advance, a way to pay me for what I was about to sacrifice. Nevertheless, I drank in the story like a thirsty traveler in our hottest desert, and I made matters still worse by asking rather eagerly, "So is that why titled Mythran leaders are legates? They are Arthmis emissaries?"

"They are Lord Daimyo's emissaries, yes, his legates. Sometimes, we also call them Daim to honor the memory of the one who created the order. Legend has it that Lord Daimyo served as example to the first Mythrans, that no one could beat him for the first fifty years of his life. But that could just be silly Xhania pride. There's plenty of that to go around."

Her tone had grown teasing again, but I could still sense her deep concern. She shifted back towards the lake and returned to her earlier observations, "Ashewe, if the insults from the newcomers continue, more and more of our people will take offense. And this time, more than four Border clans will join together and know no bounds. Arthmis would not be able to stop the blood letting even with Mythras beside it. I have no desire to follow in Lord Daimyo's footsteps, although I shall not hesitate to do so if I must. But O'bonne has centuries of experience mediating conflicts, and nothing in the universe is sharper than an O'bonne mind."

I acknowledged the oft-repeated compliment with a brief nod, and replied, "As I have already assured your Grace, it shall be my pleasure to convey her request to our Assembly. I'm sure O'bonne will be honored to offer the insights of our experiences."

"Thank you, Dragon. And what about my personal request to you?"

"Your Grace is convinced that my continued presence here would help?"

"Yes. You need time to reflect on it, of course, as I well know. And I need to get ready for my little sailing adventure."

We both rose and she took her leave. I was quite awed by her faith in me, awed and humbled, and I knew even as I accepted the offered time to consider that she had won me over with that faith. I could be of service to a people I respected and admired despite their fearsome wild streak—that promise proved irresistible.

When I got to my quarters, Kyet had snuck in and was waiting for me, sprawled across my body chair. Sneaking into my quarters went against the rules, but this time, I did not feel like reminding him of it.

"She's asked you to stay," he observed without prompting.

I activated the controls to my bed and when it slipped out of the wall, I let myself drop into it with a sigh of relief. Flashing a shy smile, he half-rolled, half-crawled out of the chair and onto the edge of the bed. We could still count the number of times I had let him share it, never more than two or three hours. And from the very first time, he had always stopped right there, at the edge, waiting for me to allow it.

"Will you stay?" he asked.

Part of me wanted to hold back, put a note of suspense into his life, but I felt drained by my interview with her Grace. I longed for the comfort of our growing intimacy, for his hug and his touch and his uncanny ability to fit right into the little openings I allowed, just fit perfectly.

Adjusting ever so slightly towards him, I stretched one arm until I managed to brush my fingertips against his thigh, "Probably."

His smile grew brighter, "Good."

"I thought you might feel that way."

He leaned forward, lifted the thigh into the bed, and flowed towards me as I burrowed under his sweater for warm skin, my Alnese substitute for the O'bonne sun.

◆ EPISODE 20 ◆

Raymond's Alnese Education Continues

After Lady Ciani and her retinue had gone off on their sailing trip around Lake Limnos, I sought out the mother of my child.

I found her in a workspace she had started to adapt into her new workshop, a big room on the other end of the first floor dominated by a magnificent loom. Picking up the sleeping Socorro from her workroom crib, I informed Leila of Lady Ciani's wishes. She had no trouble connecting the dots, "If both you and Eden return to Zyss, Goal won't let up until I follow. I might as well resign myself now. Is he with her Grace?"

"I think so."

She let out a disdainful grunt, stepped to the nearest com unit and called out, "Minguard?"

When Eden's Arthmis lieutenant answered the call, Leila told her, "I need to see my husband as soon as he is available.

Make sure he is appraised of it." To me, she commented, "I'm just getting this space ready, you know. I should have known better. You can tell her Grace you will be available for the end of Ostyx, definitely by the fortieth. You'll have to give me one week. We'll follow you before the month ends."

"All right."

I lingered.

She knew why.

Her next look made it clear she still did not want to discuss any of her decisions, but she conceded, "Everyone knows you chose her first name. I haven't changed it." And then she clarified, "It's an acknowledgment. But she needs to spend more time with Eden. They both do."

And for the second time that day, I got to practice the well-worn Alnese phrase, "As you wish."

She looked at me sharply, stepped to where I stood and gathered the baby back. Socorro yawned at her mother. Leila whispered endearments at her and rested her against one shoulder, walked around the room until the rocking lulled her back to sleep.

I screwed up my courage, "Leila."

She cut me off, "One week, Ray. Get started at Alnos House, and we'll follow you in one week."

"All right."

"I'll bring her up in the afternoon."

"All right."

I decided I might as well meet up with Dragon and Vai again, as usual. But when I climbed up to the fourth floor, I found only Vai in her office. The Alnese scientist was in her usual garrulous mood, complaining about the "unending stream of interruptions."

"That's what I get for moving into a house built by a Justiciar!" she snorted, "How could I ever have been stupid enough to buy that line about building a summer retreat? Retreat! This is worse than Zyss on market day! Have you seen all the Jotun-witted fools that have been trooping about this morning?"

"Actually, no."

"Well good for you! Half of Eden's companies must be here! If this keeps up, I am moving to Kyet's little island. If the man can negotiate a house out of Thor, he can bloody well add an island!"

Her grumblings were the perfect antidote to my anxiety, as was keeping busy. Gathering up my O'bonne reading tablet, I flipped through the index until I found the half-finished talk I was looking for, and started to read.

> The Concept of Debt in Alnese Society, by Azetmir Dragon Ashewe.
> Presentation for the Planetologist Society,
> First O'bonne University, O'bonne Year 4136
>
> Following in Ndinzi Nyemba's footsteps on Alnos, I have turned my attention to informal means of social regulation. As Nyemba himself reported in a series of recent talks, the Alnese have stuck with some traditions more common in pre-warp, even pre-literate societies. Makalanyone's recent historical research into the almost two millenia-long Alnese odyssey has provided some intriguing clues to this unique Alnese development.

Makalanyone first focused her attention on the years immediately following an eighty-year gap in the Alnese historical record early on in their odyssey, and found many adaptations to the stresses of early space travel, among them a shift towards a more mixed, more distributed system of record-keeping. I will mention that the innovations from this period included the first Alnese chroniclers and storytellers, two new roles that have endured into the Alnese present, as we all know. Makalanyone hypothesizes that the first few generations of Space Gypsies experienced perhaps a few more adventures than they cared for; the historical record, fragmented though it may be, makes it clear that they suffered heavy losses, including the loss of entire ships and technologies. It makes sense that the Space Gypsies would grow weary of relying too much on technology, and a re-emergence of more oral or more mixed-media means of cultural maintenance and transmission appears a plausible adaptation.

Like traditions in other societies, the re-emergent oral traditions that have persisted into the Alnese present are rooted in social networks. In recent months, I have started to take note of a particular concept that recurs again and again in Alnese clan affairs, a concept that, indeed, could be termed a key to Alnese clan affairs. That concept is the concept of debt.

One could say that on Alnos, everything revolves around debt. To simplify things for the sake of this discussion, on Alnos, every child is born in debt to her "eight lineages," that is, to the eight clan houses whose alliances have led to her conception and birth. That debt is reciprocal, however; the parents, grandparents, and great-grandparents are in debt to their children for carrying on their blood and their memories. Other relationships are viewed in the same terms, as unending cycles of obligations that are simply a fact of existence. I am familiar with a similar concept on Earth, where at least some groups have developed the notion that every action generates karma, or consequences. On Alnos, you could substitute the word debt for karma, and the same basic rule applies: every action generates debt, and it is the unending task of every Alnese to work down the debt, to strive for balance, and to make sure he does not generate debts that cannot be repaid and that would create a permanent imbalance.

The Alnese apply this concept with surprising even-handedness. On Alnos, I am in debt to the air I breathe, the food I eat, the wood and stones in my house, the cashmere that keeps me warm, as well as to the cook who prepares my food, the singer who bestows the gift of a song, and the friend who offers me an hour of conversation. In fact, good conversations are prized on Alnos; they are deemed excellent examples of the kind of reciprocal relationship that leads to balance. I can achieve that cherished balance by reciprocating favors, acknowledging gifts, and balancing out inevitable acts of destruction with acts of creation.

It is conceivable that the concept of debt and the ideal of balance lie at the root of the well-known Alnese love of pleasure in all things and love of art in all actions. Giving art or pleasure creates a good debt, a debt that may in time yield art or pleasure in return. Over the years, many of us have appreciated this aspect of Alnese life, not just because of the quality of their workmanship both on Alnos and on O'bonne, but also because of its influence on Alnese daily life and on their dealings with their guests. To us, the Alnese are not just hospitable, they suffuse their hospitality with many gracious little touches and little pleasures. And their routines appear thought through to an extraordinary degree. Our kinesiologists have long expressed admiration for the Alnese 'basic eight,' for example, praising not just the health benefits of the exercise routine, but its aesthetic quality as well. Of course, the Alnese swear that creating aesthetic movement further increases the health benefits of the routine.

I don't doubt that their planet's climate has further encouraged their devotion to infusing daily life with pleasurable moments, especially in winter, but there is more to Alnese love of art than simply making the Alnese igloo tolerable. Most of my Pallas hosts devote time to creative work, but a lot of that work is quite experimental and never leaves the artist's workroom. The Alnese have an interesting saying, "Some art is just for one day, and some is meant for God." On Alnos, art can be ephemeral, short-lived, frivolous, or even entirely private. Among the Pallas artists in my most immediate orbit are Pallas Leila, whose hand-crafted furniture has a reputation as among the finest on the planet, Pallas Alexander, whose tapestries are also quite sought after, and his son Pallas Kyet, a rather talented musician and dancer. His mother Pallas Vai, on the other hand, has never considered any of her compositions fit for anyone but herself, and Pallas Eden only occasionally smithies a piece of jewelry or a dagger. As a matter of fact, Pallas Alexander once told me with a wink, "The great Prophet herself thought it was good for the soul, but Pallas never pretended to do much more than dabble with the loom." I have, of late, started to follow the Alnese example and started to dabble myself, mostly with Pallas Vai's multi-dimensional graphics. And like my good friend, I find my dabblings most appropriate for God rather than my fellow O'bonne or even my tolerant fellow Alnese. I am finding that the great Alnese Prophet had a point, even if her meaning was distinctly Alnese.

To return to my analysis, Pallas Alexander's comment points to the suspected connection between art and debt. Even questionable and private results have been decreed 'good for the soul,' good because they lighten the unending burden of debt. The Alnese say, 'Just try to run out on your debts!' and 'Debts circle back.' All acts have consequences, and sooner or later, all must acknowledge and deal with those consequences. Creative and artistic activity is so widespread

> and ranges so far and wide because it provides a means of absolution, even or perhaps especially if the art is only meant for God.

After that last paragraph, Dragon's piece broke off into a series of not entirely intelligible phrases and notes.

I put the reading tablet aside, pondered what I had just learned. For a bottomed-out musician, I sure had landed on the perfect planet.

◆ EPISODE 21 ◆

Leila and Eden Talk

I should like to say...
That you are what I fear most and am least afraid of.

The lines aren't drawn very clearly. I suppose that's what guerilla warfare is all about. A collection of memories at war, no, two collections. At sixteen, I was so certain about my feelings I refused to listen to anybody else's misgivings, not even yours. I was so intent on my conquest. That refusal to listen sucked you into our cycle of violence as surely as the demons within us. And now, I'm tired of the memories.

Aren't you?

Why do I try to placate you about the child? You say with your quiet sneer, "Oh, once again it shall be as Pallas House decrees." I'm furious, stay calm. I want to take my children and leave again, but I won't run this time. Time to face the music on Alnos, as Ray would say. When you tell me what I already know, that Lady Ciani has asked Ray to join her in Zyss soon, I can see you relish that, too: You like to see me struggling with him, don't you? A taste of revenge after all this time.

I see it in your eyes, the old brooding, and I'm waiting for your anger to resurface, and I've reached a point where your pain only tires me. I even get flippant: If you loathe it all so much, why don't you just do yourself in, like Ray? I am tired of keeping the good soldier afloat, of keeping the house of the good soldier afloat, of keeping Ray afloat!

We meet in the garden. I stalk you there. Our secret dance of pursuit and avoidance, so like a courtship, winds around the rose houses and autumnal shrubs until you turn down a blind alley and I have you cornered. The morning sun in my eyes blinds me until you move a few centres and stand between it and me. This small courtesy allows me to drop my hand from my eyes, to face you, perhaps to appease our memories after all.

You signal your surrender to me, "Well?"

We look at each other.

Even in his shadow her eyes struck him as too light. He'd never gotten used to them. Now her hair flashed blue shadows, her face had changed to a more angular oval befitting her age, and a tattooed rose grew right out of the jugular pulsing under her pale neck. Once again, she seemed infinitely fragile to him, her white hands like porcelain, with yellow doll's eyes highlighted by her sepia hair.

I can't make you out until we dance gingerly around each other, and you step back out of the light spilling over your head, overshadowing your face. Except for the silver in your beard you haven't changed much. You look as weary as you did when I left you. Just …that light in your gray eyes, that liveliness … that is a change. To think that Cousin Lex would fall for you, of all people. Then again, my own desperate longing for you at fifteen came just as unexpectedly. We have a lot in common, Alexander and I. I've always known that, from the time when I first tagged along on all his adventures at Xhania House. I touch your sleeve, brush my fingers up the material until I reach your face. You don't move away. You put your hand over mine and hold it on your shoulder.

"Why?" You ask finally.

"Would you believe because I missed you?"

I free my hand, press further up, through the speckled chestnut, try to pull you closer to me until you draw back. I let you retreat the one step it takes to re-establish a safe distance.

"Hardly." Brevity is still your trademark.

I observe, "Four years with my ice master father as expiation for your assault. And you've been back, what? Another four years?"

You keep silent, still.

I add, "And Socorro was dying, so I had to return. Now Peg tells me she'll be all right. If you want me to stay in Zyss, you should just say so."

That stings, I can tell. Your anger rises, but you snap yourself back into line, "I have learned my lesson, if that's what you're here to establish."

"You like your new daughter, then?"

What possesses me to goad you like this?

"Is that it? You want assurances that I'll keep my part of this new bargain between us? Well then you can have it: I like the little bastard just fine."

Ah, you still know how to sting back!

And then you add more calmly, "Rest assured: I'll fulfill my obligations in our alliance, for both Goal and Socorro."

I turn my back to you and start to walk towards the closest rose house. Once inside, I sit down, wait for you to make up your mind about escaping. You could have taken that out. Then again, when have you ever taken the easy road?

"Well?" You repeat after you have caught up with me.

I don't answer right away, and you continue, "Why don't you come to the point of this meeting, since you've gone to the trouble of forcing it."

After gathering my courage, I dive in, "Things need to change between us."

You look at me wordlessly, encouraging: *Go on.*

"You trusted me once."

That dry bark of a laugh hurts, but I let it pass. You response is almost a speech! "After nine years? You stop talking to me, announce to the world that we can't get on, take my child to some godforsaken planet to be raised by some junkie, and now you want trust?"

"You slammed me into that wall, Eden."

Whatever it was you were going to follow up with, it's hard work swallowing it after my salvo. Still struggling with it, you squeeze out between clenched teeth, "I swear to God there is an O'bonne witch in you!"

I show no mercy, "I may not remember the fight, but I do remember the pain, later. I can still feel it in my bones some chilly days." And then I recall why I have sought you out this morning, so I try to make amends, "All right. You're right. I do know how to strike back. But I also know you have changed. I can sense it. I know it's real."

Almost a re-enactment, your hands lock onto my wrists and your voice rings savagely against me as you shake me, "How's that for a start: I still can't live with the memory of that third year. The regret of that day still haunts me. It's heavier than any of my other debts, even the killings."

I gasp, and realizing what you are doing you almost throw my hands off, cover your face. This time I let you recover, moving closer to you as you say, "Winter lows, Leila, can you sense the immense, immeasurable weight of it?" You let out a hard sigh, murmur, "I'm sorry I hurt you."

My turn. "I don't know when you stopped being the monster, but one day it happened. Yes, I needed to go that far to stop hurting, but the distance also gave me perspective. Then, almost killing Ray was the clincher. There was a part of me that wanted him to suffer." I pause, finish dryly, "Well he did. I got to taste my wish coming true."

I can't complete what I need to tell you, that indulging my anger has taught me about yours. I simply can't get it out. Instead, I say, "And I almost lost Ro. I hope you'll never know how that feels, Eden. You may think you lost Goal, but no, she's alive and she was never in danger. You have no idea." After a second pause, I ask more haltingly, "Do you think, might it be possible, for us, to find some peace, something like Vai and Alexander?"

"They started out so differently."

Without the violence of first love and first grande déception. Neither of them had the temperament for it. Cousin-brother

Lex sure knew how to choose his life partners.

A physically painful longing washed over him. Leila still had that power to re-awaken that old, fearsome rage snapping through him and out of him, to be stopped by broken bones. The self he'd turned over to the ice mentor, the self he couldn't even retrieve safely in combat. He thought back to the fateful day he had hurled her clear across their bedroom and cracked her skull against the wall, watched her crumple to the floor. Waiting for the physician he'd alerted to arrive before turning himself in to his Order, he had sworn ice penance. Arthmis had agreed, with a twist: he'd go serve his time with her ice mentor father, the former Pallas Vrezh. He had not expected the old Mythran to let him live, let alone to turn into his teacher.

"It's worth a try," you whisper finally. You look so haunted that I reach for you, twisting my wrist into my tunic so you won't see the purple marks you left there. Compassion sweeps over me and I want to give you what I withheld just a moment ago: Tell you I forgave you even before I learned the need to be forgiven.

Quieter, you say, "You already know it, but I'll tell you anyway: The stupid things I say about your going to Earth, it's just bravado. Abandoning me was the right choice."

Oh how you word things sometimes!

You continue, "And the truth is, I've gained a whole new understanding of passion. First-hand."

"Yeah?" Was I about to taste another wish coming true?

You half-nod, then half-shake your head, "How could you stand it? Where did you find the strength to get over it? To go on?"

And just like that, you've evoked my out-of-control younger

self, and I know very well how I found the strength to go on: No one wants to live like that. I say, "You just ... do. But I think, unlike so many of us, you won't have to."

"Really? That's not the conventional wisdom."

"Oh he'll test you, that he will! Lex is not used to limits. Don't you already know that? But I always knew that if and when my cousin-brother surrendered himself, he wouldn't hold back."

And he has surrendered himself, I just know it.

And I sense that despite your nagging doubts, despite the whispers you can't quite put out of your mind, you know it, too. An interesting way for your debts to come circling back.

"Truce, then," I propose, and I say quietly, "I trust you, Eden. But as you say, I'm something of an O'bonne witch. I know I can. You'll need more time."

And I see shyness come over you, an awkwardness that signals a small opening in your armor. I lean into you for a timid hug. You hold me like a porcelain doll, almost at arm's length. And I know that this trust I seek will come to pass.

◆ EPISODE 22 ◆

Raymond Starts at Alnos House

God is everything, and everything is God.
There is no beginning to God.
There is no end to God.
God is everything, and everything is God.

A steward had guided me through the maze of Alnos House right before sunrise and left me just inside an impressive carved door. Four rooms strung along a long internal balcony overlooking one side of Alnos House's central octagonal great hall. I had moved from the first to the second to the third to this the final room, and as if by design, Lady Ciani had started her chant the moment I set foot there.

I stole some glances around a cross between a small Orthodox church and a mosque. Behind her Grace, on the wall across from the balcony, an abstract representation glowed in alternating colors. Interlacing eight-sided figures flowed into each other, anchored by eight points of light whose golden warmth I found mesmerizing. Circles of eight suns appeared on the two other walls, harmonizing with stylized Alnese proverbs. A similar meditation room existed off the central hall of Pallas House, but this one outshone it. No doubt it outshone every meditation room in every Alnese house on the planet.

After four iterations, Lady Ciani looked up, "I repeat this basic observation every eighth hour. How nice to have a chronicler witness again." She rose to her feet and adjusted her cardigan, pulling it tightly around her shoulders.

It broke the spell.

We were alone. I froze at the thought, then took a deep breath, "Is there something I should do?"

"Join me for breakfast." She waved me along as she stepped through a side doorway into what I would soon come to know as her inner sanctum, four private rooms that included her bedroom, her library, her spa, and a small personal dining room. We crossed the bedroom to the dining room, where she made a small gesture towards an elegant round table surrounded by four of Alnos' finest bodychairs. I stepped ahead of her and pulled out one chair, and with a 'Thank you!', she smiled and sat down.

The moment I settled down next to her, two attendants appeared. Each set down a plate full of Alnese pancakes covered with berry-preserve, other toppings, a cup and a pot. I could smell the coffee in mine. The two attendants retreated out of sight. I poured myself a cup of the coffee and let out an appreciative sigh after a first taste.

"Ideally, you will join me in my acknowledgements occasionally."

"I don't think I understand these ... acknowledgements."

She picked up her pot and poured herself a cup of choctea, then repeated quietly, "God is everything, and everything is God. Every eighth hour, we acknowledge it. It's good for the soul."

"Good for the soul? God rewards you?"

She paused, her cup about midway between the table and her lips, then shook her head. After another moment of reflection, she elucidated, "To acknowledge God reminds us that we are boundless, and finite, that we share in the infinite light, and in the equally infinite gravity that consumes light. That's good for the soul, especially when your debts come circling back and you don't quite know how to repay them."

I repeated slowly, "God is everything, and everything is God." Then I turned towards her, "What does it mean?"

"It means what it says."

"So ... you are God?"

She smiled, "Yes."

"And I am God, too?"

"Of course. And so is this cup," she lifted hers slightly, "The altar behind us, the scent of the incense I burn sometimes. God is everything, and everything is God."

"You believe that?"

"What I believe is irrelevant."

"Oh." Relevance ... That's something I'd taken for granted. "I ..." paused again, shrugged, "Well there's this song on Earth ...," and I hummed quietly, in English, "We are million-year old carbon."

"A similar idea, yes," she acknowledged.

"Part of me believes it, but the other part ... But then again, I suppose that would be irrelevant, too."

"Obviously, it is not irrelevant to you. Now, I will tell you, I know, I know much deeper than belief, there is no beginning to God, no end to God, but when all is said and done, it's irrelevant. One of God's many gifts is my mind's ability to spin many worlds, consider, perhaps a few too many possibilities, and yes, to have or not to have beliefs. Those are simply manifestations of the infinity that is God."

We both fell silent, ate a few bites. After sipping most of my coffee, I wondered, "So, you would like me to ... join you in acknowledging God. But if I don't believe it, wouldn't it be wrong?"

She picked up my pot and poured me another cup, "Interesting. For you, God punishes and rewards. Like a parent."

An accurate observation.

"But not for you?"

"God is everything. Father. Mother. But also child. As Alnos Ciani, I have to remember the child, that infinite mind just getting started." She looked away for a moment, then back at me, "and I have to remind my people."

I shook my head, "I can't say I understand that. I can't even grasp it."

"Then we'll wait."

"You think I'll get it, then?"

"Like God, the future is unpredictable. You may grow comfortable with our acknowledgements in due time. For today, let's get you comfortable with these quarters, and get you acquainted with Alnos House. You should at least be able find your quarters. My Chronicler's apartment is right next to this one, and it will be furnished to your liking. Díaz Raymond, I know how easy it is to get lost in Alnos House. When I first accepted to serve my people, at sixteen, I must have found every possible way to get lost here. I propose we spend at least half a day getting lost together. It's the best way to learn about this house. We can work out a suitable schedule for you later, in a few days."

"Get lost together?"

A mischievous gleam practically lit up her face, "Oh yes."

"How?"

"We could play hide and seek. I haven't done it in quite some time."

Dumbfounded, I echoed, "Hide and seek?"

"I concede almost forty years of residence give me an unfair advantage. I propose that you hide and I seek. And," she lifted a slim book-sized tablet that came to life as she shifted it towards me, "here are the schematics you'll need. I've had a handheld programmed for you. It'll shift as you move so you can always orient yourself."

I couldn't help but chuckle, "All right." I took the offered handheld and fumbled with it a bit. I could read the Alnese characters with almost the same ease as human ones. I repeated, "All right," and finished off the last of my coffee.

The handheld helped tremendously in our next few hours together. During one of our breaks in the residence's western wing, while we looked out over Zyss, Lady Ciani observed with a sigh, "Too bad the children remained in Eden Hamlet. That's the right way to play this game!"

I nodded acknowledgement.

"I know what I shall do! Invite Goal and the twins to join us at the earliest opportunity. And maybe Kyet, too. Have you played together?"

I nodded again.

"Well make a note for me, will you?" She had to show me how. Once the note was recorded and sent to her steward, we played a few more rounds.

A dinner engagement gathered us back into her suite in the late afternoon. Once ready, we proceeded to Alnos House's smaller, more intimate formal dining room, where Lady Ciani met with and introduced me to three of her Councilors.

I stayed in my Chronicler's quarters in Alnos House the remainder of that week. I met with the remaining Councilors, with all of Lady Ciani's staff, and with the Kobran ambassador. And I helped her Grace's steward prepare four invitations: One for Pallas Thor Goal, one for Pallas Eng Oddysseus, one for Pallas Eng Illias and a fourth one for Pallas Xhania Kyet. When I presented the four slips of paper to her Grace, her face lit up with mischief and anticipation. It was catching.

◆ EPISODE 23 ◆

Dragon Sails into Eden Hamlet's Sunset

Before my departure for Zyss, Kyet wanted to take us all sailing, but in the end Goal caught a chill from the twins and Ray decided to play nurse, so it turned out to be just the two of us. That suited Kyet just fine. Vai explained to me once that Eden had an engineer calculate the highest future water level of Lake Limnos before the designs of the Pallas-Thor summer villa were finalized, so each time I walk down the half-mile to the shore, I count my steps to see if the lake level is rising. In my two years with the Pallases, the path has shortened maybe two paces. I fear Alnos may have reached the apex of its warmer climate, and in my nightmares I see myself enduring so many short summers and long winters that I actually grow accustomed to the cold. But I am assured that a temperate equatorial zone has established itself on this igloo planet, with less merciful sub-arctic and arctic zones to the north and south, and I am told this by O'bonne experts no less!

In the boathouse, Kyet and I helped each other into insulated sailing suits designed to safe-guard our body heat, and I immediately felt the beneficial effects. Kyet made sure the catamaran—a sleek, perfectly maintained 15-tre clan-ship—was ready, and joked, "For a ship this size I'm gonna need a crew." He directed me to take the rudder, jumped back out to push the ship off, waited until he was sure of the ship's motion, and then leapt back in. When we had cleared the boathouse, he instructed me to stay where I was and hoisted up the sails.

With a ring of excitement in his voice, he asked, "Where to?"

I looked up and down Lake Limnos, then pointed to a little island far down the lake that had always caught my eye from Eden Tower.

"Pirate Island! Great idea."

Kyet joined me, put a hand over mine, and guided my steering. With his other hand, he grasped two ropes tied to the mast and to each side of the ship. He adjusted the direction of the sail until it was braced stiffly against the prevailing wind, and the ship took off. Gradually, I began to understand the eddies and currents which determined the catamaran's direction, and I felt his hand relax over mine until it turned into something closer to a caress.

Kyet breathed a kiss down my neck and murmured, "Go ahead and explore. I'll handle it." I let go and he took over, angling sail and rudder to take advantage of a new gust. I stepped around the cabin roof to the front platform, where I could put my face into the wind. The sound of water shooting between the two keels made me feel like a great adventurer, and the occasional sprays spattering over the deck increased my delight. Though weak, the autumnal sun still bathed Lake Limnos in its equatorial light, and that luminescence was a balm to my winter-weary soul. When I rejoined Kyet, I felt wrapped in a cocoon of calm and happiness. He reached out and pressed me to him, still mastering both sail and rudder as effortlessly as if he had been born to it.

After about an hour of sailing we reached Pirate Island. We anchored the catamaran in a small bay that formed a natural harbor, and after encouraging me vainly to join him, Kyet jumped into the glacier-fed water. He swam ashore and teased me one more time, then disappeared in the underbrush. I climbed to the cabin-roof and was content to lay down and soak up more of the autumnal light (heat it could not be called, alas), and when I heard Kyet swim back, I barely even lifted my head. He crawled up a small ladder at the back of the ship, joined me on my platform, and handed me a small bag full of blue and black berries. When I looked at them doubtfully, he smiled at me with that charm he could muster, and showed me his darkened tongue. But when he approached, I held up both hands, "Ooo, get away from me, you're wet!"

Kyet laughed and shook his hair, and when I rolled myself into a defensive ball, he took it as a personal challenge and darted all over me, planting wet kisses on my neck and hands. I turned towards him and caught one arm. Kyet let himself be overpowered and I towered over his pinned-down body before I pronounced the ritual formula, "Do you yield?"

He nodded. I let go of him and he stayed down, puckered his full mouth seductively, then passed his tongue over his lower lip. I wanted to ignore the invitation, but couldn't help and reflect, "Did your father teach you how to make love, too, in addition to training you in the fighting dance?"

Kyet chuckled, then shook his head, "Uh-uh, that taboo even we Alnese libertines observe." I didn't care to continue my line of inquiry, but he felt no such reticence, "I did start early, but the usual way. With someone my age, a cousin."

Someone his age—unlike now. He saw the thought in my face and reached for me, "That came out wrong."

I seized on one of the many questions about my host clan idling in my mind as a diversion, "Why did your parents agree to the contract?"

Turning around for a lazy stretch, Kyet obliged with, "Probably because it was a good match."

"A good match?"

"Well," he rolled around again and pushed himself up on one elbow, "you know my father. At my age, he'd already scored so many conquests his Order put him into ice training to cool him off. Who would consent to give a man like that a child? His only chance was an alliance child, and he knew it. And my mother . . ." he thought about it for a minute or so, "It's always been astrophyics with her, and science. I don't think she really wants involvement."

"Does she have lovers?"

"I think . . . once. When I say she doesn't really want involvement, I mean, with anyone. Not even with me, even though she tries."

Is that why I am so attractive to you? We had circled right to a topic I wanted to avoid, and the Freudian misgivings hovering at the edge of my consciousness when I contemplated our circumstances came swarming like moths around a summer night flame.

"I did surprise dad making love once," Kyet continued as if he sensed my urge to retreat again, "Ever since passion struck he has tried to be exclusive, but . . .," he hesitated, stared out over the lake, then concluded, "Maybe it's just not in his nature." Then he turned to face me and surprised me with, "You really think I take after him?"

Oh, to be put on the spot by one's own words! I squirmed a little, considered lying, but knew perfectly well that Kyet had his own Dragon eyes in matters concerning us. I tried to save myself by specifing, "Physically, you do. The way you move, the way you use your hands." I let the words trail off.

He lay back down, "I was fifteen. His paramour was from his order. She was all muscle, and short and lithe enough to ride him. Gave me ideas."

The image he had conjured had the intended effect. When I saw him smile up at me, I shook my head, "Lithe I am not."

"Mm. We adjust. You work more, I work less."

I had a sudden urge to throw him back into the water, but he isn't particularly lithe himself. Then it occurred to me that letting him bear my full weight for a few moments might accomplish the same effect, and I rolled onto him.

"Oof!" he braced himself as I pressed down on his rib cage. "I yield! I yield!" he squeezed out between more labored inhalations.

I broke off my satisfied chuckle when he pulled me back down to him. After he let go again, I found myself enveloped in a warm blanket of desire, a stirring for him that started in my loins and ascended through my breasts, then went straight to my head. "I think it's good you take after your father physically," I hushed against him. He curved an arm around my head and kissed my temple, but made no other move.

We lay there in each other's embrace until the weak sunlight started to fade. Kyet sighed contentedly, then sat up and asked, "Ready to go back?"

Not really, but I knew it was time to return. We rode a rising wind back. To our right, in keeping with its equatorial position, the sun was setting fast, covering Lake Limnos with a golden, then an orange, then a rich carmine sheen. I felt as if I were savoring a last reprieve, both from the coming cold season and from Alnos' impending moment of truth. My entire being recoiled at the idea.

Once back in the boathouse, after the sail had been folded back, the anchor lowered, the catamaran secured, Kyet asked me to wait and not look into the cabin, then disappeared into the bowels of the ship. When he called me in, a half dozen lit candles greeted me. The whole cabin glowed softly, framing my radiant young lover like an exotic candy. I let my eyes linger on him: Wild, tangled mane, long, muscled dancer's limbs, thin, long hands like those of our tall, graceful mountain people on O'bonne. And he even had their black eyes!

Kyet closed the cabin door securely behind us, and we moved to one of the narrow bunks that lined the cabin-walls, sat and fumbled with our sailing suits. I snapped his open first, tore it clear to his navel and let my mouth follow the trail readied by my hands. His breathing caught, then he rolled each shoulder out of his suit top and leaned back against the cabin wall. I grabbed the suit sleeves and pulled, kept pulling as his second skin peeled off his arms and exposed his dark blue torso, then tackled the lower half of the suit, peeled it off his waist and buttocks and thighs. After stewing in desire all afternoon, I was hungry for him. Lucky for me, he reciprocated.

Later, my young lover whispered into my ear, "Not too bad, our adaptation." I couldn't answer. He added more audibly, "You're right about the weight." Though I took the hint, shifted closer against the cabin wall and propped myself up with one hand, I replied somewhat tartly, "Well, I'm sure your father didn't have to contend with the space limitations of a catamaran cot."

He smiled. The calm that always followed our love-making rippled through me, and I adjusted into a seated position with my back against the cabin wall. Listening to the lake waves hitting the other side of the hull, I was strongly tempted to nudge him to one side, stretch out next to him and let the lake sounds lull us to slumber. I did not want to separate, as we always did, each going off to our allotted space; yet this longing could not be indulged.

As if guessing my thoughts, Kyet sighed, "Staying here would be nice, but not very discreet. Mom's already suspicious, you know. We better be getting back." He rolled himself into a sitting position next to me and before we knew what we were doing or why, we were enmeshed again, Kyet nibbling at the corner of my mouth while I rained butterfly light kisses on his nose and brow.

"It's okay," he soothed against my efforts, "it's okay." And with a sense of dread rising I realized: That was not what I wanted to hear. Before giving in to him, I had extracted an agreement to keep our relationship private, secret even, and now, I was ready for a challenge to that agreement. I just could not break the agreement myself, not yet.

Kyet got up, disappeared towards the back of the cabin and came back with sponge and towels. Cleaning up, we almost fell several times, steadying each other with giggles and laughter. Then, in a curious reversal of our usual pattern, we helped each other into our day clothes. I opened the cabin door and braced myself against the autumnal evening chill, and Kyet blew out the last few lit candles behind us.

Our hands interlocked for half the path up from the lake, then, as we were coming closer to the house, despite the protecting darkness, despite my reluctance, I let go and stepped ahead of him.

◆ CHAPTER 24 ◆

A Call for Help

From Ashewe Azetmir through Alnese subspace channels to Nyemba Ndinzi, Director of Cultural Studies, O'bonne First University

Two reasons prompt this urgent message to you, the second a personal one. Let me start with the first: The 32nd Ruler of Alnos, Lady Alnos Ciani, has requested O'bonne mediation. Since the planet warmed and its habitable area is expanding, many immigrant-settlers have been drawn to Alnos by the promise of easy wealth, and a group has come into conflict with the native population. I am not up to the task. Aside from the obvious ethical questions raised by my long-standing involvement with the native Alnese, the problem is of such a scope and severity that a more experienced team of mediators is absolutely necessary. In addition, the immigrant-settlers coming into conflict with the natives entertain some trying prejudices about women. In spite of my long preparation on Earth, which surely should have immunized me once and for all, I find that immigrant leaders often get under my skin.

Lady Ciani counts with the support of her entire Council, and their request is urgent. Violence has already flared up between natives and immigrants in a few regions, and her Grace fears that it could devolve into something closer to a civil war.

And now the time has come for me to confess my other reason for requesting your counsel: I am no longer just an observer here. I have succumbed to one of the great temptations of cultural planetology work and have taken a native lover. It gets worse: Soon, the consequences of our dalliance will force our involvement into the open. Yes, dear friend, I have not only succumbed to my blood-fever, but I have also, in a moment of madness, allowed for the conception of my first child. I know that you will immediately reassure me that my desire for this child is to be expected, since I am in the third decade of my life and have reached our normal age for child bearing. The problem is that I am not in a normal situation. The Alnese will want the child as soon as they know of its existence, especially if I acknowledge its Alnese father. I am therefore thinking of removing myself from Alnos as soon as the signs of my pregnancy become unmistakable.

You will no doubt understand the urgency of my request. Time is running short, both for Alnos and for myself.

TWO

WINTER SCHISMS

◆ EPISODE 1 ◆

Raymond Indulges in an Earth Habit

Let's just say it's the first time you shoot up in months. Let's say it's the first time in a good four months, well, four Earth months, in any case, when your habit has already receded and when, to put it simply for those of you who don't know this mistress, it's more like you've decided to take a vacation down memory lane with the old flame. What you expect to happen that first time after the trial separation is for someone to walk in on you. It always happens, so I shouldn't have been surprised. But I was surprised.

Lady Ciani had given me the Alnese equivalent of the weekend off. An O'bonne delegation was set to arrive just as the first snows started to fall, turning Zyss into a winter wonderland every bit as beautiful as Switzerland. I had taken advantage of my free weekend to tag along with Leila and a whole gaggle of Pallases to Eden Hamlet. We wanted to enjoy the Hamlet's last mild days, but a bitterly cold early ice storm disappointed us all. Casting an icy spell over trees and buildings, it blasted up from the mountainous end of Lake Limnos the very night we landed, and we had to confine ourselves to the villa for the duration.

With Vai giving anyone who crossed her path the evil eye, most of my traveling companions steered clear of the fourth floor, and stayed mostly off the residential floors as well. Somehow, the unexpected privacy of my second-floor quarters beckoned like a rare chance to indulge.

Or so I thought at the time.

I chose my right arm since I didn't really have to hide what I was doing, and the movements came back at once: The needle filled up flawlessly, the vein just popped out. I nudged the point in and started pushing her in slowly, savoring this particular vacation, when the two men walked in.

After taking one look, Eden strolled over to a seat in front of me, grabbed the chair's back and leaned against it, "I should have knocked."

There was a sparkle to his voice.

"You should have." With one jerk I slid the needle out of my arm, untied and bent it over a little ball of prepared cotton. I shook my hair back and directed my gaze at the man behind Eden. I knew immediately who he was.

"Meet Raymundo," purred Eden.

I ignored him, "Hello." My arms relaxed completely, and I had to focus most of my energy on not dropping my little piece of cotton.

"So you're my former sister's new chronicler."

Alexander and I studied each other.

He is the one being I've met to whom the term 'chiseled features' truly applies. Everything is perfect: The shoulders, the hands, the cheekbones, the lips . . . especially the lips. He had on a long-sleeved Alnese tunic that flowed about his body, his thick hazel-golden hair hung down his back in one braid and dark lashes framed a pair of amber eyes. My jaw hung in disbelief long enough to be noticeable. I cursed myself thoroughly for it.

"Would you like to be left alone?" The latter-day Apollo asked.

I continued to stare, "What can I do for you?"

"We would like you to help us with a little mission."

Eden added coolly, "If you feel up to it."

The Alnese junk careened through me. I closed my eyes and leaned back, and almost fell off my bodychair. Alexander and Eden both caught me, guided me up and to my Alnese settee, where they tried to make me lie down. I fought them off, "I want to sit." Alexander sat down next to me and straightened me against him. An exquisite pulse dove through my entire body and I sighed, spying on Eden as I shook through it. Then, challenging him directly, I said, "I will be."

"How much time do you need?" Nothing could take the sparkle out of Eden's voice that day, and I understood him. A second rush coursed through me and I let out a slow contented sigh. With Alexander keeping me from sliding down, his wave-breaths crashed through me at regular intervals, and I thought I could feel his heartbeat. I kept looking at Eden and felt a sudden kinship with him, which I suppressed. Perhaps for the first time, I also took note him: Eden and Alexander could have been brothers, the first a more understated version of the second minus the gray-blue skin.

Alexander asked from behind me, "Do you really think we can use him? Doesn't seem too wise to me." He'd switched to Alnese. Eden replied in the same language, "He's an occasional user now. This is the first time I've seen him shoot up since he's been living in our house."

"He's still an addict."

"Yes, but I'd say that's irrelevant on Alnos. You spent too much time with the Kobrans."

"Get off it! For once I agree with them."

Eden put both hands on my cheeks and lifted my head towards him, "Tell him, Ray, would you sell your soul for a needle? That's what they teach on Kobra, on Ko, on O'bonne ..."

And on Earth. I shook him off, then shook my head, "I'm stopping again. I have stopped for months at a time. I'm not going back," I broke off, realizing I had said too much.

Eden smiled at me, then he leaned forward and whispered in English into my ear, "I know, I know what you're not going back to." I leaned back against Alexander in an effort to get away from him.

"Now, listen," Alexander chimed in behind me. "In two days, the O'bonne mediation team is scheduled to arrive. There will be festivities and," I felt him shrug, "conversations." He paused, went on, "Her Grace has an exaggerated sense of honor sometimes: If someone talks to her confidentially, the conversation has never taken place. But she can't hide anything from her Chronicler. Do you understand me?"

I nodded.

Eden continued, "Dragon and Lady Ciani do not keep secrets from one another, and her Grace can have no secrets from you. We want to know exactly what the mediators are proposing each time a suggestion is made. I also want to know what Kobran Ambassador Periasamy's investigation turns up, and long before he decides to tell me."

Eden turned around, walked over to my table and surveyed the rest of my precious drug. Alexander took the relay, "You'll report to me regularly."

I tried to pull myself together, "Like the man says, I'm an addict. Why trust me?"

Eden shrugged. "Why not? It's not a factor in my opinion." Then he came very close to me again and leaned forward, "You can do whatever you want here, little Chronicler." He paused, then repeated slowly, breaking between each word, "Whatever." Pause. "You." Pause. "Want." He straightened up. "Nothing will stop you from doping yourself up day after day until you die, or someone kills you. I think you know that." His voice was even, flat almost. I don't know why I found it so menacing.

He motioned to Alexander. "Make sure he's comfortable for the rest of his journey." Then he started back towards the door.

I felt Alexander tug me gently to one side. He lifted a pillow and leaned my head against it, then moved towards the door where Eden stood waiting. Out of the corner of my eye, I saw Eden lean forward ever so slightly when Alexander was within a step from the door. Their heads came together, then I heard a swirl of clothes and they were gone.

I would never have believed myself capable of the regret I felt then. In my head, where it counted, this vacation had lost its appeal.

◆ ◆ ◆

When he arrived a few hours later, Kyet did knock. I had come down enough to do away with the most obvious evidence of my flirtation. But after two Alnese months with my tolerant hosts, I had grown careless. He took one look at me and he knew.

And I didn't like it.

He didn't say a word. Simply threw a glance into my waste basket for confirmation, plopped down in front of me, and examined the tapestry behind me a little too obviously.

I could only endure that silent reticence settling between us for a minute. I gnarled, "What?"

"My father sent me to get you."

"Your father?"

"Alexander."

"Oh yeah, the Apollo."

"What?"

I waved him off, "Never mind. An Earth thing." Then, realizing Kyet wasn't volunteering any more, I asked, "Why?"

"He wants to talk to you."

"Well he knows where I am."

Kyet put his elbows on his knees and brought his hands together, fingertips against fingertips. He pre-empted my next cross comment with, "Privately."

"Privately." I pondered the meaning of that word on a planet where, as I was discovering, everyone discretely keeps tabs on everyone else. "What about?"

"Eden's duel last month, I think."

The petulance in my voice increasing with each syllable, I whined, "I created that report already."

Kyet countered with, "Oh dad's read it. I'm sure he's also seen the other records. Now he wants to talk to you." Then he repeated quietly, "Privately."

Kyet's eyes followed me as I got up. I know what I look like after coming down from smack, so I turned my back on him.

"Are you sure you're up to it?" The concern in his voice infuriated me, but at the same time, I felt disingenuous. My hands balled into fists. What I really wanted was for Kyet to take back his solicitude and his awareness. I wanted our relationship back the way it had been before this day.

"Let's go," he said behind me.

In the hall, he helped me into the pelt snow-coat and legging trews that served as Alnos' basic final outdoor winter-layer. After wrestling on boots and hood, the tough hide and soft, fleece-like interior turned the outfit into a cocoon of warmth. In the two weeks since Alnos entered its first winter-month, Loxi, I'd learned to appreciate that cocoon. Once outside, Kyet seated me in front of him on our sled and we shot down the incline to the boat-house.

The first thing I did at the bottom of the slope was lean over to one side and heave a little. Kyet scooped up a handful of snow and brushed it against my face. Gratitude and resentment welled up at the same time. I twisted away, wanting him nowhere near me, yet needing his steadying arm. He guided me to my feet, into the boathouse, and up the stairs to the studio and up again to the little look-out crowning that structure. A solar panel on the roof pooled enough warmth into the room so our breaths stopped misting into view. Alexander was standing by the large window and surveying the half-frozen lake. He pointed to a chair at his right and Kyet bundled me into it, hesitated, and said quite unnecessarily, “He’s not well.”

Alexander turned his gaze to me, “Looks like Eden’s right about you. You haven’t been using much.”

I was measuring each breath carefully, and didn’t bother to reply. Kyet pulled off my hood, opened my coat. I struggled on by myself and rested the coat on my shoulders, leaning back in my chair.

“Thank you. I’ll call you back.” Alexander had closed in. Out of the corner of one eye, I saw Kyet hesitate. When he straightened, he threw a weary glance at his father. Alexander nodded towards the door, and Kyet made up his mind to obey him.

Once Kyet had gone, Alexander pulled a second chair up and seated himself next to me, tugging the chair closer until he sat just inches from me. When his hands rose to my head I tilted back and as far out of reach as I could. He tut-tuted quietly and I stopped. I fought the small wave of panic rising within me as I felt his thumbs lock onto my temples. After a quick rub, his fingers burrowed over to the back of my skull, and then, just when my eyes were closing, his inaudible command jolted me back to awareness: *Focus on the memory of Eden’s last duel.*

He let go of me, explained, “You haven’t done this before, I know. I’m focusing my mind into yours, joining the two.”

I rasped, "I thought the O'bonne were the empathic ones."

"They are. I have a different gift." He'd shifted back a bit. Anticipating my next question, he continued, "Actually, it's rare. Depends on our ancestry. I have Danyx blood."

"One of the planets you gypsied by before Alnos."

"Our ancestors did, but in my case, my grandmother was a traveler. I visited Danyx after my son's birth. Spent a bit of time there. My relatives very graciously helped me perfect my mind skills."

Our brief conversation had eased me into a calmer state. When his hands moved onto me again, I stayed put.

No. Not language.

What, then?

Sights. Sensations. Let go of language.

A few false starts marred the emerging recall, then Alexander's growing approval guided it into focus. What came back first was the end, the dry crack that had knifed itself into my aural memory when Eden broke his challenger's neck. Eden's final stratagem had paralleled one I'd seen him use on Kyet: He'd let his challenger pounce at a chance that proved illusory. Then Eden spun behind him, knocked him to his knees, and got a hold of his head, snapping it up, then to the side. The sound echoed through me to Alexander. He asked me to go over it again, then again, then he nudged me along until I recalled the entire fight.

It had not been an easy contest, this duel between Eden and his Tomrys challenger. Tomrys formed a martial Order akin to Alnese forest rangers, only better armed and more lethal, and they had announced that the time had come for all 'aliens' to leave the Islands. After Eden started to close in on three suspects for nine murders of said 'aliens', he received a challenge from Tomrys. Eden accepted the challenge, and Eden's Arthmis Order agreed to end his investigation if he lost.

Eden was the stronger fighter, but his foe had a good fifteen years on him, and a grim desperation into the bargain. He'd gotten his knife into Eden twice, once superficially in the arm, the second time right in the gut. That second cut was painful, and serious. When Eden finished, he'd doubled over and practically fainted in his lieutenant's arms. Lieutenant Minguard Lauran, the same woman he'd assigned to chaperone me in the Islands, had caught and supported him until an Arthmis medic could attend him.

Alexander directed me over some scenes several times. He instructed me to bear down on one, then another detail. When he was satisfied with the particulars of the fight, he had me foreground as many reactions from the various on-lookers as I could recover. Again, we went through the cycle of repetition and focusing, repetition and focusing. Finally, Alexander broke our connection. He rubbed my temples again, stepped behind me and continued with a neck rub.

"The Tomrys challenger's death bought the lives of the other two. You know that, don't you?"

"I don't really understand that part." Without prompting, I flashed back to the challenger's accomplices, a woman who reminded me of Leila, visibly pregnant, and a kid that looked like her twin, certainly not older than Kyet. Chantico cousins all three, they claimed sole responsibility for the nine murders that started the Island Troubles last winter. The two non-combatants had stayed calm, even at the end.

In spite of the fact that no one believed they did it on their own, Eden had accepted their guilty pleas. Once he'd accepted the challenge for a duel, he had to accepted its terms: to drop any further investigation into the matter and recall any extra Arthmis troops from the Islands. In return, Tomrys had agreed to let the two surviving Chantico cousins be banished into ice, but not until after the birth of the woman's child.

With Eden out for the duration, Lieutenant Minguard Lauran had confirmed their bargain, announcing, "The Justiciar will wait to send you into ice until spring, as agreed. He will find an ice master once you begin your sentence."

"What will happen to the child?" A question I'd been meaning to ask.

"She's not allied. She'll probably take the child with her, as is her right."

"Into ice?"

"Why else ask for an ice master?" Alexander finished his ministration, tapped me lightly on one shoulder, and returned to the windowsill. He leaned against it and folded his arms in silent observation.

A slow neck roll confirmed Alexander's effectiveness as a masseur. "I don't know anything about them. All Dragon says is that they are like solitary nuns and monks."

Alexander shrugged, "Not a bad description. An ice mentor answers a call for solitude, for meditation and reflection away from the distractions and demands of our clan responsibilities. Usually this happens later in life. If you have a calling, you apprentice with Pallas-Metis, and the Order gives you a sponsor. Leila's father is an ice mentor, and I'm almost sure that Vai will join them one day."

I let his explanation sink in and drew out, "So … the Chantico cousins are getting an ice mentor when they start their sentence?"

"Yes," Alexander confirmed, "Pallas-Metis releases you from all ties, all obligations. If you choose to associate with the shunned," he shrugged again, "who can object?"

"And ice mentors know how to survive in ice?"

"They know a great deal more than how to survive." The observation rang heavy with implications. Hadn't Alexander himself just returned from an ice retreat, presumably an encounter with a mentor?

I wondered aloud, "Do many of them choose to associate with the banished?"

"Ice mentors are generous if they find you worthy."

His long gaze turned entirely too measuring for me. I got up and moved to the window, shifted away. The corners of his mouth twitched upwards. My defensiveness amused.

I clarified another point, "You think the kid's his?"

"His?"

"The Tomrys challenger's."

"Yes, more than likely he asked for that gift from her."

"That gift?"

"He was with Tomrys. He knew he was doomed once he issued his challenge to a Justiciar of Arthmis and admitted to murdering nine people without providing any justification. If he'd won, Arthmis would have given him a little time to walk into ice, and then send someone like me after him. He didn't challenge Eden to save himself; he did it for his partners." Alexander kept looking at me, concluded, "And since she isn't allied, there are no complications."

For some reason, I sought out those golden eyes. The current between us turned palpable, almost strong enough to re-establish our earlier connection. Still, I had to strain to hear his low murmur, "Don't expect too much from Eden's debt to Leila."

"I expected less than what I got."

Not quite the anticipated answer, I could tell.

Alexander fished out a communicator and keyed in a quick code. Ten minutes later Kyet appeared. "Take him to your studio in the house for an hour." And to me, "You understand that's where you've been?"

I nodded.

"You do learn quickly."

Praise for the human pet. I examined the floorboards to mask my reaction, but he picked up on it anyhow. Before I knew what was happening, I was whirling around, then I slammed into Kyet. Alexander's shove had come faster than the eye could see, exceeded only by the speed of his subsequent composure. He looked unchanged, as if nothing had happened. Except that I detected even greater amusement in him.

Alexander addressed his son, "Is he making progress with your training? His reflexes need improving."

"True," came the careful reply. Kyet steadied me. The sudden spin had almost re-awakened my nausea, and I breathed deep and hard to find my way back to the relaxed state Alexander had massaged me into before my lessoning.

"One last warning, Chronicler," this time, Alexander's voice hardened unmistakably, "Eden may not object to your drug use, but I do. I don't care for an impaired spy. You've tasted my Danyx abilities. They can be put to other uses. Less pleasant ones."

We both caught Kyet's relief. One of Alexander's eye-brows went up, then down again.

Kyet spoke the formulaic "By your leave" for both of us, and Alexander dismissed us with a quick wave.

After we had reached Kyet's studio, my young friend felt compelled to reiterate, "Take my father seriously. If you need help staying off your drugs, talk to Peg."

"How much do you know about addiction, Kyet?"

"Enough. I know it's for life. The point is, Ray, how much do you want to find out about dad's Danyx gifts?"

When he guessed the thought that came into my mind next he almost burst out laughing, "God Almighty no! I am the apple of his eye. He's never laid a hand on me."

"Then why are you so careful around him? He let you watch when he straightened out other wayward souls?"

He was taken aback. "No." He did not sound convinced.

"But you have seen things?"

He clammed up, flushed a darker indigo.

"Forget it," I mumbled. Then, peeling off my winter-coat, I proposed, "Now that we're here, why not go through a centering cycle?" He agreed with one curt nod and slipped off his winter layers. I assumed the first of the eight basic positions he'd taught me. The motion felt almost natural.

◆ EPISODE 2 ◆

Dragon Takes a Respite at Alnos House

I seized on the imminent arrival of my O'bonne colleagues as an escape, an easy excuse to move my quarters temporarily to Alnos House, Lady Ciani's residence and the diplomatic head quarters of the planet, which almost amounted to a safe distance from Kyet. I simply was not yet able to bring myself to tell him about our pregnancy, and after the second month, the only alternative was avoiding him.

Of course, the minute I started pulling back, Kyet started to seek me out more persistently, threatening to expose our secret. Had I applied some O'bonne logic to the whole situation, I would have recognized at once that our secret was about to come out, and stopped all the nonsensical limitations I imposed on Kyet. In truth, I simply needed the distance and the time to myself until I could discuss my predicament with my own people. I needed rational discussion again, needed to feel some true kinship as I explored my options. I simply couldn't communicate the news of his impending fatherhood to Kyet before then.

I practically wept with joy the day the O'bonne delegation landed. As primary mediator, O'bonne had selected Maskar Enku, whose abilities as both empath and mediator were already legendary. In response to a special request by Lady Ciani, he was accompanied by Nyemba Ndinzi, an old Alnese hand with two decades of local research under his belt, and one of my mentors. I thought them wise choices, and I am sure both men concurred, despite the fact that practically the first thing out of Nyemba upon landing in Zyss was a mournful, "Ashewe, what have you done to me? It took a decade on Danyx for me to recover from this igloo of a planet and now you call me back?" Enku Maskar winked just to make sure I would not take my old mentor too seriously, and we turned to our hosts for the first set of greetings.

Once the two men were settled in their adjoining quarters at Alnos House and we had some privacy, however, Ndinzi Nyemba surprised me. He grasped both of my hands and explained, "Ashewe, I have taken Maskar into our confidence about your delicate situation. I hope that this did not constitute a breach of trust. I did so because I wanted to give you the means for an immediate departure from Alnos if that is your wish. Our Kobran transport stands ready to take you back to O'bonne."

Before Nyemba's announcement, all had been confusion, but at the thought of actually leaving Alnos it was as if the sun broke through the haze of the tumultuous conflict within me. "No," I said after the briefest of hesitations, "that won't be necessary." Then I added, "I appreciate the choice, and the effort you all put into providing it."

"You realize of course," Maskar intoned from behind us, "this means you have already made up your mind about your child's future. At least, insofar as where that future is to be."

I had to acknowledge the truth of his observation, but I still needed to talk through my options. We took advantage of the one night we all stayed together to do just that, until the wee hours of the morning. I needed this one night of true companionship, of the kind of talk I had begun to long for without quite admitting it to myself. In a way, it was a reminder of the price paid for the years of relative isolation required for planetologist research, and it revealed to me another reason for my child's conception.

Maskar had a wonderful ability to counterweigh the strict O'bonne rationality I clung to initially. "Really, Azetmir, out with it!" He challenged me, "You want the impossible, an O'bonne child with an Alnese father. Only you're sure it's impossible, so you steadfastly refuse even to consider it. Very reasonable, and such a difficult attitude to work with."

"What do you suggest?" Nyemba asked before I could.

"Ndinzi, how often have you said that on Alnos, everything is negotiable?"

Nyemba parried adroitly, "Hardly an original observation. And like many such over-generalizations, not completely accurate."

"Well then, let us get to work: What is negotiable?"

Maskar's last question was clearly directed at me. I pondered his words, thinking aloud, "Having an O'bonne child is not really difficult, as long as I do not acknowledge its Alnese ancestry."

"That is not what you want," Maskar observed with a patient teacher's tone.

I raised both hands in a helpless gesture and zeroed in on what was really the crux of the problem, "What I want is a family, but if I own up to the child's Alnese half, I will have to deal with a whole Alnese clan."

"Ai, to have a hundred in-laws in one stroke!" Maskar commiserated.

I quipped, "One hundred? The Pallas clan is five times more numerous!"

Maskar considered my admission for a little while, then concluded, "It sounds to me like the relationship between the child and the clan is what needs negotiating, does it not?"

"As you see," Nyemba chimed in again, "My learned friend has a keen grasp of logic."

I nodded to them both, my thoughts whirling around the possibility Maskar had just woven out of the combination of my desires and my circumstances. An O'bonne Alnese? Could it be done? Could my child grow up on both its worlds and with both heritages? The unpleasant realization followed that some Alnese prejudices I so lamented were reflected in my own distaste for my prospective in-laws. *These Heshtis are crazy! They have such strange customs!* So went an almost planet-wide chorus about newcomers on Alnos. And yet, I had to admit to myself that I found Alnese alliances, their strangely elastic inter-clan marriage based strictly on joint procreation, too strange a custom for me. I had O'bonne ideas, wanted convergence between intimacy, family, and even passion, illogical as that was.

Sensing my thoughts, Maskar inquired delicately, "The man involved could . . . adapt to O'bonne customs?"

I felt the blood rise to my cheeks, and turned away from him to signal my continuing unwillingness to discuss that man. What could I possibly tell them? Taking a native lover was one thing; being seduced by a youth half my age was quite another! Maskar let my feelings wash over him, then he touched my shoulder and murmured so quietly only I could hear him, "Lovers come in such surprising shapes sometimes." When I turned to face him again, he winked at me for the second time that day.

"Yes," I stumbled forth, "the . . . man . . . could adapt, I think."

"He doesn't know? You didn't tell him?"

I shook my head.

Maskar rubbed his beard pensively, "What could turn into such a preoccupation that you wouldn't even tell him?"

Ndinzi Nyemba cleared his throat, "Maskar, you cannot imagine the intrusive quality of Alnos clan-life. It's worse than living in a small village, at least when children are involved. It is impossible to maintain any kind of distance. The in-laws will try to control every facet of that child's upbringing, and if they disapprove of O'bonne ideas, you can be sure they will find ways to subvert them."

I chimed in, "Strangely enough, though, the clan never tells you directly what to do or not to do. It is subtle, and maybe more irritating that way."

Maskar smiled, "Me thinks you two urbanites talk overconfidently of differences where I detect a universal experience, and may be particularizing Alnese customs when they in fact are quite common." He broke off for some brief reflection, and the next thing he said threw a fascinating light onto the origin of his empathic and mediation skills, "A good mountain man can tell you a thing or two about village life! But let me assure you, Ashewe, I do understand your reluctance concerning your five hundred future in-laws, perhaps better than most."

"In any case," Nyemba cut in, "you now know the next step. Is there somebody who could be a local ally in your negotiations?"

"There is." The time had come for me to draw on the store of goodwill I had accumulated with Pallas Leila, the one Alnese I knew who had successfully defied her own clan and taken her child where she pleased, rearing her on two worlds, exactly as I planned.

Nyemba concluded for all, "Then might we suggest you take that person into your confidence as soon as possible?"

I nodded again, and we switched to the Alnese problem bringing my colleagues to "this igloo of a planet." But as I gave Maskar and Nyemba a quick overview of the conflict brewing between natives and newcomes, the lateness of the hour suddenly impressed itself on us.

I proposed, "Perhaps we could go over the situation tomorrow, once you have rested? Her Grace Lady Ciani has asked me to take the lead in getting you fully briefed about the situation. She has stressed that she wants to start with an O'bonne analysis of the situation. She hopes to meet with you both soon."

"Well," Nyemba announced with a yawn, "I do declare we have all stayed up way past our bedtime. Especially considering the days that await us."

Maskar grimaced slightly to indicate his complete agreement.

"What you have done for me, I will not soon forget," I said bowing to my colleagues.

They recognized my formal pronouncements with slight nods of their own, then Nyemba replied in the same tone, "Nor will your world forget what you are contributing in return."

◆ EPISODE 3 ◆

Raymond's Bill Comes Due

As if Eden, Kyet, and Alexander weren't enough for one twenty-four hour period, the next morning Leila caught up with me. I had made sure she'd be gone before shooting up, seizing on her early return to Zyss to help with the preparations for the O'bonne arrival as a perfect opportunity. Fool! Judgment is the first thing to go in addiction.

Leila stormed into my apartment without so much as a hello. Her yellow eyes were shooting sparks. But I had the children with me, so she held off at first. Then, when I was done with Socorro's morning routine and Goal carried her off for morning child-care, Leila launched into me.

"How dare you? I give you a little bit of responsibility and the first thing you do is trip on me? I am shipping you back to Earth, Raymond. Eight years of caretaking is enough. I won't have any more of your shit."

She paced up and down my room, alternatively shooting another eye-full, then shaking a fist at me. All I wanted to do was crawl back underneath my blanket and pretend none of the past twenty-four hours had happened, starting with Eden and Alexander's unannounced visit.

I finally found my voice, "Leila, it was just a little vacation. What's the big deal?"

"I do not want my children's uncle high as a kite when he's supposed to be watching over them."

"But I wasn't. I wasn't. They were with Vai."

"They weren't supposed to be with Vai. You were supposed to take care of them. Isn't that what we agreed?"

I crossed my arms around my knees. "Leila, I've stopped, okay?"

She practically snarled, "Of course you have."

I ignored her, "Earth? You want me to go back to Earth? Are you serious?"

"Fool that I was, I thought taking you out of that environment could not just ease my debt, but actually help you." She raised both hands in a helpless gesture, then snapped around and reiterated, "Here or there, you're the same old Ray."

"Come on, Leila, look at me! I'm not knocked out the way I was. This was just a vacation!"

"A vacation!"

"Like when we started, before I hit the skids. Before," I broke off. I didn't even want to allude to that time, so I just blocked it out by recalling, "You know I took vacations for years before I got hooked."

She shook her head, more to herself than to me, muttering quietly, "I can't believe I ever bought that line. But I'm not the naive stranger I was then, Ray. Spending the last nine years on

Earth has taught me a few things." She took a deep, calming breath. "All right. Pack your things. You don't want to return to Earth, fine. You have a job in Zyss. I'll have you taken to her Grace's household."

Her grim expression left me dumbfounded. And all of a sudden, it hit me: She was serious. I was standing over the abyss again. "No." My eyes opened wide, the realization of what she proposed to do cutting through me like a dull blade, "No."

She hissed, "If this is how you want it, I'll get Eden," and turning on her heels, she made for the door.

I bolted up and slammed against it, repeating, "No. No." She tried to push me out of the way. I braced myself against the door and would not budge. Enraged, she pounded into my shoulder and grabbed a fistful of hair. I cried out hoarsely as she pulled, but didn't move. "Leila, Leila," I was panting against her, struggling with the hand tearing my hair out, "Leila, please." Still scowling, she let me disentangle her fingers. I whispered down to her, "Why did you have her? Didn't you have her for me?"

She said with uncommon vehemence, "That didn't make any damn difference!"

"For me it did. Maybe not for you, but for me it did. Leila," my whisper turned pleading, "Not again, not now." I would have promised her anything knowing full well it was useless. She didn't believe my promises. Rightly so. "You knew, Leila," I argued desperately instead, "Why else did you ask me not to make promises I can't keep? You knew I wouldn't kick it completely. Why are you freaking out now?"

“Maybe I didn’t know how I’d feel. I don’t want my children growing up with a junkie. You are leaving.”

“I raised Goal while taking vacations, didn’t I? You didn’t see a problem then.”

“Well I do now. I have changed, Ray.”

“So have I, goddamn it. Leila, we both know it’s for keeps. Leila please!”

She said very slowly, “Get out of my way.”

I opened the door behind me, inched my way into the doorframe still holding her off, then threw the door shut behind me. I sprinted down the hall, down the stairs, found the door, and stumbled on blindly outside. I stopped only when I could no longer make out the house through the falling snow.

It was dark, dark and still. The silence wrapped around me like a comforting blanket. Glancing around, I recognized the garden. The cold cut into my lungs with every breath. I wanted it to. I found a bench and sat down, waited to turn into a snowman.

When Eden found me, I had lost all sensation. He hoisted me up like a sack of potatoes and lumbered back to the house. Hovering between a welcome numbness and total oblivion, I was vaguely aware of our movements through the house, of a light turning on, of being laid out. The sound of ripping cloth was next, then I felt a burst of soft warmth over me.

The reverse of freezing turned out to be much more agonizing. First pain started needling my entire body, then it burned into my hands and feet. I contracted involuntarily, tried to grind my chattering teeth.

"Well, do you want Ray to experience the entire torment of defrosting or do I knock him out?" came Eden's voice from close by. There was no audible answer, but a welcome darkness settled over me.

When I came to, I sensed more than saw him sitting behind me. We were alone. I stirred. My hands were wrapped in some kind of gauze. Shifting to my side, I felt the same material on my feet. Cold had settled into my very bones, replacing the earlier scorching. I shook through a chill and bundled my blanket around me the best I could. A second blanket was flung over me. Eden bundled it around my feet.

"You'll lose a toe or two, you know."

I closed my eyes through a second wave of the trembling. I wanted to curl into the warm fabric beneath me.

"You'll feel better in a little bit," Eden soothed. He used the gentle tone he reserved for Goal.

Goal.

I had made her a promise I'd meant to keep.

A third wave underscored my growing misery. My teeth started chattering again. After I finally suppressed it, I cleared my throat and jerked my head to get Eden near me. He bent close. "Goal," I rasped weakly.

Eden looked surprised, "Leila took the girls ahead to Zyss. She's stepping in for me with the O'bonne delegation until you're well enough to travel. We'll join them soon."

"Both of us?"

He nodded.

The warmth of the bed penetrated into me at long last. I relaxed gradually, still clutching my blankets to me the best I could. Every time I even thought of moving a finger, a stinging pain threatened to shoot through hand and arm, so I tried to hold my hands still.

From where he was standing, Eden murmured, "What was Leila thinking? And you? Don't you two know Goal won't separate from you now? You can't just sever your relationship now! She's turning twelve. She's got her own mind."

"What did you tell Goal?" I gurgled through my thick throat.

"That you got lost in a snow drift. I didn't tell her you had no decent clothes on."

The warmth was acting like a soporific, but one of his statements had awakened my curiosity. I struggled on to get the question out, "Is this how you felt when Leila took Goal to Earth?"

He didn't answer for so long that I though he was going to ignore me. Then his voice jarred me back to attention. "Leila never told you what happened?"

Again I was at a loss for words.

He continued, "What I did to her?"

I tried to shake my head.

"What I did to Leila … If anyone ever did that to Goal, I'd kill him, Arthmis or no Arthmis. Yeah, Leila took Goal away, far away. Leila had a right to every one of her demands. What I felt was," he measured the word before pronouncing it, "irrelevant." After reflecting on it further, he mused, "My wife never threatens. She acts. Maybe you've learned that now. And maybe," his voice moved so close it practically tickled my ear, "maybe she just found her match in you."

He pulled one blanket to the side and gently touched one hand. The hum of a scanner turned on and off, on and off. "Your fingers will regenerate fully. I should think a bass guitarist would want all his fingers."

There was just a touch of the old, sardonic Eden in that last statement. I tried to nod some kind of acknowledgment as I was letting go. Drifting off, I pressed my wrist against his arm as a wordless sign of gratitude. I couldn't read the expression that crossed his face: a mixture of embarrassment and something akin to satisfied anticipation, as if he saw something in me that he'd been waiting for.

◆ CHAPTER 4 ◆

Dragon Readies Her Colleagues

It took Maskar and Nyemba until the late afternoon the day after their arrival to have recovered sufficiently from the rigors of their trip. That gave me a chance to go through my notes and summaries of O'bonne research into civil conflicts like the one brewing on Alnos, and I felt much better prepared when we got together.

"How was your rest?" I asked my colleagues after we'd all settled down to cups of local choctea. Lady Ciani had arranged for a mixture of O'bonne and Alnese dishes to be served to them as soon as they'd awakened, complete with concluding hot drinks. Both Maskar and Nyemba praised their accommodations, and we got down to business.

I provided them with a quick summary of the situation on Alnos. According to our geologists, Alnos's climate alternates between deep and moderate ice ages, and the current Alnese arrived just as the planet entered a moderate period. By O'bonne standards, the planet still comes closer to an igloo than the temperate worlds inhabited by most people, but for the Alnese, their planet is turning into a green wonderland of new possibilities. What they hadn't anticipated was that with new possibilities come new problems, like getting a lot of interest from people who would never even have visited Alnos before.

Both Maskar and Nyemba came prepared for their mission: They knew that a steady stream of immigrants had started about a century before my arrival, and that many of the newcomers on Alnos were turning into settlers, starting families and communities of their own. They also knew that the Alnese mostly ignored their 'visitors' for several decades, and had only recently considered what to do should the 'visitors' turn into more permanent neighbors.

Nyemba quickly went over his O'bonne demographic analyses showing that newcomers now made up about 15% of the planet's population, but with an uneven distribution. Most lived on the main inhabited continent, Nyheim, with regions like the arctic Borderlands still almost 100% Alnese. We were all surprized that conflict between the two communities had started in the Islands, where immigrants mostly cycled through for seasonal work. Their more permanent settlements there were small and quite isolated, and we were as perplexed by the fight that had erupted on Chantico Island as our Alnese hosts.

We soon turned to Alnese pacification efforts to date, and I told my sponsor Nyemba, "I've been studying your initial work on the Alnese martial orders, but your later reports got themselves chewed up during inter-planetary transmission. I'd appreciate a quick review."

"Again? Really, we need to discuss our Kobran communications arrangements sooner rather than later! Alright, where shall I start? With the keepers of the peace, Arthmis, or with the second wave, Mythras? Studying Mythras was something of a challenge. Mythrans camouflage their status using Arthmis symbols and Arthmis structures, and are difficult to identify. Well, I guess technically Mythrans belong to Arthmis."

"Arthmis is deeply involved in the present affair, as far as I can make out. I couldn't tell you much about Mythras." I encouraged him.

"Well, Arthmis would be involved, wouldn't it, given its function? It is the largest and most public of the martial orders, with thousands of members. And did you not report that your Alnese sponsor is involved, your Justiciar Pallas Thor Eden?"

"Yes. It's funny, but I get this odd sense that he is not just a justiciar ruling over his four companies of Arthmin. I have been observing him ever since he agreed to let me shadow him, and I haven't seen him command any other companies, and yet I can't shake the impression that he is tied into more powerful circles."

"Well, among Justiciars are some tasked with resolving specific problems by the Council of Eight. They become the heads of special investigations or special task forces. It makes sense that the Justiciar involved in this affair would have more authority. He'd be acting for the Council in this matter, and he would have the authority to mobilize whatever resources he would need to get the job done. What is Pallas Eden like?"

"Ruthless," was the first word that popped out of my mouth, but then I reconsidered. "It is difficult for me to discuss Pallas

Eden as rationally as I should," I apologized, "He is controlled, careful, very strict, at a physical peak. I recognize a bit of genius in his decisions even as I am repelled by them."

"Hm, he fits the bill. Weren't we supposed to meet him when we arrived?"

"Yes, but he was detained. Some problem in the Pallas summer compound. An off-worlder who walked into a snow drift."

"Are you sure that is the reason?" Nyemba asked. "Hardly sounds like a concern that would tie up the lead Arthmis officer in the present dispute."

"It . . . is one of these complicated Alnese family situations, involving his children."

"I see. Where were we? Ah yes, the third involved order, the Order of Tomrys. I never observed any Tomrys companies, and you haven't either, right? The Order started out almost like a hunting association, then evolved a quasi-religious mission of protecting God's gift to the Space Gypsies, Alnos. Most Tomrys units operate in the Islands region, with a few more scattered on the land bridge between North and South Chrymna. As former hunters, they prefer the wilder areas of the planet. They see themselves as the defenders of the land, and I am not surprised that members of Tomrys would take it upon themselves to fight against people they see as invaders. I can understand your Justiciar's concerns. A strong provocation could easily trigger something along the lines of a Tomrys holy war. What I would like to know is whether these newcomer settlers have any idea what they would be up against."

I observed, "I don't think they know very much about their hosts. They don't care to."

"Not good, that. Now, the Mythrans have always interested me the most, even though I had a devil of a time finding members. They are the closest the Alnese have come to a true security force, and they are much more secretive than members of Arthmis or Tomrys. Mythrans are the most warrior-like. They often become mercenaries on other worlds and thus collect a range of trainings. And they are quite sought after: They are superb fighters! I finally learned to recognize some Mythrans by watching Arthmin training sessions carefully, and identifying some unique patterns, especially speed. Mythrans used to be a special branch of Arthmis deployed primarily to end inter-clan conflict, and they were essentially the best of the best. They branched out into their own semi-independent tradition, though nominally Arthmis still controls them. You can bet that several of them were observing yesterday."

Maskar asked, "As a branch of Arthmis, are they led by Justiciars, too?"

Nyemba shook his head, "They have their own titled leaders, Legates. The way you describe him, your Justiciar could be one. Since Pallas Thor Eden is solidly Arthmin, I'd say there is another connection there."

I thought of one Mythran candidate immediately: "Pallas Alexander!"

Maskar broke in, "Lady Ciani's brother? He spent some time on O'bonne not too long ago. What would a warrior want with us?"

"That is interesting," commented Nyemba.

We both turned to him.

"Given our arrangement with Kobra, and their situation...," Nyemba paused.

Maskar understood immediately. For my sake, Nyemba elucidated, "The Alnese chose this planet because of its hostile climate, but they did not realize they landed right as that climate was warming. Now Alnos is growing more desirable. That makes it almost certain more and more people will take an interest in the planet, and with their small population, they won't be able to withstand a serious incursion. They are smart enough to know that. They know they need a new arrangement, one that provides added protection without taking away their treasured self-determination."

"You mean, they wish to emulate us?" I spelled out, rather embarrassed at my slow-wittedness.

"When you consider their options, it is an excellent strategy," Maskar answered, "This igloo of a planet protected their treasured independence for a millennium and a half. Now that it is melting, they know they need to adapt."

I sat back, "It appears I have called you not just into one, but into two enmeshed intrigues."

Maskar leaned his head to one side, "Perhaps. And your future in-laws have a hand in both. What an interesting clan you have managed to get yourself entangled with, Ashewe."

Oh, the consequences of passion! I closed my eyes and sighed, "My work is compromised. I will have to return to O'bonne after all."

"On the contrary," Nyemba Ndinzi protested, "with kindness and hospitality, the Space Gypsies have always eluded us. You are the first to get this close to them, and I shall encourage the Academy to sponsor your stay for as long as you wish. Ashewe, your training will carry you through the crises that may follow from your involvement, take an old planetologist's word for it."

"Thank you Ndinzi. I appreciate your kindness."

"It is not kindness. Just the simple truth."

After that reassurance, I transferred my observations about the most immediate conflict to Maskar Enku for further study. He wanted all my findings and field notes about Chantico House and Kuan House in the Islands, and also asked to get more information about Alnos's immigrant communities, particularly the ones with contacts with the Islands. At the end of our conference, I put both of my colleagues in touch with Pallas Thor Eden, who was planning his own visit and briefing as soon as they felt up to it.

◆ CHAPTER 5 ◆

Raymond Gets Help

When we returned to Zyss, Eden had me dropped off at Doctor Peg's clinic in the capital's main hospital. The good doctor fussed over my hands and made disapproving noises about the care I had received. She had me flex each finger, then she poked my fingertips a few times. The noises gradually turned more approving. "You realize of course that you owe your fingers to Eden's fast actions. That did more for you than that fool calling himself a physician practicing in Eden Hamlet! You must have been out there for a while, judging by the depth of your frostbite."

I hesitated, wondering for one brief moment about the extent of Eden's discretion. Doctor Peg didn't wait for an answer. "Happens all the time with you travelers. Spend a couple of weeks on the planet and presto, you're an ice master! I hope this teaches you to respect our winter!"

I put all the conviction I could muster into my slow nod.

"All right." She brushed over one hand one last time, "On the whole, you were lucky. This time."

"Doctor Peg."

She caught my earnest tone, met it with an encouraging expression.

"I . . . shot up in Eden Hamlet."

Her face turned neutral, "How often?"

"Once."

She lifted one of my hands up and murmured as if to herself, "Must have been one hell of a rush after, well, four, five of your months? Forgot to put on your gloves, eh? Too high to notice the difference."

I didn't want to lie, but I didn't want to tell her the truth, either, so I just stayed silent.

"So, why are you telling me this?"

"Kyet, Pallas Kyet told me to ask you for help."

"What kind of help do you want?"

I shrugged.

"Do you want it or is everybody on your case about it?"

"Oh," I shrugged again, "Both."

She walked out of the room and returned with a small instrument similar to a scanner. Popping two little wings out of it, she turned it into a mini-stealth bomber, which she let me handle. "You're familiar with hypnosis, of course. This med-scanner acts a lot like it. Sends a current to your neural pleasure centers and kills your desire for opiates by flooding your brain with your own endorphins. First, you use it regularly, then you taper it off. But I'm warning you, the day will come when you have to choose between it and your drug. You still have to decide which is more important."

Tell me about addiction!

She showed me how to place the little hypnotizing stealth bomber on my forehead, then had me lie down and switched it on. It tingled through my skin. Very gradually, I felt as if my thoughts were relaxing. When Doctor Peg switched the med-scanner off, I felt strangely alert, as if I'd just come out of deep sleep. I sighed contentedly and swung back into a sitting position.

After explaining and having me echo back instructions for the little contraption, she popped the two wings back and handed it to me. "Well then, it's yours. For what it's worth, I hope you make the right choice when the time comes."

And what choice would that be?

Our eyes met, and I could have sworn she read the thought.

She pointed to my recovered hands again, "Have you tried anything complicated yet?"

Not a bad move. I smiled, just couldn't help it. "I did some riffs right before leaving Eden Hamlet."

"And?"

"Not too bad. Guess I was lucky."

"And you've learned your lesson?"

"Absolutely."

"Such a good patient!"

I thought she was going to pinch my cheek.

Upon my arrival at the Pallas compound after my doctor's visit, anxiety replaced the light-hearted mood generated by Doctor Peg. I was barely able to cross the threshold into Pallas House's vestibule. After peeling off my snow clothes, I sat in the cool little antechamber, ruminating over what to do next. When I heard steps, I looked up and saw Kyet and Goal approaching.

"Hello," he greeted me, "Uncle Eden wanted us to meet you."

"But we're not going out into the cold, so you better come inside," Goal added.

I stood up and hesitated one more moment, scanning her face. If she suspected anything, she wasn't letting on.

When I crossed into the warmth of the compound, Kyet continued with, "We'd both like to chew you out over your carelessness, but Peg probably beat us to it."

"She did."

I kneeled and hugged Goal to me. I had an overwhelming need to apologize, but I knew better. Instead I joked, "Stupid uncle, eh?" She wanted to see my hands, and I gave her one for a close up. She ended her examination with a shrug, commenting, "Looks the same to me."

"It is. It really is."

I didn't want to let go, but forced myself to rise, looking from her to Kyet, then back to her.

"Dad also told us to get you into some decent clothes for tonight," Goal announced.

"There's some big to-do about the new mediation effort. Alnos House is hosting a traditional feast, and Lady Ciani wants her Chronicler at her side," Kyet informed me.

They led me through the Pallas labyrinth to an apartment in the southeastern wing. The whole suite was almost bare, a desk and chair in a paper-filled study, a hammock strung across what I deduced to be a resting corner, a chest of drawers and a lean, low bed in the bedroom, that was it. Goal slipped right into a walk-in closet behind a wall of mirrors in the bedroom and dove among one row of neatly hung outfits. She emerged with black fabric draped across her arms. When laid out over the bed, something akin to a uniform took shape. She turned right back into the closet and groped until she found a matching open tunic with a triumphant "Ha!" She countered my doubtful expression with a commanding, "Put it on! Put it on!" and retreated to the study with Kyet.

The uniform fit surprisingly well. The cashmere-soft material wrapped around me like a warm cocoon. I swung the tunic about my shoulders and checked the effect in the mirrored closet-door. The cut of the black suit lent me an unaccustomed air of elegance, but something was missing. When Goal peeked, I was undoing my braid. She clapped her hands and disappeared into the bathroom, returned with a brush. Leaning forward, I threw the loosened hair over my head. When she was done brushing, I threw my head back and together we checked the effect in one mirror. With my black eyes, my toasted skin, and my black tresses settling over my shoulders, I looked like a Plains Indian.

Goal nodded approvingly, "Black is your color."

Behind us Kyet said, "All you need now is a little silver. I have exactly the right belt for you."

To confirm my suspicion, I asked, "The suit belongs to your father?"

"M-hm, but he looks terrible in black."

I threw another look at my reflection. I had thought of him as taller than me, but the difference appeared not so great: The sleeves and pant-legs were just a fraction too long, the tunic comfortably loose.

Pushing the thoughts that came into my mind to the side, I asked finally, "Is Socorro here?"

I was informed that she now spent her mornings with the other Pallas toddlers. Kyet and Goal took me back to my own quarters, then went to retrieve her while I changed back into regular clothes.

When I saw my child again, practically the first thing she did was to grab the hair about my shoulders. She pulled as forcefully as she could. Kyet came to my rescue, uncurling my daughter's little fists and holding them so Goal could gather my mane into a safer pony-tail. Gurgling happily, Socorro turned towards him and reached for his locks. She was obviously discovering something about shape and texture.

Kyet said quietly, "She was upset when you disappeared." Socorro settled into my arms and scanned the room for other interesting shapes. I felt as if our second separation had lasted longer than the first. Apologizing silently to both sisters, I squeezed her to me, humming a low, "I'm back. I won't disappear again, I swear it." I wanted a renewed trust between my daughter and myself, an encompassing trust between us all, even between her mother and me. With Leila, that prize was eluding me.

Goal startled me out of my wave of self-condemnation with a wry, "Then you had better learn more about snow."

"Look who's talking," countered Kyet. "You haven't spent a winter here since you were three years old."

She stuck her tongue out at him, and hid behind me when

he lunged towards her. Socorro squealed when Kyet's hair came within reach again, and we all ended up tripping over each other. "Kyet, Goal, cut it out!" I wheezed as quietly as I could after steadying myself. I shook my head, more to myself than for any other reason, and made a determined move towards my settee, where I could release Socorro for a little bit.

"Goal, I promise I'll learn everything there is to know about snow, okay? Kyet, you can teach us both, all right?"

"Teach the little princess? Me?" Kyet settled himself in front of a bodychair, "You can't be serious!"

"This fog brain? You're joking! I'll get one of dad's aides to do the job right." She sat down next to me.

"Arthmis doesn't know a glacier from a snowdrift in winter!" Kyet challenged playfully.

"I'll tell him you said that!" she spat back.

"Ooo, I'm scared."

She leaped up and landed squarely on top of him. They wrestled and he let himself be overpowered, only to sit up suddenly and tumble her to the ground. She giggled so hard she couldn't squeeze out her next sentence. Socorro crawled towards the edge of the settee, and before I could grab her, she climbed down. In a flash, she reached Kyet's hair.

"Ouch! Goal, control your sister!" He tried to lift his head and poked a finger into Socorro's side, making her squirm until she let go of him again. Goal rolled over and shooed the baby back towards me. I leaned to pick her back up, asking, "This feast tonight, when is it?"

"Oh I suppose we should get ready," was Kyet's not overly helpful reply.

"You're playing tonight?" Goal wanted to know.

He nodded. "And your uncle has to get there early because of his job." His next comment was addressed to me, "Leila and Eden will take the children. The feast is also Socorro's introduction as a Pallas." As if to detract me, he continued, "Tell me, Ray, what are your clan names again?"

I put the baby in my lap. She seemed satisfied and ready for a short rest. "One of them …" I stopped, started over, "In my culture, we only have two, one from the father, one from the mother. My father's clan is called Díaz, my mother's Ruiz. So together it's Díaz Ruiz."

Kyet intoned solemnly, as if he were introducing me, "Díaz Ruiz Raymond."

Close enough.

When I made ready to take the girls to Leila's suite, he leaned forward and whispered in my ear, "So it's Pallas Thor Díaz Ruiz Socorro, isn't it?" And he smiled the most innocent smile.

◆ EPISODE 6 ◆

Dragon Confers with Leila

The time had come for me to, as Ray would say, face the music with Kyet, so the day of the feast, I tapped my private ally Pallas Leila. I declined an offer by my fellow O'bonne Maskar and Nyemba to accompany me, stressing to them that I expected better results from a more discreet conversation and promising that I would call them after Leila and I had formulated a strategy. Still, when Leila turned her questioning stare to me after meeting me in my temporary quarters in Alnos House, I regretted having to do without their comforting presence.

"Leila," I started without further ado, "I have called you here to request your assistance in a matter of great importance to me."

Her eyes registering mild surprise, she countered with the formulaic, "To help a friend is a great honor."

Taking a deep, calming breath, I made my announcement, "I am expecting my first child."

Her eyes widened perceptibly, so I rushed on with an invitation, "Please, have a seat. I have prepared some choctea for us."

She took the offered body chair and her face changed again while I completed the final touches of our choctea service. She ran through a series of mental calculations as I served our drinks and sat down, trying to relax a little. Then, she murmured quietly, as if to herself, what to me was quite a shocking pronouncement, "Like father, like son."

She must have seen the astonishment on my face, because she went on without prompting, "Well it is Kyet, isn't it?"

"But ho- . . .," my voice died within my throat.

"Who have you spent any time with, especially in Eden Hamlet? Who has been in a state lately? Not to mention how strange for him to be without a lover. The clues all point to Kyet. And, well, you may not know it, Alexander entered an alliance very early. He was twenty when his son was born."

"Alexander is that young?"

She nodded, "Thirty-eight."

I shook myself out of my ever-present interest in Pallas trivialities, and confessed haltingly, "Yes, Kyet and I, are lovers, and he ... is my child's father, but he does not know."

"You didn't discuss it with him?"

I bowed my head and didn't know what corner of the room to crawl into to avoid her gaze.

"Oh, he is not going to like that!"

She had hit on a major fear, and hearing her pronounce her opinion with such conviction, I sighed deeply and unhappily. She lifted her cup for a sip and studied me in silence while the steam wafted about her nose. "Is that the help you need? You want me to talk to him?"

"No, I need your help dealing with your clan. You must understand, Pallas House is the reason why I did not talk to him. I did not plan this pregnancy. The morning came when I was supposed to suppress conception and I was lying right next to him and I just could not fight my longing anymore. Of course it was an irrational decision. I truly do not know what possible relationship between myself and your clan I would find acceptable, and until I can at least think of a possibility, I cannot acknowledge Kyet."

Commenting, "I see," she continued to study me in silence.

"And yet, I do not want to shut him out. Only … I need to work out how to acknowledge him and still raise an O'bonne child."

"That is what you want?"

I nodded.

"I was hoping, well . . .," I took another deep breath, "You seem to have had success in negotiating a special status. I was hoping to profit from your experience."

"My success was," she hesitated, "due to special circumstances."

I had the distinct impression she had been about to say something entirely different, and her own mutated Danyx empathic ability must have helped her sense it. After some reflection, she added with unusual intensity, "It was paid for, first by me, then by Eden."

I pressed my lips together and focused on my own cup of choctea, tried to channel my peaked curiosity out of my mind, knowing she would not say more. She sat back, and her weary expression faded into a second calculating look. Finally, she advised, "You should seize on the advantages of your situation. Pallas would be eager for an O'bonne alliance, and since you are already expecting, you can practically guarantee a link between Pallas and an O'bonne scholar. What more could my kinspeople ask for? I would advise you to ask his parents to help you, particularly Alexander. What specifically do you want?"

I repeated, "An O'bonne child."

"Would it be good enough if the child grew up on both worlds? If you really want Kyet to assume his role," her face brightened, and with a smirk she concluded, "you'll have to put up with some of our Alnese nonsense."

I guffawed and gulped for air at the same time.

"Well, that's what you think, isn't it? Why else insist so much on an O'bonne upbringing?"

I nodded, hiding my embarrassment at my own xenophobia the best I could.

"Anyhow, I'm reasonably certain you could negotiate a half-and-half arrangement. Half the time here, the other half back on O'bonne."

"I would like Kyet to come along, but I wonder how he would adjust. It must be trying to be so recognizably alien all the time."

She shrugged, lifting her hands to underscore her implicit "Who knows?" Then she said, "I've never heard anyone complain about O'bonne. Your world is not like Europe. But ask Alexander, he's spent enough time on O'bonne, and he sticks out a lot more than his son."

"Mm," I acknowledged, "that he does." Another sip later, I resigned myself to what I knew I had to do, "I'll speak to Alexander, then." It was easier to start with the parent I hardly knew than with Vai, after deceiving her for half a year. As fellow scientists, we had spent many hours in conversation and become quite good friends, and I felt more than a twinge of guilt about carrying on secretly with her son.

Sensing my unease, Leila rescued me, "I'll speak to Alexander, and to Vai. You should begin with Kyet before he hears it from anybody else."

She was right. Trying to control the stricken expression on my face, I nodded wearily.

◆ EPISODE 7 ◆

Leila Executes

Finding Alexander is easy—all I have to do is follow Eden's movements. Judging by how much time Alexander devotes to doing so himself, his summer of abstinence built up a healthy appetite. A few hours after Eden has returned to Zyss, the time feels right.

"Enter," Eden's voice calls after I identify myself.

We meet in his study. Alexander is rocking gently in Eden's hammock, his tunic off, hair and shirt undone. For no particular reason, my eyes follow the shape of the Mythran snakes winding up each side of his torso. The snakes continue and transform into stylized hawk feathers down his still covered arms, tattooed with the blackest blue against his gray-blue skin.

Folding Eden into one of our still awkward embraces, I tell him, "I need to talk to Alexander about a private matter."

As I knew he would, Eden holds in his surprise. I turn to Lex and repeat, "We need to talk about a private matter."

Continuing to rock himself, he replies, "Well then, by all means, let's."

"It is private."

"Do either of us keep secrets from Eden?" He goads.

I move closer and lock into him, Danyx to Danyx. *You certainly do, and I can ascertain their names for him.* I sense him flinch ever so slightly and add, "Other people do."

Sitting up, he scans the dim room. I step over to Eden's dresser and gather up a brush, then hesitate. Eden doesn't move. I throw the brush at my cousin. Lex swings out of the hammock and steps into Eden's bedroom.

Eden says graciously, "I think I'll visit my new daughter. Maybe she'll get used to me before tonight."

Lex comes back out, looking quite regal in a cream-and-silver suit, eclipsing Eden in his casual gray sweats. He has fastened his hair into a high pony-tail that accentuates his angular cheek-bones and full mouth. His eyes brush over Eden as he turns to me, linger just the one or two seconds it takes to caress without physical contact. I almost feel sorry for Eden. My husband heads towards the door, informs us, "As you can guess, my study is always secure. Even from me."

"Thank you."

Eden nods to us both before leaving.

"Well then, cousin," Lex accentuates each syllable. I prolong the pause between us to let him know I'm not about to let him rush me. He walks over to the room's narrow window and, with one of his incomparably fluid moves, swings himself into the seat-like nook beneath it. "You might as well take the chair," he indicates with a nod. Taking him up on the offer, I drag the chair closer to him. My approach only kindles amusement, so I stop playing games. “Actually, what I have to tell you is really good news. You are about to become a grandfather.”

His left eyebrow arches up, then he performs the same mental computations I have.

“The little bastard! I always hoped my wife’s steadying influence would outweigh my wild streak.”

“Oh, I think the combination turned out quite well on the whole.”

“Is it the O’bonne?”

A curt nod confirms his deduction.

“He was . . . resonating to her presence before I left, but then it stopped. I attributed the change to the wrong ending.”

“You thought it had come to nothing?”

He lifts his legs to the nook and wraps his arms around his knees. “So,” he continues in a more businesslike tone, “my son has seduced an O’bonne scholar and fathered a child. At least Dragon’s not allied with anyone. Or is she? Is that why you need privacy to tell me?”

“No, she’s not allied. She’s . . . particular about what kind of alliance she’ll agree to.”

“Aah!” He smiles, “I wonder if my son has any idea what he got himself into.”

“He doesn’t exactly, how shall I put it, know about the child.”

Incredulously, “He doesn’t know? How could he not know?”

“Dragon described it as a spontaneous decision on her part.”

After a moment of reflection, Lex observes, “Makes sense, considering their prejudices. Does she regret it now?”

"Maybe a little. Mostly, she is apprehensive, but not enough to end the pregnancy."

"Of course the clan will like it."

"What about you?"

He shrugs, nestles his head in his arms and directs a penetrating gaze at me, "An alliance with passion . . . You know more about that than I do."

Touché!

"But if passion has struck, Kyet won't let go. In that he takes after me. I know my behavior belies it, but I am not afraid to pay the price for loving, and he won't either."

And what price have you paid, cousin Lex? Did you have any idea what you got yourself into when you fell in love with Eden?

After a short silence between us, I reach for one hand, "He can't love unconditionally."

Lex knows who I mean.

A very quiet sigh brushes against me, "Part of the price."

I squeeze his hand gently, let go again.

His head still resting on one arm, he returns to our principal concern, "So, Ashewe Dragon will not agree to a traditional alliance? My son will have to adjust, won't he? And the clan had bloody well do the same."

"Would you enter into negotiations? One of the other O'bonne will probably represent her. She wants the child to be raised on both worlds."

"That's downright generous for an O'bonne."

I smile.

"How long is this to remain private?" he asks.

"Give it a few more days. Dragon has to tell Kyet, and she wants to tell Vai, but I suspect that of all of us, Vai is the one who already knows. You can discuss the matter with her. And with Eden, if you want."

He lifts his head, nods slowly.

Lowering his legs, he starts the Danyx current between us again, quite deliberately. He leans forward and probes for the memories he seeks, the memories of both my happy year and my bitter one with Eden. Smiling at his retreat, I sense for one fleeting moment how he, too, is keeping secrets.

"Thought I'd give it a try," he says with mock-resignation.

"Why do you always want to know about that time?"

"I want to understand Eden."

I get up. He follows suit, towers over me, his golden eyes glowing like cat eyes.

"Then get into his memories. Join with him."

"He won't let me."

"Do it when his guard's down."

"Are you testing me?"

"Just being sensible, Lex."

Turning my back to him, I head towards the door. He catches up and opens it for me. As I pass him, he says, "I'll talk with the clan elders and with Vai after the feast," and I nod acknowledgment.

◆ CHAPTER 8 ◆

Raymond Witnesses His First Feast

Maybe it's the long winters, but Alnese parties are spirited affairs. What's more, they cut across generations, include everybody from babies to great-grandparents, like the parties of my San Antonio youth. When I reported for work the evening of the feast, I could have sworn that the entire city of Zyss had preceded me to Alnos House. The compound's usually wide-open spaces overflowed with early visitors in festive suits and gowns. Many of the suits matched my own, dress uniforms with elegantly cut open tunics, though most alternated two matching colors. The weave of the gowns blended different colors and threads into complex, layered patterns that seemed uniquely designed to complement each wearer. I worked my way between knots of people loitering about, their children scurrying playfully between them. Most of the guests didn't pay any particular attention to me, though the flowing hair attracted notice here and there.

A knowledgeable steward rescued me and guided me to Lady Ciani's private apartment, to a dressing room where she was enduring the ministrations of her personal attendant. Pallas Alexander, in a cream-and-silver version of my suit, lounged in one corner. He nodded greeting, examined me with undisguised interest, then loped over and sat down next to his sister. He undid his pony-tail and shook out his hair, watched the effect in the mirror.

"Oh stop it!" her Grace said sharply, "Ray will think you're making fun of him." She grabbed a brush and pulled it through his mane quite forcefully.

"Ah!"

"Besides, I don't want people to confuse us." She laughed, and twisted his hair back into a ponytail, brushing it into order. Her attendant completed the operation. Brother and sister examined each other in the mirror. The family resemblance did not lie solely in skin color, though all the small differences between them favored him. "All right," he said finally, moving aside.

The attendant started to work on Lady Ciani's hair, transforming it into a complicated raised chignon threaded with silver and white. "You'll stay with me tonight," her Grace instructed me, "Ambassador Periasamy and I need to discuss Kobran proposals for Alnos tomorrow." Nodding, I tried to catch her brother's reaction.

"Lex, I don't like it when your Mythrans are too obvious, especially at a feast. You should at least try to hide your lack of confidence in my own guard."

"If they are obvious, they're worthless," Alexander replied.

"They are obvious to me."

"Don't exaggerate. Maybe you can spot Ixchel Aria, but only because you already know her."

Finishing with the hair, the attendant moved to a cream and silver gown laid out next to the dresser. Lady Ciani stepped into it and let herself be draped in its folds, then stood still as the attendant fastened various hooks and laces. When she sat back down, the attendant nestled what looked like a chain of opals and moonstones across the sides of Lady Chani's hairdo, adjusted it until one luminous white stone rested against her gray-blue forehead. Lady Ciani was taking on some of her brother's Apollonian radiance. Directing a long look at his reflection, she said, "I don't like to repeat myself."

He bowed to her ever so slightly, then planted a kiss on her cheek. "Your wish is my command."

She slapped him lightly. He caught her hand and pressed her palm to his lips, then he got up, twirled around, and strode out. She remained seated, adjusting only slightly in my direction before asking, "You have recovered?"

"Yes."

"I'm disappointed in Pallas Eden. I specifically instructed him to orient you to the dangers of winter."

"Oh, he did. I grew overconfident."

The look she returned made me wonder if she shared her brother's mental abilities, but I retained my calm expression.

"I have invited the two chief Heshti negotiators tonight. They'll be seated at our table, along with the O'bonne. I would like to ask you a favor."

"Your wish is my command."

Another probing look almost made me apologize for mimicking Alexander.

She continued smoothly with, "Would you attend me? I prefer not to have my regular waiter butting in and listening."

"Is there a protocol I need to learn quickly?"

She shook her head ever so slightly, added, "Thank you." Rising, she guided my left hand to her right elbow.

When we reached the huge stateroom at the center of her residence, we were greeted by a solemn hush. She stepped forward and nodded greetings to her left and right, slowly worked her way to a table by a central fire pit. Neither the Heshtis nor the O'bonne were difficult to spot. My attention was drawn to one man in particular, a lanky giant with skin so black I expected it to reflect the lights around us. The other, older O'bonne man bowed in Lady Chani's direction and spoke, "Your Grace has troubled herself far too much. We can't ever hope to repay her."

A mischievous smile lit up her face, "Nyemba, old friend, don't get ridiculous! When have we Alnese ever missed a chance to celebrate?"

She made the round of all her personal guests, then positioned herself, with me standing behind her. A second hush settled through the hall. She lifted both hands and announced with a solemn voice, "God is eveything, and everything is God. There is no beginning to God. There is no end to God. As our great Prophet did the day of our arrival, so do we give thanks for God's favor."

A rumble flowed through the assembled crowd as her hands fluttered down. I lit a long match and passed it to her.

Murmuring "Blessed be!" each time, Lady Ciani lit a circle of eight candles. When the eighth wick took, a more enthusiastic rumble greeted the completed circle.

Lady Ciani called out, "I bow to my people," grabbed a hold of my hand, and curtsied deeply. When she pulled herself back up, the entire hall clamored, "Alnos Ciani, Alnos Ciani." A rhythmic chant washed over us, and all assembled, O'bonne and Heshti guests included, bowed to her. I pulled her chair back, and seating herself, she officially opened the feast.

My attendant duties kept me occupied from then on. I hadn't waited since leaving San Anto, but the moves came back easily enough. Among the stream of people delivering our dishes and drinks, one woman kept popping up. I noticed her because, apart from her short stature, she looked like family. Hair, eyes, and skin tone were a close match, though she was rounder where I was angular. Lady Ciani fairly scowled at her the one time she caught sight of her, and the woman faded into the attendant corps without further ado. Scanning the room between courses, I figured out that guests clustered according to their clan affiliation. I made out the Pallases by recognizing Alexander and Vai. It took a little longer to find Leila and Goal. Eden was standing behind them, rocking Socorro.

As the meal came to a close, her ladyship pulled me down to a stool next to her and insisted I eat. Kyet's musical group struck up a first melody about midway through dinner. The rhythms sounded North African, but strong vocal and choral flurries jolted through at regular intervals. The pattern piqued my interest. Matched voices would weave complicated parallel harmonies, then flow into the more rhythmic instrumentals.

The sometimes competitive, sometimes harmonious, sometimes deliberately interrupted relationship between the two currents built an intriguing tension. Eventually, the vocal eddies retreated, and a more danceable blend asserted itself.

Sitting right behind her ladyship, I didn't immediately catch on to the increased restlessness among the Pallases. By the time the buzz caught up with me, Socorro's ceremony was already under way. Leila had joined her husband, and she was lifting my daughter up as far as she could. He took over and raised her even higher. The Pallases were alternately clapping their hands and drowning their corner of the hall with high ululations. Eden passed the baby on to the nearest relative, who did the same, and she rode a crest of raised hands until she reached a beaming Vai, who announced, "Socorro." The clan's voluble pride continued for quite some time. Finally, Lady Ciani rose, and after the clan finally calmed down, she said, "God has blessed the House of Pallas. Welcome, Pallas Thor Nambo Renan Socorro." I held my breath, I was so sure the clan would get going again, but only a few satisfied grunts sputtered up.

Some of my anguish must have come through, because Dragon leaned over behind Lady Ciani's back and reached for me.

We only had time for the most fleeting touch. The dance music reprised and the clan groups surrounding us started to get into it. Lady Ciani let her own cry rip through the hall, like an invitation spurring the dancers into action. When her Grace repeated her call, I had the impression it was directed at someone in particular. Across from us, Alexander divested himself of his tunic. Raising her hands to join in with the rhythmic clapping of her guests, Lady Ciani threw off a bone-piercing ululation.

Alexander met his son in the middle of the hall. They started with a slow, almost languid rhythm, then worked up a more strenuous pace. The dance was like a combative courtship, a more playful version of the fighting practices I had seen Kyet and Eden engage in. Only Eden couldn't begin to move like Alexander, and even Kyet, with his youthful power and grace, barely matched his father. They spun into the more contentious part of their performance, a routine that reminded me of Brazilian Capoeira. Increasingly aggressive skirmishes built a delicious tension. Flying at each other as they were, I expected one of them to be struck any minute. Then all of a sudden, they stopped, sauntered towards each other like the best of friends.

Alexander turned to her ladyship and bowed. She clapped her hands, and new dancers joined father and son in a reprise of the slower routine. Gradually, the space filled with people. I recognized my short Alnese twin among the new dancers. She sidled up to Alexander and, under the watchful eyes of both Lady Ciani and Eden, they melded into the crowd together.

The music remained danceable throughout the night, the floor stayed crowded, and the guests kept drinking and dancing, occasionally signalling more loud approval. Around midnight, Lady Ciani pulled me to her and said into my ear, "Enough of my selfishness, Díaz Raymond. Join in with whoever you wish. My steward knows where to lead you when you tire." Even though I didn't mind attending her, I appreciated the chance to roam a little. I mouthed the customary "By your leave," knowing full well that only lip readers could communicate in the general auditory ruckus of the party, and set off on my own explorations.

I ran into pretty much everybody I knew. Almost immediately, as if she had been waiting for it all evening, Goal met up with me. She grabbed my hand and meandered her way to Kyet's group, where we got to congratulate him. "I didn't know you were that good," I shouted in one ear. His face darkened quite noticeably. We were almost back to our old selves, before my last dalliance with heroin. Next, Goal led me to her parents. Leila pointedly ignored me. Eden was more civil; he handed Socorro over for a brief reunion. Our afternoon together had stilled my separation anxieties, so I didn't mind when Vai gathered her back. I stared at Leila until she gave in and returned one look, then I blew her a kiss. We left it at that. Neither of us had the right words just then.

Goal and I kept moving, exploring the hall and various adjacent staterooms until the early hours of the morning, at which point her parents called her back. During that time, I gradually grew aware of a surreptitious shadowing. Somehow, my Alnese twin just happened to appear in many of the less traveled paths Goal and I discovered during our roaming. Her way of moving reminded me of Lauran, the Arthmis lieutenant that shadowed Eden.

After Goal had rejoined her family, the shadowing grew more pronounced. I went to hang out with the musicians. After a little while, the woman had joined in with some of the percussionists. When I looked her way, she sauntered by. We danced around each other like that until the band started packing it in.

As if for one final libation, she offered me a mug of the ale-like brew that had been flowing generously all night. I took the offered mug and she let her fingers slide over mine. I finished the draft, and we retreated to a more quiet niche I had discovered during my meanderings with Goal. She lifted a hand and skimmed over my hair, barely touching it. Then she shrugged, jerked her head in a direction I did not know. I brushed against her hair. The texture, too, was very close to mine, down to the soft waves. She pulled my head down with one hand while standing on her toes to close in. Anticipated though it was, the kiss jolted through me, and I broke it off. I threw my head back and avoided her steady black eyes. She sought out one hand and tugged me gently in one direction. When I hesitated, she waited.

"I'm Ray," I mumbled.

"I know who you are." Her low, husky voice clashed against my expectations, "Aria will have to do for you."

The name clicked. I directed a questioning gaze at her, "Alexander mentioned an Aria."

"This has nothing to do with Pallas Alexander."

When I continued to hesitate, she moved to scan the hall beyond our niche. "I know where they've put you up. I'll take you there," she volunteered. She stepped out, and I followed her.

◆ EPISODE 9 ◆

Dragon Confesses to Kyet

"How could you?"

That one verbal assault cut me down like a sickle blade. It had taken every ounce of fortitude not to shrink into myself beneath the fierce coffee eyes of my lover, and in the end I still crumbled. His accusation signaled a turning point, a moment of decision when we would either start a new, public phase in our relationship or flounder into an awkward parting whose very real possibility terrified me.

"I did not," I swallowed my fear the best I could and started over, "Kyet, I did not plan this."

"You certainly did plan two months of evasion!"

"I just couldn't face your clan, not alone."

"Alone! What am I? What have I denied you since we started? Which one of your conditions did I object to? Which one did I fail to observe?"

My months of indecision and anxiety had worn me out, and his anger overcame me. A great bubble of misery burst inside me; I struggled mightily against it, but my eyes filled with tears. Biting my lower lip, I leaned my head back to try and hold them long enough so they would get reabsorbed and not start running down my cheeks. I failed. Kyet watched my silent struggle without moving until the tears started to gather at my chin, then he lifted one hand and brushed against one cheek.

Blinking in a vain effort to repress further tears, I stammered, "Do you want this child?"

He turned to a recess behind him and rummaged in it until he found a kerchief, then he touched it against my chin, patted up one cheek. "You can ask an Alnese this?"

I struggled on stubbornly, "I . . . am . . . asking . . . you."

He stared at his hands, "I can't believe you couldn't trust me, Dragon. I just can't believe it."

A second wave of misery closed my throat completely. I blinked back more tears the best I could, repeating wordlessly, *That isn't it at all, that isn't it at all!*, even though I knew that all the rationalizations in the world couldn't offset the basic truth of his observation. Finally, I wheezed, "I felt . . . I wanted . . . too much."

"So you just took without asking? I don't think an Alnese would ever do such an underhanded thing."

Taking the kerchief from his hand, I began to clean up my face, and resigning myself to his anger, I was able to speak a complete sentence reasonably coherently, "Well, now I have told you." Sniffling one last time, I swallowed my sadness the best I could and prepared to leave.

"Where are you going?"

I shrugged, avoided his gaze. With one hand, he sat me down again, turned me around and leaned my head against his shoulder. When he put his arms around me, nothing could prevent another sob. I pressed against him, hungered for the familiar sounds of his breathing and heartbeat.

Caressing my stomach with both hands, he murmured in my right ear, "Don't you ever do something like that again. Not ever. I'm dead serious, Azetmir."

"I won't."

I closed my eyes, wanting this moment between us to last a millennium. I let the blanket of our renewed intimacy wrap around me. Gradually, the paralyzing fear within me retreated, giving way to a mixture of serenity and hope that had evaded me ever since the moment of conception.

"Is it a son or a daughter?" My lover asked, an undercurrent of anger still biting into me.

"A son."

After one further moment of contemplation, I inquired, "Will you stand with me against your clan if it comes to that?"

"We'll have to see, won't we."

It was his moment of revenge. Without admitting it to myself, I had set out to get the passionate, consuming O'bonne relationship with him that I had always wanted. I accepted it.

◆ EPISODE 10 ◆

Another Bill Comes Due for Raymond

I have always been something of a chameleon in sex, absorbing and reflecting back the respective enthusiasm or inhibitions of my partners. In Germany, this had served me well, while it had invariably turned disastrous Stateside. Since the Alnese were, if anything, even more pragmatic than Northern Europeans, my dalliance with Aria promised nothing but pleasure. Only I hadn't yet finished paying for my other love affair.

We stopped at the threshold to my suite. Aria looked up and I looked down. When she closed in a second time, I stayed put. Her soft lips moved up and down my face. As I started to inhale her perfume, the first stirring she had evoked in the hall strengthened. Letting the door fall shut behind us, she backed me into the room until I stumbled against a low, Alnese-style settee in the dark. I sat down, hoisted her onto my lap. She pulled off my tunic with one hand and burrowed under my suit with the other until she made contact with my skin. When my mouth opened to drink in some air, she slipped her tongue right in. I let desire ripple through me as I unfastened the low cut bodice of her pantsuit. Both my hands slid down her smooth back. Under her layer of winter-fat, the woman was all muscle. I pushed each thumb across her sides until I felt the softer orbs of her breasts, leaned forward to bite one nipple through the silky cashmere of her suit. She purred with that strangely low voice of hers, started to pare the upper part of my suit off me even as her bottom was pressing against my rising periscope.

After nearly two years of deadened passion, the sensual current keened through me. When we both finished with our clothing, I felt her naked legs rub along mine as she rolled into me, closed my eyes. She stroked my pride, waking lovely sensations that made me lust for more. Reversing our positions, I sat up and went after her, savoring one divine moment of intimacy. Then, before I had even found a decent rhythm, my treacherous wand bucked and spewed off.

I wanted to cuss in every language I knew, but was too embarrassed to utter one solitary sound. I wanted to disappear, but lying pretty much on top of Aria nixed that option. Avoiding eye-contact, I swayed to one side. Her heavy breathing told me plenty about the state I had left her in. I sat up. She pulled her legs up and peered at me until I cast a quick glance her way. On one side of her leg, I caught sight of a scaly, dark blue shape winding up from her ankle.

"You're staying?" I ventured finally, hoping ardently for the contrary.

She stretched out the tattooed leg, nudged my thigh with her big toe. "How long has it been?" she asked finally. Her breathing had calmed, and her voice sounded almost normal.

"Almost two years."

She gathered herself up. As unobtrusively as I could, I traced the tattoo on her leg. The same shape wound up her other leg as well, and both continued up the sides of her torso, around her shoulders, and down her arms. Both finished in a flurry of feathers reminiscent of the ones I had observed on Eden's forearms, but with a thin forked tongue licking each wrist. "Let's take a bath," she proposed. After a moment of struggle, I gave in. Hadn't the worst already happened?

Alnese tubs are huge, layered, recessed affairs. The hot water bubbles up whirlpools, and warm steam can be regulated to transform the room itself into a sauna. We plunged in and re-emerged dripping wet. I shook my hair back and she splashed me. Then Aria waded to the controls and played around with them until she established a pleasant contrast between cooling water and steamy room-temperature.

She waded back and nestled herself into my lap. Calling up some courage, I told her quietly, "I'm not ready to risk another spectacular failure tonight, Aria."

Between kisses, she murmured back, "Before you stopped, it was always women?"

I nodded.

"And at least one Alnese woman?"

"With humans, it's not the best idea to bring up the cuckolded partner, you know."

Her laughter matched her voice, deep and husky. I relaxed a little. Her black eyes narrowed and she slid up, planted her knees inside my thighs and lifted herself up. Her breasts pointed straight at me. Moving to caress the snakes up and down her torso, I nuzzled one dark nipple. A contented sigh echoed through her. My hands glided down. I spread my fingers when I reached the curves of her bottom, squeezed. She wriggled out from my embrace, stepped up on my seat and sat on the tub's rim, legs dangling into the water. Turning about myself, I anchored one arm around each thigh. When I reached our target, one leg splashed up and wrapped over my shoulder and her earlier fire came back. Her breathing turned ragged and when she started to shake and twist, I savored my vindication.

I waited for her to open her eyes again before lifting myself to the rim, then kneeled next to her, leaning against the wall behind the tub. I said, "I can leave it at that."

Smiling, she said, "Lean back more." She shifted herself over me and impaled herself, then moved with me as we rolled into our third round. And when I came that second time, it was full and sweet and left me feeling wonderful.

◆ EPISODE 11 ◆

Dragon Enters Negotiations

With Lady Ciani's welcome reception and my confession to Kyet out of the way, I had run out of all excuses to put off negotiating my formal alliance with the House of Pallas. I invited my colleagues to breakfast to recruit one of them as my intermediary and reiterate my most important requirements.

As soon as I broached the subject, Nyemba urged, "Take my advice: Have Maskar represent you with the Pallases. Nobody bargains tougher than a mountain man." Maskar shrugged and, looking a bit embarrassed, asked, "And who will I start with, if I may ask that now?"

I replied, "Pallas Alexander," whereupon both of my colleagues tried very hard not to look puzzled, forcing me to reveal, "My future father-in-law. He probably will represent the clan elders."

Nyemba kept his even expression, but a brief moment of surprise did flash across Maskar's face. "His dance partner?"

He inquired delicately, and averting my gaze, I confirmed the inference with one nod.

As I anticipated, Alexander arrived that very morning, announcing after a brief round of introductions, "I am on my way to the meeting between Kobran Ambassador Periasamy and her Grace. I decided to drop by privately because my cousin Leila has brought a concern of a more personal nature to my attention."

"Nyemba and Maskar have been appraised," I cut in.

"Then, Ashewe Dragon, let me be among the first to congratulate you," he continued smoothly, "Which one of them will represent you?"

"Maskar."

Alexander nodded acknowledgment and Maskar bowed back, then Alexander explained, "You may know this already, and of course it is understood that my son's alliance is a special case, but in one form or another the House of Pallas will gain two new members. According to our custom, we need to compensate Ashewe for this gift. Nyemba, and even Ashewe, knows enough about us to tell you that at this point, you hold all the winning cards. What Ashewe wants, Ashewe gets."

Maskar let a little smile play itself out on his lips, then answered, "I can't yet tell you just what that might be, Pallas Alexander. Having just been appraised of this forthcoming marriage, I have only consulted briefly with Ashewe."

"It will take time," Alexander agreed.

The two men closed in on each other, looking into each other's eyes and obviously testing each other's empathic waters, though without physical contact, Alexander could only follow Maskar's lead. When they broke contact, Alexander invited Nyemba to accompany him to his next meeting, and they left together.

Maskar turned to me, "His Danyx mind-sharing abilities are well-developed, comparable in some ways to those of a full-blood. His predisposition must be interacting with something else in that genetic stew of his to have reached such full fruition."

I gave it some thought, shared, "Let's see. His great-grandfather was O'bonne, and at least one more ancestor came from Ko, but could have been Danyx originally. That's from Nandez House, the other side of the family."

"And what about his cousin Pallas Leila? Didn't you say she also inherited the powers of the Danyx grandmother?"

"In a very different way. Hers is a wild, unhoned talent. She reads strong emotions, even without contact, and she can make herself quite receptive."

"And your lover?"

"He's sensitive, but it doesn't go much beyond instinct."

"Still, your child will be eagerly anticipated."

I snapped, "However my son turns out, Maskar, he is first and foremost my child, mine and Kyet's." Projecting my irritation, I concluded, "O'bonne better learn to respect that as much as the House of Pallas."

He backed off, "Of course." Still, I sensed him struggling with his curiosity, so I scowled at him a bit longer.

Later that day, Nyemba returned full of news. Our collective deductions about the Alnese dealings with Kobra proved correct; they did wish to emulate us in their quest to join the

Kobran Commonwealth. Using us as a model, they hoped for Kobran protection, but wished to retain complete autonomy in all internal affairs. Naturally, the sticking point lay in finding a mutually agreeable return for the Commonwealth. Nyemba concluded, "Pallas Alexander said it quite plainly, 'We cannot offer O'bonne intelligence'."

Maskar folded his hands together, "Alnese can be so disarmingly frank."

"Indeed," Nyemba agreed, "and Legate Alexander nailed the Ambassador. What do you think Kobra is after? Mythras! After that comment about O'bonne, Legate Alexander dropped quite casually, 'So, besides Mythras, what do you want?' Imagine Ambassador Periasamy's consternation! He wasn't about to owe up to it, not in front of me, which is no doubt the reason why Alexander called him out on it, but Ambassador Periasamy had to admit it. To use his words, 'The Commonwealth hopes to borrow Mythran warriors from time to time.' I'm reasonably sure the Order will agree to occasional missions, and possibly help train a Kobran complement. Close enough to satisfy their sponsors, in any case."

"Well, it is a logical exchange," Maskar observed.

"Indeed," repeated Nyemba, then he continued thinking aloud, "Especially since settlements or a substantial population increase are out of the question. Of course Kobra is interested in all the usual resource extraction, the new mining possibilities and such, and this is practically a virgin planet. But they'll proceed at their usual, quite reasonable pace with that."

For the next few days, the three of us shuttled back and forth between on-going negotiating efforts. Maskar divided his time between Pallas and immigrant leaders, I assisted Ray in chronicling the developing Kobran-Alnese treaty at Lady Ciani's request and helped the Alnese Council of Eight draft proposals, while Nyemba juggled all three. The schedule became the more exhausting the clearer it became to us all that the principal reason for the O'bonne participation in these negotiations, the conflict between natives and new settlers on Alnos, was turning intractable.

◆ CHAPTER 12 ◆

Raymond and Leila Hash Out Their Differences

Leila chose precisely the little niche where Aria and I first retired that night to confront me. I don't know what arrangements she made with Lady Ciani's staff, or who else she conspired with. An errand brought me down to the hall, and by last night's little alcove, I found my Leila barring the passage. She looked magnificent in a black suit that matched my borrowed clothes, her eyes huge and bright, her mouth flushed a red pink to sound an immediate warning. The sparks were about to fly.

Why did I choose you eight years ago? Why do I now turn Ixchel Aria into a rival? Why do I feel cheated? Why do I even care about what you do? "You and Eden are so well matched!" observes Alexander after I order him to keep her away from you. How can I contradict him? The moment I step across your path, I accept everything, I forget everything, I let the law of desire wash over me like a cleansing fire. But first I have to get even with you.

"Whore!"

"What?"

"You heard me. Putain!"

"Ten days ago you wanted to ship me back to Earth. You wanted me gone. I'd say that counts as a break-up."

"After two years your dead wood suddenly comes to life? For that Mythran bitch? I saved your goddamn life. Twice. Your ass is mine!"

"Well you don't want it!"

"Oh? Who smothered his balls in junk? You don't have any idea what I want or don't want. You haven't been sober enough to formulate a single coherent thought about what I want or do not want."

She spat that last barrage up at me from as short a distance as our different heights permitted. I took a step forward. She retreated. I backed her up against the wall. She kept glaring, but gave in. I placed both hand against the wall, one on each side of her head. She didn't blink. I said, "Why the hell do you jerk me around like a fucking yo-yo? Up, down, up, down. What am I, huh? Your human toy?"

Still glaring, she replied, "Oh right, it's been such fun with you these last two years! It's been such fun carrying our baby not knowing if you would live long enough to see her born! Such fun having you check out as soon as she sickened."

Words. All I have left is words. I've given up other means of payback. Even Eden is on your side, though he might still break a few of your bones.

I slammed my fist. She jumped a little. "Whatever my failings, Leila, I never used Socorro to get back at you the way you have."

Your eyes close. You press your mouth into a thin line. You swallow. I reach for you, pull your head down, taste the cottony softness of your lips. I've forgotten the sensation, forgotten the charge building between us. I want to get a hold of your braids and turn them into a curtain. Run my hands over your skin and take back every milotre of you.

You whisper, "Don't fuck with me, Leila."

And I tell you, "Don't fuck that Mythran bitch again."

Your eyes fly open, but you don't ask the question. When I move in for a second kiss, your arms finally come around. After we break it off, you turn my chin until you have me eye to eye. "You're sure?" Nodding, I conclude, "Just don't ask me where we're going. I've been through hell and purgatory, and that should be enough for one life time, but you never know."

◆ EPISODE 13 ◆

Raymond Eases Back into a Routine

Socorro did not weather her colds as well as the other children. Catching one, she'd suffer through it plaintively through the day and then sleep only fitfully, mewling through half the night. Maybe it was her age. It's what I like to think. When she caught another cold on a week-end trip back to Eden Hamlet between rounds of mediations, Leila and I soon worked out a routine that took advantage of my night owl tendencies. I stayed up with Socorro, and Leila took over during the day. After two sleepless nights, Vai, the only other certified night owl in the lakeside Pallas Summer Compound, volunteered to help me out. We moved the baby from my quarters to hers, hoping for better luck the third time around.

We spent a good deal of time comparing San Antonio and Alnese lullabies that night, deciding in the end that both were about equally successful with Socorro. With her good ear for sounds, Vai caught on to the similarities between my lullabies and Socorro's name, and immediately moved to test her hypothesis, "You named her in your language?"

"One of my languages."

"Ah yes, Earth is so interesting in that respect. We only have dialects."

It occurred to me that not too many Earthlings felt that way.

"Actually, I don't speak that language too well. I named her after my grandmother. Her name was Maria del Socorro, but everybody just called her Socorro."

"Is she also the source of the songs?"

"Yes."

Socorro piped up again and I picked her up, started to walk her back and forth. I hummed one of my grandmother's melodies to my daughter, one of the ones for which I couldn't remember the words. She kept having trouble breathing, and we regularly had to clean out her sinuses. Even so, she was getting better, whining less.

In the early morning, right before dawn, she finally sank into an agitated slumber. Bone-tired as we were by then, the smallest sign of improvement felt like a major victory to Vai and me. We were on our second wind, not really ready to sleep, and tip-toed to the other room. I offered to go prepare some coffee for the two of us, and Vai nodded enthusiastically.

Maybe because of the villa's quirky combination of Earthly and Alnese design, each staircase between floors connects to one end of a hall, then you crossed to the other end of that hall to reach the next stairs down. I climbed down to the second floor and made my way along the hall. Since my eyes were adjusted to the dark, I chose not to turn on the light, and simply brushed against the wall to be sure of my bearings. Moving as noiselessly as possible, I sensed something and stopped to listen. Hearing nothing, I was just about to continue toward the staircase when suddenly I was slammed against the wall to my right. At the same time, all the air was knocked out of my lungs. I heaved, simultaneously trying to relax every muscle to show no resistance. This wasn't the first wall I'd kissed in my life, and I knew what had caused my lungs to contract, a special, not particularly painful, but very disabling blow between the shoulder blades. I winced as my left arm was twisted and pushed into my back. Between two gulps for air, I squeezed out, "Take it easy, man."

"Oh, it's you." The lock on my arm loosened just a little bit. I stayed put. "Why are you stalking about?"

I said slowly, articulating each word, "I'm on my way to the kitchen to make some coffee. I don't want to wake anybody up." The lock loosened a little more. I rolled my left shoulder up and down, straightened out my left arm and set it against the wall for a slow stretch. I didn't move any more than that, waited for the man behind me to retreat first.

He didn't.

Continuing to face the wall, I commented a little more recklessly, "You are one of them." I was almost sure of my assailant's identity.

"One of them?" he echoed, still not moving.

Yes, that was Alexander's voice.

"Mythras," I hushed as quietly as I could.

He took his sweet time answering, "Yes." After a second pause, he moved back just a little more, "I obviously made a mistake here."

Another voice behind us almost made me jump, "If this was a mistake, you've been in ice too long." This time I recognized the voice immediately. It reinforced my reluctance about turning around. Then all of a sudden I heard the distinct thump of another body slamming into the wall opposite me.

When I finally stole a look over my shoulder, Eden was standing behind Alexander, who was sucking in a big lungful of air. I made damn sure my satisfaction wouldn't show on my face in spite of the dark. Turning around slowly, I leaned against my wall.

Eden's voice was barely above a murmur, albeit an intense one, "Not here. Not in this house."

"Oh Eden, you have no sense of play," Alexander replied, managing to sound both petulant and mocking.

Eden's voice dropped even lower, almost to a growl, "You're playing with fire."

Alexander was recovering, turning about. His hands started to move up Eden's torso as he whispered something that sounded like "Only yours." When Eden stepped away, brushing Alexander's arms off, Alexander held him back. He reached for Eden's head and clasped his face in his hands, leaning forward slowly.

When their mouths met, I did start moving towards the next stairwell. Making my way to the end of the hall, I heard a smothered sigh behind me, then Alexander said more audibly, "Sorry."

I didn't know which one of us he meant it for.

I cast one last look their way while rounding the landing. Eden was giving in to Alexander's advances.

When I crossed the hall again, coffee pot in hand, I was strongly tempted to stand and listen, but I resisted.

Socorro had stayed asleep all the time it had taken me to get our morning brew. Vai and I raised our first cup in quiet celebration.

Maybe it was the night spent together. I had a strong need to unburden myself, and Vai was right there across from me, sitting on her sofa, so I commented, "Maybe Eden will want me out of the way after all."

She looked up, registering first mild surprise, then a clear invitation to go on.

I told her what had happened in the second floor hall, concluded, "Eden seemed convinced that Alexander had just made a pass at me."

"What makes you think that?"

"The way he reacted. From the sounds, I'd say he slammed Alexander against the wall almost exactly the same way Alexander did me. And Eden said some things."

She waved me to her and ordered, "Let me take a look. Take off your tunic." When I complied, she sat me down next to her and started to rub my back. Under her fingers, the muscles between my shoulder blades relaxed in the most heavenly way. She tackled the knots around my neck and spoke up, "Eden's suspicions are certainly not groundless. That husband of mine can be such a whore. Still, there's room for doubt. How did you feel?"

"What do you mean?"

"Did he come on to you? What does your intuition tell you?"

I reflected on it. When Aria had come on to me, I had known it. "It felt more like . . . playing. His way of having fun."

A disapproving grunt burst over me, "At your expense! Lex is up to his usual mischief. He just can't resist a target like you. But as far as Eden is concerned, you shouldn't worry. I've never known him to blame anybody but Lex for his behavior."

This time I had to ask, "It doesn't bother you?"

"What?"

"Well . . .," I didn't quite know how to put it, bumbling, "On Earth, if your spouse is going to fool around on you, the least they could do is not do it in your face."

Vai finished with my neck. "Oh, if passion strikes here, we also want exclusivity." She sounded amused, "Look at poor Eden." Then her fists started to rain all over my back, "But passion is personal. Alliances are a clan matter. It's not the same relationship. In fact, it's not considered wise to try and mix the two. Leila was passionate about Eden and the predictable ensued: They almost wrecked the alliance."

She switched back to open hands, long strokes gliding from each shoulder down to my waist. I breathed out a contented sigh.

"My alliance was never passionate," she continued, "Lex and I have always been good friends. It helps that as a lover, he's second to none. Focuses completely on you."

She stopped.

I got up, put my tunic back on.

She smiled, "You know what's funny? Alexander fell for Eden first. He was in love! I told him not to go after him. I told him: 'You're a player, and he can only be exclusive, so leave him alone.' Of course that made Eden irresistible. Lex stuck with it, and it took more than a year to complete his conquest. And Lex has stuck with him ever since."

I went back over my encounter with the two lovers. Alexander's moves had been smooth, but something stuck in my mind: He just didn't seem the type to let himself be pushed around, and if he really matched Eden in Alnese fighting, as everyone kept hinting, then his close encounter with the wall didn't make sense. Eden had not surprised him. He had announced himself.

As if reading my thoughts, Vai added, "If only love were enough for those two. Lex submitted to Eden out of love. He always has. Then he goes off after another flame of his and hurts him terribly." She shook her head lightly, "Jotun-witted fools!"

Vai's philosophical conclusion made me think about Leila, about our relationship. We hadn't moved beyond civil exchanges after clearing the air at Lady Ciani's residence. I made up my mind to progress further. When Leila arrived a few hours later, I sought out one hand. She let me pull her to me. I put my head on hers, caressed the back of her hair, pressed her to me with my free arm. A sweet calm settled between us.

"Tired?"

"Mm-hm."

Vai brought out Socorro, still asleep. Leila walked up to her and they shifted the baby into her mother's arms. Then, she turned to me again, "I'll walk with you."

At my threshold, she leaned against the door frame. With the baby between us, I had to crane my head to reach her. My hair fell over Socorro. Leila brushed it back, then slid her free hand over my cheek. I blew lightly against her fingers, craned my head a little harder to reach her lips. Between kisses, she whispered, "Good night."

I broke it off, "You mean good morning?"

Smiling, she replied, "Maybe good afternoon. In a little bit."

◆ ◆ ◆

ALAS, IT WAS NOT TO BE.

Leila did come and wake me up that afternoon, but only to announce right off the bat, "All hell has broken loose, Ray." She gave me a minute to stretch myself awake before continuing, "You have to return to Zyss with Maskar and Dragon. The Heshtis have blown up Chantico House."

I stared at her, mouthed slowly, "The Heshtis have blown up . . . what?"

"The Chantico clan house. In the Islands."

Alert, I sat up, "When you say blown up, what do you mean?"

"I don't know the details. Just, a bomb, and deaths."

My mouth opened for a silent "oh," then I finished aloud, "Shit."

"You can say that again."

"When did this happen?"

"Last night. Eden's already on his way. But he said there's nothing he can do, that it will just have to run its course now."

"Meaning?"

"The Island clans . . . ," she drew her finger across her throat,

"Nothing will stop them from going after every last Heshti remaining out there. Eden is aiming for containment. Let the Island problems play themselves out as Island problems."

I started to pull together my clothes, "What does Dragon have to say about all this?"

"I haven't asked her."

I returned to Zyss that evening, with a glum looking Dragon and Maskar for company. Landing there, we were immediately hustled to Alnos House, briefed more fully, and started a series of essentially useless conferences to try and mitigate the violence unleashed on Alnos's Islands territory. Eden's assessment of the situation was no doubt the most realistic, but Lady Ciani was not content with mere containment.

◆ EPISODE 14 ◆

An O'bonne Progress Report

From the 1676-1677 Alnese Fieldnotes of N'dinzi Nyemba, Planetologist and Mediator

Upon us descended the dark days of the 1676 (Alnos Calendar) massacre in the area of Alnos known as the Islands, a region I had only visited briefly in my prior investigations. Towards the end of that year, two immigrants managed to smuggle powerful explosives into the heart of the Chantico clan house in the Islands and set off a devastating explosion. Chantico casualties were heavy (see below), and the other Island clans immediately united with the Chanticos to fight back. They rallied members of the Alnese martial Order of Tomrys, an order particularly popular with Islanders, to hunt down and root out all "Heshti invaders." The Order of Tomrys is also the patron of hunting on Alnos, and members are all skilled trackers. There was soon no place to hide for immigrants remaining in the Islands as Tomrys members went about their grim task of finding and killing them. Thankfully, most immigrants had already left the Islands.

The Alnese Regent and Council of Eight re-appointed Justiciar Pallas Thor Eden to continue investigating and attempting to resolve what everyone eventually came to call the 'Island Troubles.' Appointed the prior winter to investigate the murders of nine immigrants in the Islands, Justiciar Pallas had dealt with a group of Chanticos who eventually took responsibility for the murders. During the investigation, he also contended with a Kuan House-led attempt to intimidate Island immigrants into leaving by shelling one of their settlements during the summer. In both cases, Justiciar Pallas had sent perpetrators into ice without hesitation, but these actions apparently were found insufficient by some immigrants.

Justiciar Pallas knew of course that he would not be able to stop Island reprisals for the attack on Chantico House. Abandoning Island immigrants to their fate, Justiciar Pallas convinced the Arthmis elders to let him deploy several hundred Arthmin as an Alnese shield around settler-camps and communities elsewhere, strangling almost all contact between them and their Alnese neighbors and potential antagonists. He succeeded in talking his clan of origin, Thor House, the only non-Island clan affected by the attack, into an uneasy neutrality, thus staving off the spread of the Island Troubles. While the Island slaughter raged, no incidents marred the forced peace he achieved in this manner, and even after the Island bloodletting had presumably run its course and the planet entered a period of great danger, calm prevailed. The Order of Tomrys did renew its declaration of war against all "Heshti invaders," but did not challenge the Justiciar's Arthmis shield directly.

I'm enclosing a more detailed report about the attack on Chantico House kindly made available to me by the Alnese Regent, Lady Alnos Ciani.

From: Pallas Eden, 12th Justiciar of Arthmis
To: Lady Ciani, 32nd Regent of Alnos
Report on Island Developments

As far as I have been able to make out, Chantico House suffered extensive damage. The explosives were smuggled into the clan room, and detonated in such a way as to blow out the center of the structure and set off a wave of collapses to practically the outer walls. Since the explosion occurred at night, the effect on the residents was devastating. One question I have not resolved satisfactorily is how the Heshtis ever got all the way into the clan room. The remains of the two pulverized Heshtis there do indicate a suicide mission, but Chantico survivors do not recall any sounds of mayhem before the blast. It is true that the Chanticos with knowledge about the two Kamikaze Heshtis are all dead, a considerable hindrance to my investigation.

The toll stands at 97 dead. Besides the Chanticos, there were five visiting Minguards, four Kuans, two

Ochumares, two Akhmin, one Sin'Odras, one Heytens, and one Thor. The worst appears over, and I expect the remaining survivors to pull through.

As we all thought would happen, the Island clans have united and called on Tomrys to rise against the Heshtis; a swift and thorough retaliation is now in progress. Fortunately, only a few hundred Heshtis remained on the Islands at the time of the attack on Chantico House. I'm hoping that maintaining a neutral course on the Islands will defuse Tomrys fury enough so the Order will choose not to expand its actions to other areas on Alnos. I'm also doing my best to talk Thor House out of joining with Tomrys. I shudder to think about the consequences if I fail to keep my native House out of this fight.

In the meantime, the Heshtis would be well advised to keep their people out of sight, and to stop their silly little incursions into the Islands. I knew the ungrateful jotun-witted fools would not appreciate your protection. Have our two O'bonne mediators, Nyemba and Maskar, get it through their leaders' thick heads that sending more of their men here is tantamount to killing them, and that they're liable to lose the core of their clan structure if they keep doing it (not such a bad idea from our perspective, of course—they'd be so much easier to integrate without their men to carry on the way they have). They'll just have to cut their losses. We may get some of their children back once all the adults have been hunted down, but before then, there is nothing they, or Arthmis, or anyone can do.

◆ EPISODE 15 ◆

Lady Ciani's O'bonne Guests Visit Eden Hamlet

Quite incredibly, during the bloody month of the Island massacre, my colleague Maskar and Pallas Alexander forged ahead with my personal contract with the House of Pallas. Even Maskar agreed with Pallas Eden that any further mediation was futile for the foreseeable future, so he refocused on, in his words, 'two parties willing to come to an agreement'. I railed against everyone's pessimism to Kyet, only to be upbraided by him, "The Heshtis brought it on themselves." This casual judgment from my usually sweet and reasonable lover was far more shocking to me than Eden's practical reasons for giving Tomrys free reign in the Islands, and I protested sharply, "A small band carried out the attack on Chantico, not the entire Island immigrant population. How can you even think like this?" Our disagreement degenerated into a full-blown fight with no resolution, though both Kyet and I agreed to drop the subject after his mother, my old friend Vai intervened.

I was faced with two momentous failures, one public, the other private, and both were bitter pills to swallow. I couldn't believe Kyet's willingness to let hundreds, maybe even thousands of people be massacred, and even considered dropping everything and returning to O'bonne after all. The prospect of rearing a son in a society so suddenly transformed into a bloodthirsty and vengeful collection of savages left me thoroughly chastened. Oddly enough, I confided in Ray, whose human perspective often turned out strangely comforting.

"Oh, Dragon! You can have some distance. After all, it's not your family they took out. But hell, they killed half the people in that house. That was crazy! You can't just blow away a house full of people and expect their homies to sit on their hands! You know they're gonna come after your sorry ass! At least here they're only going after the adults. In my Texas hometown San Anto they'd be spraying bullets a lot more indiscriminately."

"And why should this rule only apply to immigrants?" I harangued back, almost repeating my opening salvo with Kyet, "After all, Kuan Kim and her followers blew away a house full of people last summer."

"I see your point, but if the Heshtis had really wanted to go after the people who blew up their settlement, they knew where to find them. Would the Alnese really have minded if some of Kim's followers had suddenly gone missing? But no, the Heshtis had to take it to a whole new level. Well, ninety people have a hell of a lot more relatives than eight."

"Exponentially more!" I shot back, my bitter anger coming to full fruition, "And how many relatives will get into it now? A few thousand? Or will Tomrys have succeeded in neatly wiping out entire families?"

Ray returned a long gaze, "Would you fight Tomrys? Even if they had killed a relative?"

I shook my head, "No doubt some immigrants will want to, and no doubt the Tomrys militia members are just waiting for that."

"And finish the job. Convenient." He took one look at my face and pulled me to him for a comforting hug, then asked "When are you getting married?"

"In the spring," I answered, adding more to myself, "If I go through with this alliance."

"Second thoughts?"

"When I contemplate that my son, too, could turn into a murderer here, I feel like running as far and as fast as I can."

He mused, "My old man killed at least a dozen people that he knows of. So did my grandfather. And then my cousins started getting into it. Dealing tar. I did run away."

"Did it work?"

"Well, I'm here now. I suppose I could have stayed in Switzerland."

I had to laugh, the kind of laughter that ends in a few stray tears.

"Kyet will understand eventually," he continued, "Remember what you told me on the Islands? Most Alnese don't have any experience with this kind of conflict. He doesn't know where it could lead."

And weren't the ones who did know, like Eden, acting very differently indeed? The irony at hearing my own words circle back to me through Ray was not lost on me, but I drew a little comfort from his fatalism with a silver lining.

Soon after, Maskar and Alexander worked out the finishing touches of a contract between my Ashewe family and Pallas House that committed Pallas House to facilitating regular visits to O'bonne for me, any children, and anyone else I cared to take along. A little amused, Maskar noted, "I suppose whether or how often you wish to include your future husband is up to you."

I reminded him, "An Alnese alliance concerns itself with forming families with children. The relationship between husband and wife is up to them, as long as they fulfill their obligations to their children and their families."

"I know, I know," my colleague acknowledged. "It's just that I keep expecting them to look out for the best interests of the husband, since he's the one they're negotiating for, and instead it's like that thought never even crosses their minds. Quite unusual."

"Ahh, I understand, Enku, but what you need to realize is that they're negotiating for our child and our future children."

And he said, "It is a different perspective, yes."

We then went over the contract together, with him pointing out that Pallas House had even agreed to fund our O'bonne stays for as long as I wanted as long as I agreed to return the children to Alnos for an equivalent length of time. Though I had my own means on O'bonne, I was pleased. Pallas House was signalling that it was serious about my most important desire, to have my son, and any future children, grow up both Alnese and O'bonne.

Kyet and I retired to Eden Hamlet to have some time to ourselves. The strain of the past weeks could no longer be ignored, and we both hoped that the principal site of our secret romance would provide a better milieu for our personal conference than Alnos' tension-racked capital. Maskar and Ray joined us, the first at Alexander and Vai's invitation, the second to visit Goal and Socorro.

Once in Eden Hamlet, Kyet turned sweet and lustful, but our discussions did not progress far. "Azetmir, you want me to be O'bonne. I am Alnese. Our son will be O'bonne. That'll just have to do," Kyet summed up in frustration before we once again opted for silence. His stubborn refusal to listen to my ideas about how to move forward with Alnos's new immigrants grated on me, and all my nagging doubts about our alliance came circling back. Reflecting on our future together, what stood out more and more was the folly of my having embarked on an O'bonne relationship with my Alnese youth. I obviously did not lack the capacity for obstinate irrationality, and at night, when I not only allowed, but encouraged Kyet to reawaken the fires of our physical passion, I could only conclude that my quest was transforming me instead of changing him. This rare insights into myself I did not fully accept until the dreadful moment a few days later when my heart filled with vengeful hatred and I felt its poison howl through me.

It all started on the fourth night of our stay in Eden Hamlet, when a knock on my door awakened Kyet and me both before dawn. My lover answered the call and found my O'bonne colleague Maskar, whose preoccupied expression sounded an immediate alarm.

"I apologize for the intrusion, Ashewe, but I am compelled to ask for a conference. I have not been able to sleep because with each hour, a sense of danger grows more and more defined."

"Danger? For whom?" asked Kyet.

"I cannot tell. What I do know is that it is approaching, as if something were encircling this house. Judging by its steadily growing strength, I'd guess that a relatively large number of people are involved."

Kyet's eyes widened, "Who? The Heshtis?"

"I cannot tell that either."

Kyet motioned Maskar in, "I'm calling dad. And my bodyguards. Come in for now." Then he disappeared into the darkened hall.

Twenty minutes later my future mother-in-law Vai called us down to the clan room, where the other residents slowly assembled. When Leila and Ray joined us with their children, I felt a distinct quiver go through Maskar. "What is it?" I hushed against him in our language.

"It's focused around the two children."

Vai caught my puzzled glance at Goal and Socorro, and almost immediately dawning understanding crossed her face. "Goodness, they're after the Justiciar's daughters!"

Judging by the way all the color drained from her face, Leila must have grasped Vai's meaning immediately. The rest of us did not get enlightened until Kyet appeared among us and shook his head at his mother.

Vai breathed a deep sigh, and proceeded to explain, "All right, our guest Maskar has sensed approaching danger, and heeding his warning, Kyet and I have both attempted to communicate with Zyss, first through ordinary channels, then through some special channels maintained by my science Order, Lann. We have not been successful. All our channels are blocked. Maskar, if I may ask, what is it you sensed just now?"

"A focus, on them," he jerked his head in the direction of Leila and her family. As if reacting to his pronouncement, Leila pressed Socorro against herself.

"On the children?" asked Kyet.

Maskar nodded.

"My God, it has to be Tomrys." A grim expression settled on my lover's face.

"What the . . . Would anyone care to tell me what's going on?" Ray interjected.

"Apparently, the sense of danger picked up by Maskar has a particular focus on Justiciar Pallas Eden's daughters," Vai said calmly.

"Someone means harm to Goal and Socorro?" queried Ray.

We all turned to Maskar, and he shook his head slightly, "No, not harm, that doesn't describe it correctly. It's more ...," he closed his eyes briefly, "what they want, what they're after is these two."

Vai spoke up again, "Well, let's examine the facts and apply a little logic to the situation. First, apparently a group of people with a particular interest in Goal and Socorro are approaching this house under the cover of night. Second, our communications have been cut off, blocked from somewhere outside this residence. Now, who has the capability to block our communications, down to my own confidential channels with my Order? Arthmis and Mythras, of course, but I can't fathom any reason why either Order would cut us off or try to surround Eden Hamlet secretly. That leaves only a few possibilities, particularly our other martial orders, and of those, I can think of only one with a reason to want to tangle with Pallas Eden."

"Tomrys," Leila concluded for her.

Vai continued, "Tomrys has been fighting Justiciar Eden's Arthmis shield. The Order seems determined to carry on its lethal mission in other parts of Alnos. I'm told Tomrys plans to lodge a formal protest with the Council of Eight. And now, Tomrys appears to have added a new strategy."

Taking the words right out of my mouth, Ray knitted his brows and echoed, "A new strategy?"

Vai nodded, "Yes. Compel the Justiciar to back down. And there's only one way to achieve such an outcome: through his children."

Leila added, "If Tomrys succeeds, it can pretty much dictate its terms to Eden."

"Well I say, let's do our level best to keep these summer slugs from succeeding!" Vai declared, and then she addressed Maskar again, "Can you guess how close they are? Are they ready for their assault?"

Maskar closed his eyes again and breathed deeply, then concluded, "Not yet that close."

"All right," Vai turned towards Kyet, "You must get the girls away from here. The only chance you have is to try and reach

Thor House. If you head for Nambo, they'll be waiting for you, so try Thor. You'll have to take the solar sails, anything else will give you away."

"Even with solars they'll be able to track us."

"That's why you'll leave now." Sighing, she angled an apologetic gaze towards Leila, "Which one of you will go with my son?"

Leila squeezed her eyes shut, "If they find me gone, they'll know right away. Ray's connection is less well known."

Vai and Ray asked almost simultaneously, "You're sure?"

Pressing the baby to her, Leila threw them a quick nod.

Vai made a hand signal to Kyet, "Go. Get the girls to Thor House."

Looking at me pleadingly, Kyet backed out of the clan room. I followed him to the vestibule, fighting my sense of dread, and latched onto him after he said, "I don't want us to part in anger, Azetmir."

I could not respond, just hugged him to me.

"They won't hurt us if they catch up. They might even turn me into an additional hostage, to keep dad in check," he soothed, kissing my hair. I still could not respond verbally, though I extricated myself and stood ready.

Maskar and Vai joined us, then Ray and the girls arrived, all securely bundled in the best snow clothes. Kyet gathered his mother to him for a brief final hug, and the four took flight.

CHAPTER 16

Raymond and Kyet Escape Towards Thor House

Oddly enough, my most vivid memory of our escape that night is Kyet's breathtaking beauty in the rising sun. First, he parked me and Goal ahead of him on the wide board, then he leaned into the rudder and we shot off down the darkened Lake Limnos. The ice crunched beneath us as the board gathered steam, and despite the solar's force-field around the passenger area, I could still feel the cold wind whipping around us. I gathered Goal to me and we cradled Socorro between us. Time flew as fast as our solar sail. I looked up to take in dawn's early light, and caught sight of Kyet's auburn hair flapping in the wind. With his hood down, all he used for protection were his sunvisor and one of his multicolored earbands. The sun bathed him in a golden radiance. There could be no doubt as to Pallas Kyet's antecedence: His resemblance to his father stood out.

Shortly after dawn, he shifted the solar close to the shore, and after we flew by Pirate Island, he stopped it completely. "We can't stay on the lake with the sun up. We'll have to try and make it along the shore." He leaned over Goal, "Ready for some bumps?"

She nodded shyly.

"Come on, sweetheart, help me."

She rose and he guided her in the art of counterweighing his moves. The solar sail climbed up the steep shore. We straightened out between snow-covered firs. "Now I need a copilot," Kyet announced cheerfully. Goal adjusted and they started to rock the sail back and forth as we slalomed through firs.

I thought we were making excellent time. Perhaps we were. Our Tomrys hunters just made better time.

Socorro woke up and started to protest her snow-clothes-confinement vigorously, and for a few minutes, I was completely distracted. When I looked up again, Kyet was leaning back, looking over his shoulder. I actually saw the solar about to slam into us first, and by the time Kyet jerked back, it was too late. The other solar, a thin one-man board, crashed into our bow, and our board pitched up, then shuddered to an abrupt stop. I clutched the baby to me and rounded myself the best I could as I hit the snow. My left shoulder plowed into a drift and I came to a mercifully soft stop. To my right, I heard Goal scream. I swear to God I've never scrambled to my feet as fast as I did then. I was standing next to her in two seconds flat, and still clutching Socorro to me, I folded her into my free left arm.

Pressing her trembling body to me while rocking my much angrier daughter, I looked around. As I had suspected, more than a dozen Tomrys members had already surrounded us. Goal let out another terrified yelp, and when I followed her fixed gaze, I froze. Kyet lay just beyond the circle of people surrounding us, inert, a trickle of blood seeping out of a corner of his mouth. I started towards him and the circle of people around me adjusted into a more elliptical shape. When I kneeled down to him, I heard Minguard Lauran's distinct voice moving closer, "Jotun-witted fool, do you want to die? Don't you know who this is? What the hell did I tell you?" I could not believe my ears. Eden's lieutenant? I looked up, "Minguard Lauran?"

The two boards lay crashed in the snow a good four or five meters from us. Between us and the boards, a snow-clothes-clad figure trudged towards us. When she reached us, Minguard Lauran crouched down opposite me, pulled off her hood, and surveyed Kyet's unconscious figure, "The fool injures the Legate's son, the Legate's son!"

She rose again and sighed, "And we didn't bring a physician." She moved to the back of my guarding ellipse and conferred with two other snow-clothes-clad figures. When she moved off, one of them came over. As soon as his hands reached for Kyet, Goal screamed again. He backed off and waited for me to calm her, then we both waited for Socorro to pipe down. He took off his hood and soothed over Kyet's still body, "I'm here to help him. Will you let me?"

Goal started to cry, quiet little hiccups racking through her body. "Here," he said, offering her his scanner. She looked up to me and I confirmed, "It's a scanner."

"May I examine him now?"

Still shushing Goal, I gave my permission, "Go ahead."

I sat up and switched to French for greater effect, "Goal, what happened to Kyet was an accident. You needn't be afraid, nobody here will hurt you, or your sister. No one!" The hiccups died down and she wiped away her tears. When I surveyed my surroundings again, Kyet had been secured onto a stretcher, his neck and entire torso wrapped in a foam-like material, and one person was shaping a blanket-like snow-cover over him. The man with the scanner was conferring earnestly with Lauran.

She came strolling back, and after an unhappy sigh, she asked me, "Will you follow us without resisting?"

I wanted to ask, *'What the hell are you doing here?'* But since the answer to that was obvious, I skipped forward to, "I won't let any of you bastards near the children. You can break my neck if you want to."

Her face impassive, she replied, "Your death would change nothing."

"I don't care." My bravado was almost nullified as I spoke by a wide-eyed Goal, ready to start her next volley. I pressed her to me.

Lauran tried a different tack, "If everyone keeps their distance, will you follow us?"

"Huh, as opposed to freeze to death in this beautiful landscape?" I nodded wearily.

"Agreed then. They'll keep a distance of one tre at all time."

Rising from my kneeling position, I pulled Goal close to me. It took a little while to find the right balance with the two unequal weights on my right and left, then I trudged in the direction indicated. The Tomryns settled us on another solar, one jumped on to pilot, and we headed east even as the sun started to shadow our backs.

I lost track of time as we slalomed through the firs. We reached our destination as lengthening shadows and dropping temperature announced imminent sunset.

Climbing down from our solar, we surveyed a lodge almost completely buried in snow. Several of our captors had to dig a path to its door. Keeping their one-tre distance, two Tomryns walked me and the girls into the lodge. I recognized an Arthmis insignia on the mantle of a large fireplace once inside the main hall. One man was busy starting a fire in the fireplace. In one corner, one woman was working the controls of the lodge. Our escorts pointed towards the lodge's sleeping hall, and we progressed to a cozy little suite. One room was empty, in the other we found Kyet. His attendant had kept him knocked out throughout the trip, and he hadn't regained consciousness.

Goal and I were each served stuffed Alnese pancakes. We practically fell on the food. Neither I, nor Goal had eaten all day. Only Socorro had been fed whenever she started to cry.

When Lauran appeared at our doorstep, she signaled for me to join her. Making sure Goal couldn't hear her, she whispered, "Pallas Kyet is not well, and Pallas Vaideh's program has surely alerted her husband by now, so I cannot risk a call to my allies, certainly not from an Arthmis training lodge. If anything should happen, can I count on you to keep the Justiciar's daughter distracted?"

"What do you mean, if anything should happen?"

"The other board hit him across the lower abdomen and the lumbar region when it crashed into yours. Our medassistant thinks he stopped the internal bleeding, but we cannot be sure. Kyet remains in shock. If he comes out of it, he may make it. If not," she shrugged.

I hissed with uncommon vehemence, "You better fucking make sure he pulls through, Lauran."

Without batting an eyelash, she continued, "He needs surgery. Maybe tomorrow."

"You don't know what you've done, do you?"

"On the contrary, Díaz, no one knows it better. What's more, unlike my Tomryns I know exactly what awaits me because of it. I hope the Justiciar catches up with me first. I prefer his rage over the Legate's pragmatism."

"You speak as if you had already lost."

"Whether I win or lose this round, one of them will get me. It's just a matter of time."

◆ CHAPTER 17 ◆

Dragon and Maskar Face Tomrys

After we watched Kyet, Ray, and the girls sail off using the carriage house camera, Vai instructed, "Everybody, back to your suites. We must all appear to be sleeping, or we'll give everything away."

She turned to me, "I hope and pray that your contract with Pallas House has not yet become common knowledge. I don't know if Alexander's status will protect you or turn you into a new target once the Tomryns find the Justiciar's children gone. And Maskar has been brought here as Eden's mediator and honored guest. Each of you makes a desirable hostage."

"We haven't discussed Ashewe's new connection with anybody besides the elders," Maskar replied. "As for my desirability, well, it could lead to an interesting new chapter in my life."

Vai brightened, "Perhaps we could pass it off as an O'bonne pregnancy."

Maskar shrugged, "Always worth a try." Then he broke into a conspiratorial grin while he gingerly put an arm around my shoulders.

Vai said, "Do it, then. I'll climb back to my office and write a program to hack the Tomrys communications black-out. I only hope it breaks through in time."

I nodded to Maskar and we retired together. In my quarters, he sat me down for a session of joint meditation, calmed me gradually until I could face the coming confrontation with something akin to equanimity. When my door opened an hour later and two silent figures slipped in, I was even able to fake sleep.

Maskar jerked up quite convincingly, mumbling curses in O'bonne that netted him a rough blow on the chest. He switched to a bedraggled Alnese into which he continued to mix a good deal of outraged-sounding O'bonne, "Who are you? What is going on?"

"Quiet," hissed one of our aggressors. The other stepped back out to the hall. Maskar put his arm around my shoulder again and we waited in silence. A quarter of an hour elapsed, then a whistle sounded and the young woman in our room motioned to the door, "Let's go."

Maskar mustered up some convincing indignation as he repeated, "What is going on?"

"You'll find out."

We were all herded into the clan room. A dozen figures surrounded us, half of them still in snow clothes. Maskar and I sat down next to Leila, whose face wavered between hostility and blankness. Ten minutes later, Vai was pushed roughly into our midst.

The man who had brought her down sidled over to one of the

snow-clothes-camouflaged figures and they spoke in whispers, after which the figure turned to us and called, "Pallas Vaideh."

I froze, as did Leila next to me. We weren't the only ones to have recognized the voice. "So, Tomrys chose you to lead these scorpions, Minguard Lauran," Vai answered with considerable equanimity. "What a pitiful end for a proud member of the Order of Arthmis to turn into a criminal."

The figure pushed down her hood and took off her snow-glasses, then acknowledged, "You Pallas Vai, on the other hand, have proven worthy of Legate Alexander's alliance, judging by that bit of programming we just interrupted." Minguard Lauran directed her gaze at me, and both Maskar and Leila pressed closer, as if their physical contact could nullify her next pronouncement, "You are doubly precious to us, Ashewe Dragon. We'll take good care of you." My heart almost leapt out of my throat, but I managed to maintain a calm expression.

A new man entered the clan room and called out, "One to two hours, towards Nambo."

Minguard Lauran threw him a quick look, "How?"

"Solars."

Minguard Lauran made a short hand motion and her sentinel grabbed Vai and nudged her closer to his leader. "Nambo?" Despite the questioning tone, we all knew it was not a question, and she confirmed our understanding with her next pronouncement, "No doubt that's a ruse. We've cut off that route and surely you must have anticipated that."

Vai shrugged.

"What is your estimate, Pallas Vaideh?"

"My estimate?"

"How much time will it take for your message to get through?"

"It is difficult to estimate how soon an unknown reader may catch on to such a buried message."

Minguard Lauran barely moved her head and Vai flinched. None of us had seen anything.

"I do not wish to hurt you."

"Go tell a snow dervish your concern!"

Vai flinched again. Maskar stood up. Two flying figures stopped him long before he got anywhere close to Vai, who yelled out, "Stay back." Following Maskar's cue, I rose and stepped very slowly between her and Minguard Lauran. She snapped her fingers and no one else moved. Wrapping one arm around Vai's shoulders, I murmured, "Well, since they're about to add me to their list of hostages, I might as well protect you, old friend."

Vai's breaths came in careful bursts, but with my help she straightened out. The look that met us when we faced Minguard Lauran communicated temporary capitulation. She turned to confer with two associates, "We will assume the message has already gone through. We need to speed up our time table. Kuan, take the O'bonne in the small glider. Cochecpa, you pilot the other one to the listening post." Then she looked around, and directed, "Lock the others in the kitchen. The hunt is on. On my signal!"

Another woman poked me and I flashed a loathing eyeful at her, but Vai smiled briefly and I retreated. Maskar joined me again, moving as slowly as I had when I intervened. With a conciliatory shrug, Lauran gestured a final order to her troupe and left the room. The Tomryns made no further attempts to separate Maskar from me. After they had driven the other residents from the clan room, all but three of them vanished. One warned us, "Resistance is futile, O'bonne. Your companion has no protection. Attempt escape and we will kill him." I nodded understanding and we found ourselves back in the vestibule, where we dressed ourselves for winter under the watchful eyes of our guards.

They took us to the top of a ridge above the house, where I saw two gliders parked. Once we reached the crest, I tried to look far into the distance, but there was no sign of anybody, just a resplendent blue sky over the snow-covered landscape at my feet. Repressing my multiplying fears, I turned my back on Lake Limnos and climbed aboard the smaller vehicle. A short period later, we watched the larger one hover up above us. One abductor directed us to sit in the back, while the other went to the cockpit. I felt the engines hum on. Closing my eyes, I leaned into Maskar, and when I was once again ready to cope with what was happening, I made a mental note of our westward direction. Though our pilot was taking a circuitous route to avoid all settled areas, we were headed towards the Islands.

Sensing my renewed calm, Maskar murmured in O'bonne, "You know this woman, the leader?"

"She is . . . was one of Pallas Eden's lieutenants."

After a moment of contemplation, he continued, "And the others? From Vai's words I gather they are from the infamous Tomrys."

"No doubt they are."

"What is an Arthmin lieutenant doing leading a band of

Tomryns on an outlaw mission?"

"Minguard Lauran is an Islander. Her clan must have called her back."

"Ah yes, I do recall there were Minguards among the Chantico dead. Five? I can't remember, exactly."

Raymond's words echoed through me: Ninety people did have a hell of a lot more relatives than nine. I sighed, and Maskar, sensing the cocktail of dread and sadness within me, tried to comfort me with a gentle hug. Fighting the reawakened morning sickness induced by the flight, I closed my eyes and tried to breathe through it, while Maskar focused on infusing me with his relative calm.

No doubt it was my debilitated condition, and the effort we both put into countering it, that distracted Maskar and kept him from sensing the presence of the fifth passenger on our glider until right before she chose to manifest herself. When he did pick up on it, he pressed against me slightly more and whispered in O'bonne, "Remain as silent as you can." And just as he finished his warning, I saw a blur shoot by us and almost simultaneously heard the distinct crack of a disabling blow. I bit back my shocked reaction.

Our Tomrys guard rested unconsciously against his seat, his face not even registering surprise. His attacker had melded against the wall, and was alternating darting glances to the piloting area and in our direction. Maskar lowered his chin. The woman shot us a quick grin, as if she and Maskar had reached an understanding, then crept forward silently. One moment later, her voice rang out to us, "Come now."

Maskar helped me stay on my unsteady feet until we both

reached the piloting cabin. Our last guard sprawled before us, while our liberatrix was seated at the controls. "We'll be setting down now," she said, "I'm sorry, but I could not act sooner without alerting Tomrys."

I slid down into the seat next to her, toed our last guard gingerly.

"Careful. I let them live."

I examined our liberatrix as we landed. She resembled Raymond, though she was shorter and rounder. Her voice had an androgynous quality, a deep and melodious fullness that clashed with her short stature. Beneath her winter fat, I suspected more than saw the distinct build and conditioning of a martial Alnese fighter, and I wondered which order she belonged to. I didn't have to wonder long.

Having brought the glider to a complete stop, she focused on an area of her panel that was blinking intermittently, then she instructed Maskar to hold the pilot up. "Carefully. If she kicks, drop her immediately." Maskar nodded and did as he was told. She pressed a miniature scanner against the Tomryn's head and the woman's eyelids began to flutter. When she came to, our liberatrix bored her black eyes into hers and moved her sleeve up. We all made out the stylized, elongated head of a snake partially camouflaged by feathers on her forearm, and I sensed a distinct shudder run through our former guard. Our liberatrix belonged to the Order of Mythras, Alnos's most accomplished warriors. "I let you live for one reason. I can disable your alarm, but I do not wish to. Bypass it."

A second shudder traveled the length of the pilot's body,

and she swallowed hard.

"Refuse and I will tell Legate Pallas to make an example out of you." The feathered snake-tattooed warrior nodded to Maskar and he shooed our Tomrys pilot forward.

"Explain every move before you make it."

Moving with exaggerated care, the pilot complied with our Mythran warrior. After she finished, she placed both her hands on a panel in front of her and crouched down between me, Maskar, and the warrior. The latter snapped a small communicator open and dialed a code into it. A minute passed, then a sharp whistle hissed through a speaker above the steering controls.

Our benefactress addressed herself to Maskar, "You should sit down. It will take my troupe at least an hour to reach us."

Eyeing the crouching figure between us, Maskar slipped into the seat immediately behind mine. I could sense his burning questions, but I was loath to break the silence.

Our liberatrix divided her attention between watching over the crouching pilot and sending out new codes at regular intervals. Her prediction proved quite accurate: About an hour later a hum announced the approach of another glider.

"Up," the Mythran warrior commanded. Moving with the deliberate slowness we all gravitated towards in the presence of hostile Alnese warriors, the Tomryn placed herself facing the wall behind Maskar, her hands clutching a rail above her head, her legs slightly apart. The deep and melodious voice of our liberatrix managed to chill us all, "Remember: he'll make an example of you." Then she moved to open the glider.

When Alexander and his two-man escort stepped through

the open portal, I was not surprised, having suspected his involvement the minute I recognized our warrior's Mythran tattoo. Torn between relief and apprehension about the fate of our two kidnappers, I let my face be an open book when I turned to greet him. He nodded to Maskar, inquired, "You are well, Pallas Ashewe?" His choice of names certainly was not lost on any of us.

"Yes." Casting a look at the still figure facing the glider wall, I emphasized, "They did not touch me."

"Such a generous woman, my new daughter. However did my foolish son choose so brilliantly?" He smiled, then, without looking, reached for the pilot's arm with his right hand and turned her around. Her face looked semi-frozen, and when he finally glanced at her, she stared down to her feet.

"Another Kuan?" he asked pleasantly.

Continuing to stare at her feet, she moved her head up, then down.

"Kuan?"

"Kemir."

"Kuan Kemir, Ixchel Aria tells me you complied quite nicely. You are wiser than your Order. Who leads you?"

I stirred, but he raised one finger of his left hand, shook it at me ever so slightly.

"Who leads you?"

The Tomryn pilot's breathing hollowed as Alexander waited. Suddenly, she buckled almost exactly the same way Vai had. Maskar and I both scrambled to our feet. Alexander angled his head towards us and continued in O'bonne with his pleasant tone, "Do you wish me to take her outside? You won't hear a thing—she's well trained."

"Don't spare us. Spare her. At least from the questions we can answer," Maskar shot back in our language.

Alexander's left eyebrow went up. "Agreed," he replied, an amused note in his voice.

"Minguard Lauran," I said.

Both Alexander's and the pilot's face remained impassive. Drawing in a deliberately deep breath, he prodded her with a more authoritative tone, "Tell them."

She looked at me in particular, "Thank you, but I answer for my Order's challenge to Justiciar Pallas Eden. For Tomrys, for Alnos, I give my life." Then she directed a steady gaze in Alexander's direction, "My mind if I have to."

Maskar looked from her, to me, to Alexander and asked, still in O'bonne, "What does she mean?"

Alexander said to her in Alnese, "What you know is not important enough." He made a hand signal, and an aide stepped forward, then guided the unresisting Tomryn pilot away. Alexander switched back to O'bonne, "She means I join my mind with hers, and scramble her brains to break down her resistance. It's an appalling form of rape; half of those subjected to it never recover."

"You have done this?" Maskar blurted out.

Alexander looked straight at me, "Yes."

"You will do this to her?"

Alexander shrugged, "She's safe enough. What do you want me to do with her?"

Both Maskar and I were completely taken aback.

"Know that as a good Tomryn, she'll fall on her blade before she'll betray her Order," Alexander continued. "A forced joining would be the only way for me to get anything out of her."

Alexander took a look at our second kidnapper, who was still out cold. Two other Mythrans came in, grabbed the unconscious Tomryn, and removed him from our glider. Then, Alexander called out, "Ixchel," and our rescuer reappeared. She informed him, "Justiciar Pallas Eden is tracking them east. Since the safest course once we get close is on solars, we won't reach them until early morning."

"So they'll have them one night. I do hope the Arthmin scorpion is as careful with my son and my cousins as she was with you, Ashewe Dragon. We'll drop you off in Eden Hamlet. My First Lieutenant Ixchel Aria is an accomplished glider pilot. Perhaps by then you'll have come up with a interesting idea about what to do with our little waif."

I was incredulous, "You would do as I ask?"

"To the letter."

"What is the catch? Will her Order be after her?"

"More than likely."

"Goddess!"

Maskar coughed behind us. When we turned towards him, he suggested, "Sooner or later I will have to run down Kuan Kim and the two Chanticos sent into ice by Justiciar Pallas to find out what started this whole thing. As one who probably knows them all, this young Tomryn would be an ideal escort."

"Mm." Alexander looked amused again, "Not a betrayal, only a service to Justiciar Pallas Eden and his mediator as you dig through ancient history. It might work. Ixchel."

"My lord."

"I claim Kuan Kemir as Mythran servant to Maskar. Make sure Tomrys is appraised of it in due time."

His First Lieutenant bowed to him.

"What of the second glider?"

She drew her finger across her throat, "On the Thor high plain. No alarm."

Alexander nodded to himself, then he turned glittering eyes to me and pronounced with grim satisfaction, "We have them! Their escape routes have been cut off. That will teach Tomrys to go after a legate's family."

◆ EPISODE 18 ◆

Mythras Thwarts Tomrys

It took me half the night to settle Goal. Despite all my assurances and the careful distance maintained by all, she was in an absolute terror. In the early hours before dawn, she finally sank into a deep sleep, and I breathed a sigh of relief. Socorro's obliviousness to it all remained the one small favor to be thankful for.

Of course I had slipped back into insomnia myself. I woke up every fifteen minutes or so, tossed a bit, and cursed myself thoroughly. I wanted, needed to be alert in the morning. Finally, I gave up. After reassuring myself about both girls, I slid to the next room and joined the medassistant in his vigil. Kyet was slipping. His hands felt like ice, and his clammy skin had taken on a much grayer tone than usual.

"Still got a slow bleed in there somewhere," the medassistant sighed. "That Jotun-witted fool Sin-Odras will have gotten us all killed, charging at your board the way he did."

"I can always tell his father it was an accident."

"Hmpf! Doesn't absolve us. A hunter better prepare to accept God's price for his quarry."

A completely unexpected voice made me jump with, "How well spoken."

The medassistant next to me grew very still. Mythran warrior Ixchel Aria advanced from the door to Kyet's side, obviously unconcerned about the Tomrys medassistant. She took one look, then asked me, "The girls?"

"Asleep. Next door. They're unhurt."

A second Mythran woman appeared at the door and Aria indicated the other room with a quick side-nod. She moved back to the entrance herself and said quietly, "Get Tzalque Peg." Something akin to relief stole over the medassistant's face.

Unlike the two Mythrans, the good doctor made plenty of noise approaching our suite. I guessed that Eden and Alexander must have joined forces for their pursuit, and their joint Mythran-Arthmis assault must already have reached its successful conclusion. Doctor Peg swept in and launched into fairly frantic examination, cussing out everyone in the room. "I'll have to cut, it's too late for anything else," she concluded, "And he needs blood. No time for matching. Who's compatible, besides his father?"

"Argen negative?" asked the medassistant.

Peg confirmed with a nod.

"I have collected some already. Will you let us offer it as reparation?"

"If his father objects, tell him to get lost in a Jotun storm. Go get it. When you come back, assist me." She threw off her open snow suit and discarded another layer of clothes, started to roll her hair into a tight bun. "All of you, out!"

The medassistant followed Aria and me out of the room. When we reached what looked like a central hall, Aria motioned for me to stay and disappeared with him out another door. Lauran was standing by the fireplace, very straight, her arms crossed behind her. I don't think I've ever seen anybody looking quite so vulnerable.

Eden and Alexander entered the hall together. The first walked right up to Lauran while the second moved to one side. Eden closed in. She stayed put.

Looking down at her, he said in a low, neutral voice, "When you asked me to release you, I let you go without conditions. I . . . was . . . generous."

She averted her face, "I won't fight you, Pallas Eden."

He hit her with the back of his hand, so hard her entire body flew back and hit the wall next to the fireplace. He grabbed a hold of one arm and tossed her back again, and again. I could hear bones breaking the third time she hit the wall. Finally, he locked one fist in her hair and the second around her wrist and twisted her into a back-breaking angle. Alexander stepped forward, "Enough."

Eden stopped tossing her about, "Not nearly."

Alexander snapped her right out from under Eden's nose and put his arms around her protectively, "Get a hold of yourself. Yes, she was your lieutenant, and that is precisely why Tomrys chose her."

Eden glowered at them both, his hands balling into fists.

"Go take care of your children," Alexander directed.

Without another word, Eden stalked off in the direction of my night's accommodation. Alexander lifted up Lauran and carried her to a settee next to where I stood. Curling up, she whimpered through gritted teeth. Alexander snapped his fingers and a figure by the entrance jumped to attention. "Bring the medassistant."

When the man appeared, Alexander ordered, "Make her comfortable." As soon as the medassistant went down on one knee in front of the Lieutenant, Alexander added, "And don't let your knife slip."

The medassistant blew a burst of air from his cheeks, "Lieutenant Minguard ordered us not to interfere with anything that might happen."

"Almost makes you want to defy her, doesn't it?"

The medassistant nodded once as he dug a vial out of one pocket and several patches out of another. He moistened the patches with the liquid in the vial and applied the patches to her wrist, under her tunic, and on her forehead. I could practically make out the progress of the pain killer through her body as the medassistant finished, got back to his feet, and announced, "Your physician has asked for my help."

"Everyone is developing a streak of O'bonne generosity today," observed Alexander, his eyes on the still grimacing Lauran, "Well, off with you!"

Alexander seated himself on the settee's arm by Lauran's head. Looking down to her, he said, "All but one of my questions . . . can wait. You know what I want. I urge you to give it to me."

She shook her head.

"I will know his name."

"I won't have given it to you."

"Minguard Lauran, you're good, almost Mythran. You don't have anything to prove."

She shook her head again, grimacing at the effort, closed her eyes.

He sighed, called out, "Ixchel."

Aria stuck her dark head into the hall a moment later. He motioned her to him, moved closer to Lauran, then positioned Lauran's head in his lap. "Make sure she doesn't injure herself further."

His fingers fastened into place, and at first nothing happened. Gradually, tremors started coursing up and down Lauran's body. Her head jerked from side to side and he pressed it down more forcefully. When she started to thrash about, Aria caught a hold of her arms and pushed them down, eventually climbing on top of her. One anguished cry cut right into me, then a second one. Alexander's breathing grew as choppy as Lauran's, and he threw his head back, eyes pressed shut. A low, drawn-out wail shook me to the core. Eyes still shut, Alexander bent down to her and pushed her trembling figure up with one knee until he could press his forehead against the top of her head. When he broke contact, he breathed, "That's it. Enough."

Almost mechanically, his hands moved to her shoulders, and he started a slow neck rub. Her eyes darted about wildly. Tears started running down her cheek. Cupping her head in his hands again, he brushed away the tears with his thumbs. Aria got back to her feet and stood at attention. When a low moan bubbled up through Lauran's bloodied lips, Alexander hushed her almost tenderly, "Shshsh. Perhaps I won't have to violate you a second time for my other questions." Then, right as he turned to say something to Aria, two men burst in on us.

Slightly ahead, a young man stopped dead in his tracks and surveyed the scene. His pursuer stopped just behind him, but did not touch him. Alexander remained seated, now casually rubbing Lauran's temples, but Aria assumed a more defensive posture. The young man had the most remarkable jet black hair and freckled white skin. A range of emotions played themselves out on his face as he stepped closer slowly, hopeful apprehension replaced by horrified comprehension, then stern determination.

"Too late," Alexander confirmed. He slid out from under Lauran's head and gestured to me, "Make yourself useful. Continue until she blacks out." I slid down onto the settee to do as I was told. Careful not to put pressure on her broken ribs, I hugged Lauran to me. Waves of tremors moved through her body. I found myself imitating Alexander, rubbing her neck, lulling her into a merciful swoon.

Alexander stepped towards the young man who'd burst in and directed towards the man who'd followed close behind, "Was he delayed?"

With one nod, the Mythran pursuer replied, "He's been trying to get to you from the moment he recovered, my lord."

"Well he's here now. You may stand down."

The pursuer bowed and backed away. For a moment, Alexander stood perfectly still. Then, in what seemed like slow motion compared to his usual speed, Alexander thrust forward and planted a very deliberate kick in the young man's gut. The man went down to his knees. Alexander grabbed a hold of his hair and forced him up, then he kicked one leg out from under him, spun him around, and shoved him into a contour chair on the side of the settee. The young man dug into the chair's back to hold back a groan. Alexander didn't even look ruffled.

"All right, Sin'Odras, like so many of your clan, you act before you think, but you have the courage to face me. I'm sorry you were delayed. I would much rather have spared Minguard."

The young man succeeded in straightening himself against the chair, beads of sweat collecting on his forehead.

"You tied your life to my son's," Alexander continued, "If he dies, you bleed to death."

His head lowered, the young man gritted out, "Will that . . . be the end of it?"

Alexander seemed just a touch taken back, "My, concern for the team! All right, I absolve anyone but you of this debt. If my son lives, he will decide what to do with you. And I did not raise him Mythran."

Turning back to the settee, Alexander bent down and gathered the passed out Lauran into his arms. Lifting her as if she were a feather, he turned to Aria for a last set of instructions, "When Tzalque Peg is done with Kyet, send her to me." Pointing to young Sin'Odras, he ordered, "He stays."

She nodded once.

He turned towards the hall's entance, then paused in mid-turn to add, "If he faints before we know, you may keep him alive."

Ixchel nodded a second time, and queried, "What do I tell the Justiciar?"

"Give him the Tomrys message." Alexander shifted his gaze to me, then nodded his head towards the vestibule exit as he directed, "Chronicler, accompany us."

We walked outside. Alexander led the way to a glider, carrying Lauran with little effort. Once inside, he stepped towards a three-seat bench behind the cockpit and deposited Lauran onto it with the utmost care. "Your beneficial effect may help her recovery."

He pointed to the third seat and I lowered myself next to Lauran, threaded my fingers into hers, "What will happen to her?"

He straightened up and leaned against the pilot seat, "She fought me like an ice-cat, all for that Jotun-witted fool who injured my son. Why should she protect him from the consequences of his rashness? She deserves better than to get ground up between Arthmis and Tomrys over the Heshtis." He sighed.

I stole up a quick look. Paying no particular attention to me, he continued, "I'll have to continue what I started, get the other names from her. Particularly any other Arthmin who has chosen to betray us. If she fights me again, I'll probably injure her quite badly." His eyes lingered on Lauran, but he didn't seem to see her anymore, as if lost in thought.

I'd never resisted his forays into my head, so I didn't really know what punishment he could inflict on someone unwilling to share information. But I didn't doubt that his counter-measures would be punishing.

With another sigh, he mused, "If she survives her next interrogation, maybe I can convince Arthmis to let her choose ice penance. She won't have any trouble surviving an ice sentence. But Eden is furious."

"Meaning?"

"You saw him! He wants to tear her to pieces."

He shifted himself into the pilot seat and one panel next to him came to life. His fingers flew over it for several minutes, then he leaned back and looked out the front window into the distance. The sun had just come up; another splendid winter day announced itself. A sharp whistle jarred me, and Alexander's fingers danced over the control panel again.

I stayed put, stroking Lauran's hair with my free hand. Slowly, slowly, her unconscious tremors subsided.

The sun had climbed up a few notches when a blood-spattered Doctor Peg peeked into the glider. She was uncharacteristically quiet, and I waited with baited breath. She plumped herself into the seat opposite me. Alexander swiveled to face us, and brought his fingers together one by one.

"Too late for the nerve damage down his right leg. I'll be able to improve it, but there's a limit."

"He lives?"

"Yes, with Tomrys blood to spare. No more dancing, though."

Alexander closed his eyes for a moment. I exhaled. When he opened his eyes, he gestured toward Lauran. "See what you can do about her. Ribs, collar bone, concussion … Eden didn't hold back. And she'll need a neural tranquilizer."

"Couldn't *you* have held back?"

Shaking his head, he said matter-of-factly, "Nope."

Doctor Peg rose, stepped to our bench, and bent over Lauran. I got out of the way.

Alexander continued in the same tone, "Work on Sin'Odras when you're through with her. He's in the hall."

"I saw him. Why should I patch him up, Legate? So you can smash his spine after I'm done?" Doctor Peg challenged sharply.

He threw a studied look at her over his joined fingers, "Kyet will decide his fate. I don't go back on my word."

"And what about your people, when they find out Sin'Odras has lamed Kyet?"

Alexander smiled up at her, "What a strategist you are, Tzalque Peg. I will tell them to lay off."

She straightened up and mumbled one of her favorite curses, then ordered brusquely, "Have the medassistant bring my kit."

Alexander turned back towards the control panel, brushed over the com unit and relayed, "Doctor Tzalque needs her tools. Have the medassistant bring her kit."

Alexander turned to stare out into the distance again. He placed finger against finger once more, then drew his joined index fingers up to his lips. His face grew perfectly still. With the blue radiance of the morning sky behind him, his golden hair framed his Apollonian features like a halo.

◆ EPISODE 19 ◆

Dragon Struggles to Reconcile her Alnese Self

A little more than a day after his forced run, Kyet was restored to me. That same day, I learned how thoroughly Alnos had changed me. Having suffered insomnia more than half the night, I had sunk into a heavy, dreamless slumber from which Vai roused me. Instantly alert, I tried to still my beating heart by clasping her hands in mine, and she told me right away, "Kyet suffered an accident. He was hurt. Seriously. My husband had the foresight to take Tzalque Peg with him on this morning's mission, and she saved Kyet's life, but it was too late for some nerve damage."

Kneading her hands, I whispered, "He lives!" I collected myself and entreated her, "Tell me the worst."

"The nerve down his right leg was crushed, and Peg could not restore it fully. He'll be lame."

I nodded understanding. Though the loss of even a whole leg would not cripple me, I did not doubt that his loss would change the course of Kyet's life.

"He'll spend the rest of winter recovering, that's certain," Vai added.

"If he lets me, I'll work with him."

"I hope he does."

We traveled back to Zyss with what looked like a full Mythran guard, though I did not inquire about the status of our companions and they did not volunteer any information. Once we reached the City of Learning, one of the silent figures escorted us all the way into Kyet's intensive care unit, where he relieved another guard.

Kyet looked ghastly. Asleep, wrapped in a body cast, his skin had turned ashen and his face had hollowed. "Don't let his appearance impress you too much. He's quite well, really, his metabolism just hasn't caught up yet," Doctor Tzalque Peg reassured from behind us.

We took turns waiting for Kyet to waken. It was during one of my breaks that I overheard our Mythran escort conferring with—judging by the air of collegiality between them—another young warrior.

"It's really hands off Sin'Odras?"

"That's what the Legate said."

"Maybe someone should discuss the matter with his mother, Pallas Vaideh."

"You hope for vengefulness from a Lann scientist? Besides, how would you explain it to the Legate?"

I corralled Vai the minute I stepped back into Kyet's sickroom, "Who is Sin'Odras?"

She hesitated and kept silent at first, and almost

automatically, I tuned my empathic sensibilities. After about a minute of hesitation, I felt her give in to me, "Oh, I suppose you'll find out sooner or later anyway. Kyet was injured because a solar board crashed into him. I am certain the pilot did not mean for it to happen."

The uncertainty I sensed in her belied her words, and she knew it. A bright, hot rage flamed through me, so strong that I could barely contain it as I proclaimed, "I shall ascertain that for myself!"

Thank Goddess Vai is an astute player in the game of passions! "Why?" she asked simply. She didn't need an answer, of course; her question was designed to make me realize the shocking direction into which my passion was carrying me. A growing Alnese soul had just overwhelmed all my treasured O'bonne rationality, and my seething rage confirmed how far I had gone native. What's more, no surprise accompanied my rage, as if I had long since anticipated this personal turning point into the savagery of my new tribe.

I knew I needed to let the flame burn itself out, no matter how hard.

In an attempt to comfort me, Vai put an arm around my shoulders and told me quietly, "His father already extracted payment enough for an accident, and left the rest up to Kyet. Let his wishes prevail."

Struggling with the Alnese-O'bonne cauldron within, not yet able to let go of my hatred, I nodded. Finally, I moved to a body chair in the corner of Kyet's sick room, closed my eyes, and began to murmur an O'bonne meditation chant to regain a little calm.

◆ EPISODE 20 ◆

Raymond Witnesses Negotiations to Re-establish the Peace

Three days after our return to Zyss, Lady Alnos Ciani brokered a meeting between Eden, Alexander, and Prodyn Akhmin Julia, the leader of the Tomrys complement that had tried to kidnap Eden's daughters. Crested coats and a joint protocol (that nobody bothered to explain to me, mind you) marked the formality of the affair.

Her Grace Lady Ciani sat on her throne in her audience room, with me standing behind her. Eden and Alexander positioned themselves to her right and left. The Tomrys Prodyn, a tall, auburn-haired woman with honeyed skin and a dancer's body, arrived last with a company of eight.

As the losing party in an inter-order skirmish, Prodyn Akhmin slipped into a little opening ritual. First, she formally handed over command of her Tomrys escort to Lady Ciani; then, she divested herself of her rich maroon cloak and presented it to Eden. Accepting the offered garment wordlessly, he moved to the window on our right, towards the back of the audience room. Her Grace nodded in the direction of her own eight-member guard, convened for this occasion. Their leader sprang to attention and both guard and Tomrys fighters filed out of the room together.

Once the five of us were left alone, Lady Ciani spoke up, "Alnos cannot afford to have the keepers of our land, Tomrys, fight the keepers of our peace, Arthmis. I do not wish to hear either your justifications for your challenge to the Justiciar, Prodyn Akhmin, or the list of grievances resulting from the challenge, Justiciar Pallas. I shan't even entertain the voice of the most injured, though I feel for your son, Pallas Alexander. Alnos needs a swift resolution. Arthmis shall restore its captured prisoners to their Order, and Tomrys will agree to reparations. That is my wish."

The three leaders bowed almost simultaneously.

Rising from her seat, her Grace concluded, "I leave my Chronicler. Send him when you have reached your agreement."

This netted her another string of bows. I stepped forward and went to open the door for Lady Ciani's departure, then returned to my witnessing duties.

It turns out the Alnese have something of a knack for disagreeing with each other, and plenty of their disagreements escalate. They've learned to settle their differences as soon as a clear winner emerges. In this case, Akhmin Julia had challenged Eden's authority and his policies in the Islands conflict. To back up her challenge and gain some leverage, she had tried to get his children as hostages, but she'd failed.

According to Alnese custom, not only was she now forced to accept his authority, but she also had to yield up herself and her four Tomrys companies for a period of time.

Alexander motioned Akhmin Julia to a chair around a small, round table to our left as he seated himself. She accepted the invitation. Eden stayed back. A moment of awkward silence followed. The Tomrys leader's almond gaze moved from Eden to Alexander and back to Eden again, then she said, "How long does Justiciar Pallas wish to keep his authority over my companies?" Her voice reminded me of Aria.

Alexander replied, "The customary season."

Keeping her attention on Eden, she concurred with the formulaic, "As you wish, my lord."

Eden acknowledged her consent by raising one hand slightly.

She continued with, "And what of the personal reparations?"

Alexander replied again, "You know of my claim on Kuan Kemir? The one involved in the kidnapping of our O'bonne guests?"

During their counter-offensive, Alexander and his crew had taken a young woman prisoner after she'd flown off with his future daughter-in-law, my O'bonne mentor Dragon. Both Dragon and her colleague Maskar had expressed concern over the young woman's welfare, prompting Alexander to turn them into her guardians.

"Our O'bonne mediator, Maskar Enku, expressed an interest in having her assist him with his inquiries. He would appreciated an Islander guide," Alexander informed the Tomrys Prodyn presently. "One year should satisfy the O'bonne. They might even finish earlier."

Akhmin Julia nodded slowly, "That's acceptable. I'm sure Kuan will benefit from her new association."

A longer silence marked the greater sensitivity of the next matter to be settled. Akhmin Julia broached the topic with, "A hunter accepts God's price for her quarry, Legate Pallas, but I do want to express my regret at your son's laming."

Alexander's face stayed expressionless.

"Is it true you will leave the fate of his attacker in his hands?" The Prodyn asked.

Alexander nodded, maintaining his neutral expression.

"What can Tomrys offer your son?"

He drew out the next pause, then said slowly, "Ice discipline."

Puzzlement filled her almond eyes.

"Now more than ever," he added.

"We don't have many companies in the Borderlands."

"Some time on the southern Islands will work just as well."

"With our elders?"

"That would be acceptable."

"Agreed, then."

Ice discipline is an Alnese expression for a retreat to one of the planet's more isolated arctic areas for special training and meditation. I remembered that Alexander had spent half the summer with ice mentors in the southern arctic Borderlands. He had returned just before Lady Ciani's welcome celebration for her O'bonne mediators. I still didn't know much about ice mentors, but Alexander clearly valued their company, and thought it would benefit Kyet.

After reaching their agreement with regards to Kyet, the most difficult issue could no longer be avoided, but Alexander and Akhmin Julia each retreated into a few last moments of silence. As a member of Arthmis who had joined with Tomrys to challenge her own Order, Minguard Lauran had landed in the Alnese equivalent of a legal twilight zone. She'd asked for and been granted a release from her Order before taking action against Eden, but Arthmis membership was as permanent as the Arthmis tattoos on her body. Any way you sliced it, her actions constituted a betrayal. Unlike the Tomrys members of Akhmin Julia's expedition, she couldn't just be returned to her Order.

Prodyn Akhmin finally bit the bullet, "To abandon the Arthmin would be dishonorable. I humbly remind my lord Pallas Thor Eden that he released Minguard Lauran without conditions."

Eden did not answer. Instead, Alexander commented, "And is that the argument you used to sway her? Where was the honor in that?"

Prodyn Akhmin's face changed ever so slightly, flashed a glimpse of annoyance, "What is to become of her?"

"Release her," said Alexander.

This time, she showed unguarded puzzlement.

"How much do you know about me, Prodyn Akhmin?"

She shook her head, "I don't understand the question, Legate Pallas."

"You know I have interrogated Minguard. Briefly. I need to question her much more extensively. She will put up a futile resistance. It won't keep me from getting at the information I want, but it will injure her. I do not wish it. Release her. Free her of any and all Tomrys obligations she has assumed."

"That is a highly unusual request, Pallas Alexander. You are asking me to expose Tomrys."

"I ask nothing, Akhmin Julia, and you know it. One way or another, Lauran's knowledge will be mine. I prefer to get it without violating her as badly as the first time."

Eden suddenly came alive, walked over to where she sat, and stared down to her over folded arms, "I agree to let my former lieutenant be disciplined and claimed by Mythras. I'm willing to let her choose ice penance if she survives her interrogation, and Legate Pallas has agreed to find an ice mentor for her. Four years, with her son as hostage for the duration."

She sat back and looked away. I could almost see her assessing the ultimate outcome of Alexander's proposal. She must have known enough about Alexander's mind-probing abilities to understand the danger run by Mingurad Lauran. Then, she said slowly, "In view of what happened, a Mythran claim does have parity with yours, Justiciar Pallas Eden. Who would guide Minguard in ice?"

Eden replied, "The Legate has notified my father-in-law, whose honor is surely above question."

"How do you know she will accept my release?"

"She may not," Alexander conceded, "but I can sometimes argue persuasively."

She shifted back towards him, "You obviously have with Arthmis, for the Order to agree to relinquish her."

Alexander's lips twitched, then he let a smile break through.

After a final deliberating pause, Akhmin Julia formally pronounced, "Tomrys releases Minguard Lauran from all obligations."

"Your generosity is noted."

"It only matches yours, Mythran."

"Well, as I have observed before, we all developed an O'bonne streak that fateful day. God knows why. Chronicler."

I snapped to attention, "Sir?"

"Would you notify her Grace that we have resolved our differences?"

I nodded, and did as I was told.

Lady Ciani returned to the conference and seated herself back in her throne. She listened to my summary of the agreements. Prodyn Akhmin Julia had formally accepted the loss of her challenge to Justiciar Pallas Eden and had turned her Tomrys authority over to him for one year. Justiciar Pallas Eden had agreed to free her warriors and let them return to the Islands with the proviso that they would now follow his orders through her.

The three exceptions to this prisoner-release were Kuan Kemir, who would start to work for the O'bonne mediators, Sin'Odras Daniel, who would remain with and work out his personal debt towards Pallas Kyet, and former Arthmin Minguard Lauran. As agreed to by both her former and her current commanding officers, Mythras would claim Minguard and send her into ice. Tomrys had also agreed to settle its debt to Pallas Kyet with sessions of ice discipline.

Nodding, Lady Ciani proceeded to close the conference, "Good. I know you all will stand by your obligations to each other, and to Alnos."

Alexander coughed lightly, "Madam."

She turned to him.

"May I borrow your Chronicler? I will soon need a corroborating witness."

After pondering the request, she called to me, "Díaz Raymond."

I stepped closer.

"Would you do the Legate this favor?"

"Yes, Madam."

"Thank you."

She aimed her eyes at her brother again, "It is a favor, Pallas Alexander."

"I understand, Madam."

I stole a glance at Eden. He looked gloomy, but no more than before. As I lengthened my secretive examination, both her Grace and her brother caught on to it. She did not react, but a sly smile crossed Alexander's face. I could only hope Eden remained impervious to it all.

◆ ◆ ◆

THAT EVENING, LEILA CALLED ME TO HER SUITE. THE invitation surprised me; movement between our two accommodations had always been the other way around. My surprise doubled upon arrival, when I found myself face to face with a tall, older man. But even before she introduced him, I guessed his identity. He had her sepia hair, though streaked with white on the sides, her pale skin with the blue shadows, and tawny eyes only slightly darker than hers. And he was thin. The only notable difference lay in their heights. Over a foot taller than Leila, he outgrew even Eden.

"Ray, this is my father," Leila confirmed, "Since he took to the path of Pallas-Métis and retired into ice, his name is simply Vrezh."

"And Ray is?" he rumbled with a deep baritone.

"My lover."

Not a word I would have chosen at this stage.

As if picking up on the thought, he asked, "In what sense?"

I mumbled uncertainly, "Sir?"

"What do you love about my daughter?"

Leila intervened, "Ray, have a seat."

I stepped over to the body chair she indicated. Vrezh and Leila also sat down.

"Dad is here for Minguard Lauran," Leila explained, "She'll be going into ice in a few days, and he has agreed to harbor her. I wanted you to meet. And apparently, dad has a question for you."

Vrezh observed, "But my present question is much more interesting."

Father and daughter engaged in a short, wordless duel. When he turned his tawny eyes to me, I knew Leila had given in.

I shook my head lightly. What could I possibly say?

"Discretion! Your judgment is improving, daughter."

I looked away, "What was your other question?"

"Did my nephew rape Minguard Lauran?"

Leila did not bother to hide her irritation, "Dad, Ray isn't Alnese and you know it. Besides, he is not acquainted with our third circle."

"All right, explain it to him."

His regal bearing and voice reminded me of Alexander. What's more, his exchanges with Leila possessed the cocky, playful quality I had come to associate with our Mythran Legate.

"My father means, did Alexander force his mind into Lauran's."

I answered with an uncertain nod, "I think so."

A smile hovered around his lips, "You are right. We are a lot alike," he pulled one of his sleeves up enough so I could discern the conversion from Arthmis feathers to Mythran scales on his lower arm. "I'm afraid I inspired him twenty-five years ago, during his Pallas visits."

He rose and strolled to the window, put one foot on the low sill beneath it once there, and continued, "The hell of it is, we were all so pleased! Such a perfect direction for our wild Xhania boy and his Danyx gift! Lex could slip into your mind as easily as I could, just needed a little more focus."

Leila interjected irritably, "I did not ask Ray here to play father confessor to you. What of Lauran? You want to back out of your agreement?"

"On the contrary, God gives me an opportunity to atone for my crimes."

"Using Lex as a vehicle? God has a fine sense of irony!"

They fastened onto each other again. I think Leila won that round. In the silence that followed, Vrezh leaned forward and rested his arms on his raised knee, further increasing his resemblance to Alexander in my mind's eye. He might have changed Orders, but he had kept his Mythran bearing. I found myself wondering what I would look like pushing sixty. If I made it to that age. Later, I found out Vrezh was closer to eighty.

He cast another glance my way, "What about Eden?"

I cocked my head to one side, "Eden?"

"Justiciar Eden is her lord, and she tried to steal his children. Her disciplining falls to him. Why did Eden relinquish her?"

I flashed back to the beating I had witnessed, and to Alexander's well-timed interference. Relinquish was hardly the appropriate term. "You haven't seen Lauran?"

His bronze eyes searched my face, "Ah, so my son fell right back into his old self, did he?"

Acutely aware of my words' origin, I echoed Alexander, "He wanted to tear her to pieces."

I caught Leila's brief shiver.

"You know," I directed at her, "I would appreciate more explanations about what went down. With Dragon tied up, I'm navigating without a compass."

Leila brightened a little, "Where should I begin?"

I shrugged, "Tomrys challenged Arthmis, because of the Heshtis?"

"Not quite," Leila corrected, "Akhmin Julia challenged Pallas Eden. Of course she did it with her Order's full knowledge, and doubtlessly with the elders' approval, but the extent of the challenge was left ambiguous. Deliberately."

"I don't understand."

"If she had succeeded," Vrezh fell in, "Tomrys could have claimed Akhmin's challenge. She failed. Now it's up to Eden to call it a personal challenge or grounds for a conflict between Arthmis and Tomrys."

I had the answer to that already, "Lady Ciani ordered a settlement."

"Even if she hadn't, Eden would never fuel a conflict between Orders," Leila observed.

I continued, "The Tomrys Prodyn gave Eden her coat today. That's to formalize his new status as temporary leader of her Tomrys complement, right?"

Leila nodded, "He won the challenge, so not only does his Arthmis shield stay in place, but he can use his Tomrys authority to change the course of the Heshti conflict."

Vrezh spoke up again, "Yes, instead of forcing him out of the Island Troubles, Akhmin ended up handing Eden even more authority to settle the conflict as he sees fit."

"Now, how is Alexander involved in all this?" I wanted to know next, "He's not with Arthmis. And yet, he did all the negotiating today, and he claimed Minguard Lauran."

Vrezh smiled, "Well, technically, Mythras is a special branch of Arthmis. More importantly, Minguard abducted Dragon, who is about to become Alexander's daughter, and you could say Minguard kidnapped his son as well."

Vrezh swung his leg down and returned to his seat, "Minguard took a risk there. I don't think Prodyn Akhmin wanted to go anywhere near Mythras, but Minguard played her cards rather well. Dragon's status is ambiguous. She hasn't formally accepted a Pallas tie yet, and she has worked with the Justiciar. And Minguard didn't specifically target Kyet. He just happened to be there."

Vrezh paused briefly, adjusted his body chair for a moment, then continued, "The ambiguities limit what Lex could do in response. Of course he got involved helping Eden, but he did that as his clansman and lover, for personal reasons. He can only claim a personal challenge. Mythras is not involved after all."

"The personal reparations discussed today seemed . . . reasonable." I groped for the right words, "Except for Lauran."

Vrezh shrugged slightly, "Minguard turned against her Order. She's a full member, not a journeywoman. Even if the Heshtis did kill her mother, even if Eden did release her, a betrayal is a betrayal. I doubt that anything short of an expulsion would satisfy Arthmis. And now my nephew has maneuvered up a solution: Get her out of both Arthmis and Tomrys by asserting a Mythran claim." He angled his head so he could observe his daughter. "Some day, he'll maneuver himself into a corner."

After that, he once again seemed to get lost in his thoughts.

I appreciated knowing more, but I had one more question, "Vrezh?"

When he looked at me, I almost swallowed that last question, "What will you do to Lauran?"

He let a slow smile play itself out, replied, "I will guide her through a transformation."

Leila chimed in, "She's going into ice with my father for four years. We have a saying: Living in ice forces you to confront all your demons."

Vrezh confirmed, "It does."

For some reason, that made me reflect back on my second attempt to give up the ghost sitting on that bench in Eden Hamlet, letting the snow blanket me into oblivion. The silence of winter had peeled away my elaborate deceits in a few hours. That silence and the memory of Goal's eyes after the first time. I wondered what demons awaited Lauran.

We let silence re-establish a modicum of equanimity between us all.

"Are you ready?" Leila finally directed at her father.

He nodded, murmured back, "And you? You finally came home. Ready for the next step?"

She went over to him and wedged herself into the narrow space between him and the armrest. He cradled her to him, put his chin on her head. She closed her eyes. I could hear their breathing synchronize. "What next step?" she hushed.

His eyes sought me out again. I averted mine.

Stroking her hair, he repeated slowly, "What next step."

It was not a question.

◆ EPISODE 21 ◆

Raymond Assists with Alexander's Persuasion

Wouldn't you know it, Alexander had his Lieutenant Aria roust me bright and early the next morning. Another goddamn Alnese lark! Aria waited for me to pull myself together, then flew me through Zyss to an unknown compound. We progressed through its labyrinth to a smallish sitting room where Alexander sat waiting. Like me, he had slipped on a comfortable Alnos winter jumpsuit and was wearing his hair loose. He dismissed my guide and we proceeded to an unremarkable suite I guessed to be Lauran's cell.

Lauran looked ghastly. Physically, she was on the mend, her wrist securely bandaged, the bruises on her left cheek reduced to a faint though disconcerting lime trace. Still, misery radiated from her. She got to her feet from a low, short sectional when we entered. Alexander waved her back down, and pointed me to a body-chair opposite her sectional.

"It's time," she said.

She said it with perfect calm.

Inclining his head my way, he answered, "First, Lady Ciani's Chronicler has something to tell you."

I took my cue, "Prodyn Akhmin Julia has released you from all obligations."

He let my words sink in.

At least two minutes passed before we got a reaction, "She h-has released me?"

Alexander stepped over to where she sat, moved behind her seat, and placed both of his hands on her shoulders. She flinched. He started talking, "Now you have a choice. Work with me. I won't hurt you again. I'll guide you. I'll go as slow as I have to." He stooped down, his hands still resting on her shoulders, his lips closing in on her left ear, "I won't pretend you consented, but it will be easier, easier on you, Lauran. Fight me again, and I won't hold back this time. I'll take it to the end, your end. I'll destroy you."

Another prolonged pause followed. He stayed down with her, eyes cast to the ground. She stared off into the distance.

"You h-h-held back?"

He wrapped one hand around her good one and lifted it to his face, nodded slowly, "How much I hope you never find out." He straightened up, stepped away from her. "Choose life, Lauran. You have no reason to fight me now. You never had anything to prove." He rounded the sectional and turned his back to her, "Please."

Her face stayed blank, her eyes fixed on a distant point. Alexander folded his hands behind his back and stood at attention. Minutes passed without a sound. Then, just when I was ready to give up, she whispered almost inaudibly, “Okay.”

He let some relief show. Not nearly as much as I felt, and with his back to her, “Good girl.”

“The Chronicler stays.”

He turned around, “Fine.”

He sat himself to her left on her sectional, waited until she slid closer, then adjusted until their bodies touched. With his right arm, he maneuvered her head onto his right shoulder, then started to massage her neck with the left hand. Suddenly her eyes smoldered into me. She lifted her good wrist slightly. I looked to Alexander. He threw his hair back, pointed his chin in her direction and nodded me over. When I laced my fingers into hers, he murmured, “This is going to take time. Better get comfortable.” Without letting go, I kneeled down, leaned against the sectional, settled on the floor. She tugged at my arm until it rested against her thigh.

“All right.” Alexander’s right hand brushed lightly against her chestnut locks as he placed it into position. His fingers disappeared into them. Her breathing hollowed and she started to shiver. “Shshsh.” He stopped, rubbed her temples with both thumbs, then put his right hand back into position. Again, several minutes passed. At some point, her eyes sought out his, and her shivers subsided. The grip of her hand on mine relaxed. They started to breathe in rhythm. So slowly it was almost imperceptible, her whole body went limp. Alexander leaned back and closed his eyes. I folded her hand in both of mine and waited.

In the long silence that followed, fighting the stiffness that settled into my legs soon became my biggest concern. Alexander's second foray into Lauran's mind differed unquestionably from the first. Occasional sharper intakes of breath and a few tremors were the only indications of his progress. The hand in mine stayed relaxed, the body slack. I lost track of time.

At long last, he opened his eyes again. He stared unseeing for a few moments before fully coming to, then he peered sideways at her. The fingers of his right hand slipped up and he tousled her hair, dropped the left hand. She didn't react at first. His touch grew more caressing. Her eyes narrowed to thin hazel slits, and using my hand as leverage, she jerked herself away the best she could.

Alexander flowed up and sat himself on the low back of the sectional. Lauran inched away to the outer edge.

I got up and returned to my chair.

Alexander said, "If Akhmin Julia had consulted a strategist before embarking on her challenge, she might have kept you out of more planning sessions."

"The challenge was to the Justiciar."

"Everyone knows we're lovers. You think I'd just let somebody kidnap his children and do nothing? And if the Prodyn didn't know, you of all people could have enlightened her."

"The Justiciar doesn't let others f-f-fight his b-battles."

"Ah, so Prodyn Akhmin and Tomrys counted on Eden's reaction to your betrayal, and you accepted that death sentence. Didn't consider more than one price for failure, did they? Just let you conveniently solve their security problems by throwing your life away. Tomrys hubris!"

"I'm ready."

"I don't doubt it. I don't doubt you would long since have cracked the mirror or bashed in the window to finish the job if you didn't know the absolute futility of trying to kill yourself here."

Her mouth set in a thin line. She folded her legs up and wrapped her arms around herself as if to transform into a tight bundle. She hunched her shoulders.

"Well, time for you to meet your ice master."

She turned her head just enough to catch sight of him out of the corner of her eye, "M-my what?"

"You're going into ice, Lauran. Eden also has released you, or maybe I should say: he's released you again. Technically, he's relinquished you. He's letting my claim for my son's kidnapping and injury take precedence. And I have decided to send you into ice and arrange for a little ice discipline."

Alexander flipped on his handheld and punched in his codes. Lauran brought her good hand to her eyes, covered them, and uttered a low sob. Shaking her head, she whispered hoarsely, "Not kindness. Not from you."

"You were ready to let Eden beat you to death, and for what? So Tomrys could get at a few more Heshtis? Tomrys may think nothing of wasting good people on frivolous ends, but I won't have it. After a bit of persuasion, even he could see reason. We agreed on four years."

A soft hum announced an anticipated arrival. Alexander called out "Enter!" and Vrezh came in. The ice mentor examined the still bundled Lauran, then stepped forward and stood next to my chair. When she took her hand off her eyes, I caught sight of one tear gliding down her right cheek.

Without taking further notice of Vrezh's entrance, Alexander continued, "You want to keep your feelings pure. I can hardly blame you. Understand, though: your options have narrowed. Whether you accept your release from Arthmis or not, you're still ours. Mythras would prefer to keep you alive, but if you insist, I'll finish what Eden started." He concluded by brushing against her again. This time, she twitched quite noticeably.

"Leave us." Vrezh's deep rumble broke in.

"As you wish." Alexander scrambled to his feet.

I followed suit. I reached the door first, opened it.

"I'll have a word with you later," Vrezh's deep voice announced just as Alexander stepped over the threshold, and Alexander returned one of his most graceful bows, "I'll be expecting your call."

◆ EPISODE 22 ◆

Leila Tallies Some Debts

How appropriate that I should sing your passion, Eden! We gather at my father's call, you, me, Cousin Lex. My father ascertains how our broken triangle is faring, then turns to the judging he's reserved for this occasion.

"So," dad starts, his scorn targeted at the gray-blue cousin-brother who succeeded where I failed so long ago, "you continue to transform our gift into an abomination."

Without batting an eye, Lex counters, "Name your penance."

Dad slaps him without any particular grace or speed, just hard. Alexander does not avert his face. He licks a blood drop off his busted upper lip.

"Wouldn't you like to be let off that easy."

Lex shrugs. Dad slaps him again. This time, Lex fishes a kerchief out of one pocket to wipe off the blood.

And I used to wonder where you learned to associate your blows with release, Eden. I fervently hope my father went through some sleepless nights when you presented yourself for judgment.

"How could you possibly atone for two rapes?"

Ever the trickster, Lex baits back, "More than two, ice master."

Dad charges, with a closed fist this time. Lex edges aside just enough to avoid the full force of the blow. Dad grabs a hold of him, hesitates, shoves him off. Lex crashes against my sofa's arm and sucks in a breath. What I feel most strongly, though, is neither my father's anger, nor my cousin's cunning. It's the distinct strands of your ambivalence that wash over me, maybe because in the end, my connection to you is still the strongest. Repulsion at Alexander's pragmatic cruelty competes with a protecting impulse, with deeper emotions.

Dad says, "I want you to stop it."

"You know I won't." Lex lets the tiniest note of hurt manifest itself as he grumbles, "By all the lows of winter, man, nobody knows it better than you!"

My father ignores the buried accusation, "Why? You can never excuse your abominations."

"Shall I quote you?" Lex responds, "Alnos is not an excuse."

"You did not rape her for Alnos," counters my father.

Briefly taken aback, Lex finally admits, "No. Not the first time."

Dad grunts disapproval and moves to seat himself. After a moment of reflection, he waves Lex down onto the settee and mock-questions, "Oh, so the second time was for Alnos?"

Sliding down to the settee's arm, Lex shrugs again, "That, and most of the others."

"I suppose the Justiciar requested the information?" My father continues with the same sarcastic tone.

Lex does not answer.

We all know your views on mind rapes.

But then it comes. The utterance from you that changes everything: "I . . . did."

I know you lie.

So does my father.

And your lover.

What I sense from you changes, resolves itself into a still unfamiliar, timid acceptance. What a mighty step you're taking! Then it's drowned out: Alexander's wild, pure joy jolts through me like a raging torrent. His arousal engulfs me next, a hot current of desire that radiates towards you.

"You . . . did?" There's resignation in dad's voice.

You nod slowly, "And I'm ready to answer for it."

My father's eyes narrow as he hisses, "Sooner or later you will pay, make no mistake about it."

You lower your gaze. Your body has already adjusted in Alexander's direction.

Dad sighs, "Oh, go, the both of you."

You're all stiffness and embarrassment next to my cousin-brother's fluid grace, but this once, the two of you are truly matched. Before the door fully closes behind you, he has snatched you to him, is giving his joy free expression with a dozen exuberant kisses . . .

Dad says more to himself than to me, "Is this how God punishes a man, by flailing him with his students' successes? How brilliantly I triumphed with each, first as Mythran and later as ice mentor! Got Lex to dedicate his Danyx abilities to our Order and taught Eden how to control his passion by turning into a quasi-Mythran. Makes me fear how this next one will turn out."

I tear myself away from the two successes in question. I already know Lex won't settle for your Spartan accommodations this time.

"Ever the Mythran, dad!"

"What do you mean?"

"Your son is closer to Métis right now than you are. He has just learned to accept what he cannot change while you fight mightily to change the past."

Dad sighs as he relaxes against his body chair, repeats slowly, "Acceptance."

"Eden and Lex show you who you were. You fought with Mythras for forty years, and you were just as cocky as Cousin Lex. If not more so."

"Yes, God holds up a mirror for forty years of arrogance as my debts come circling back."

"Well you're not done with arrogance yet! How do you know whether what circles back to you is debt or merit? How do you know which of your accomplishments were really abominations, which abominations salvations?"

Dad smiles, "Of all people, my daughter reminds me that God is everything, and everything is God."

"Come on, dad. Let's go visit your granddaughters."

At the door, dad hugs me, and we continue down the hall interlaced. Our connection flows into the others, mixing with the thoughts and desires that impress themselves on me as if on a Sumerian tablet.

◆ EPISODE 23 ◆

Sable and Flame

After the first flush of his exuberance, Alexander edges in the direction of his suite. Eden holds back. Alexander slings back and plants his next kiss squarely on his lover's lips; encouragement enough to tug the reluctant man along.

In the study, the two men circle each other. No one had been more surprised by this passion than Alexander. He hadn't even noticed Eden until after Eden's return from ice penance. Shy, jealous, inexperienced, and at first not particularly skilled, Eden continually irritated. Yet Alexander simply could not keep his hands off him. And besides sheer physical ardor, Eden inspired the most blissful and most burning love. Soon, Alexander needed to possess him body and soul. To his consternation, he was turning as jealous as Eden, though he could not match his lover's exclusivity.

Alexander steps into Eden's path, nudges him until he backs him into the bedroom. Only when Eden's legs are caught against his bed does Alexander stop, give him one chance to turn away.

The skin of his first ice-cat on the wall opposite his bed sets the tone. Over the years, Alexander has accumulated other pelts—the large, mottled coat of a snow-bruin offered by Tomrys thrown over the carpet; a blanket assembled from the warmest, most luxuriant sable tossed on his bed, a memento from a former flame. Thick cream brocade covers the wall behind the bed. Matching curtains complete the cocoon effect. The room is tailored to skin and sensuality, and Eden invariably draws back from it.

Resentment sparked by the ghosts of too many other lovers battles against Eden's own slow burn. On the rare occasions when Lex corners him into this room, Eden has always fought an intense desire to slap him around first, to tear into his sable blanket, to shred every suspected gift. But this time, after putting Lex above his own misgiving, after lying for him, his flash of anger feels silly. Eden slides down, towards the center of the bed, plants both arms behind him, leans back. The challenge in his posture is unmistakable. Alexander kneels in after him, climbs into his lap. He lowers his lips while his hands slip into his lover's gray tunic. He moves over Eden's face gently, holding back, little flicks of the tongue skimming over eyes and cheeks, and only once tunic is off and shirt open does he seek out his lover's mouth. Eden parts his lips, shivers.

Eden's response vibrates through Alexander. With Eden, even the most artful move is imbued with feeling, with his intense desire to pleasure. Every response keens through him. Eden shifts his weight forward, brings first one, than the other hand, around, unbraids his lover's hair. Alexander leans into his embrace, his hair brushing against Eden's hands. Eden kisses his throat, licks his way into the half-opened cashmere cloth. Alexander closes his eyes. Every contact sparks through him like bursts of electricity. Eden starts to divest him. They wrestle with each other, rolling in and out of several embraces until only Eden's open shirt is left. Alexander climbs back into Eden's lap. His tongue invading one ear, he rocks against him. Eden shudders, tumbles him on the loathsome sable, kisses his way down Alexander's torso. Engulfed by fur, Alexander arches under Eden, lets himself be swept off. Before letting go, Eden swirls his tongue, savors a last writhing. One of Alexander's early lessons, delicious in the giving or receiving. Then he waits.

Alexander stretches, grabs a hold of Eden, pulls him up. They roll around on the sable. Eden's kisses grow rougher, his strokes more aggressive. They rise together. Eden catches one arm, swings Alexander to the brocade at the head of his bed. Alexander's reflexive buttresses against the wall when Eden pins him against it, braces himself, presses against his lover. Eden's arms snake up Alexander's. Biting through the golden hair into Alexander's neck, he flows right into his slow, forceful rhythm, moans deep in his throat. His release rips through them both. With a strangled cry, he presses against his lover. When the last wave ebbs, Eden holds Lex in his arms and sighs.

Once both are stretched out on the sable again, Alexander rubs against Eden's beard with his own chin, "Why does it always have to be rough with you?"

Eden scans Lex's face, detects a playful smirk, doesn't answer.

"How many fucks have I modeled for you by now?"

As usual, Eden starts blushing.

Alexander loves to see the pink flush spreading beneath Eden's freckles. He lets his hand slip down to his lover's buttocks for a lazy caress.

"But today, you made up your mind. You chose me!"

Eden stills him with a shy, gentle kiss. Alexander responds with his flicks of the tongue. He moves his lips to within a hair's breadth of one ear and whispers, "My love . . . I'll never get enough of you." And the tightening of Eden's arms around him is response enough.

◆ EPISODE 24 ◆

Dragon Meets Another Alnese Father

We were making ready to return to Eden Hamlet when the elder Sin'Odras came to make his plea. In my humble opinion, Physician Peg's care was accomplishing miracles with Kyet. After his arrival in Zyss, she had him up in only a week, and two weeks into his rehabilitation regimen, she urged him to start a modified version of his exercise routine. "Get him to assist you. Might as well make himself useful," the doctor indicated with a nod towards young Sin'Odras, who, in accordance with Alexander's instructions, had been turned over to my lover the day Kyet regained full consciousness. Kyet had once again looked towards the glum-looking young Tomrys warrior for a prolonged if silent examination.

From the first, Sin'Odras had been scared. He hid it well, and I never let on that I could sense his apprehension, but scared he was and scared he remained. I had tuned into him the moment he set foot in Kyet's sick-room. I simply couldn't help it, needed to account for his motives for myself, needed to know if even one hint of maliciousness lay behind his accidental encounter with Kyet.

Once I'd given in to temptation and tuned in, his emotional storms mesmerized me. His fear mixed with anger and resentment, and gradually, with a deep and unrelenting shame at his inability to come to terms with his fate. Gradually, with no act of retribution following any of Kyet's long, silent examinations the first two weeks, he had managed to let go of some fear, but it flared anew each time Kyet's attention was drawn to him.

"What am I going to do with you?" Kyet concluded after Doctor Tzalque had gone.

Young Sin'Odras' covered up his fear with cockiness, "Whatever you fancy, my lord."

"Don't call me that. There may be a debt between us, but I am not a Legate . . . nor a Prodyn."

Sin'Odras' voice died to a whisper, "As you wish."

"I suppose we might as well start with Peg's suggestion. What do you know about rehab?"

"What I don't know I will learn."

The third week they started working on a suitable routine, not too strenuous, yet challenging enough to enhance Kyet's recovery. It soon became clear that his attacker could also benefit from rehabilitation. While going through one session, Kyet dropped, "Your leg. My father's the one who broke it, right?" Sin'Odras jerked his head down and turned away, his shame overwhelming him—shame at his own relief that Alexander, knowing full well the nature and extent of his son's injuries, had contented himself with a broken leg. Sin'Odras wanted to be courageous but kept feeling like a coward, even if he managed to put on his brave face. Kyet didn't press him further.

The elder Sin'Odras arrived at the Pallas compound in the middle of the fourth week, requested an audience with "Pallas Kyet's parents," and was shown into Vai's office. Maskar and I shared the office in our renewed mediation effort. Balancing a wicker-basket from one hand to the other, the old man looked about him shyly and directed at me, "Pallas Vaideh?" whereupon I introduced us both properly and Maskar volunteered to find her. During the ten minutes it took, I seated our guest and offered him the customary welcome choctea, and he warmed himself with it. About my height, he sported grizzled braids, a bushy, still black mustache, and the most unusual, deep blue eyes. He wore the heavier clothes customary in the Islands, fleece-lined pants and a thick, knitted sweater with Sin'Odras clan designs. He rose to his feet upon Vai's arrival and announced with quiet intensity, "I've come for Daniel."

"Daniel?" Vai repeated with a puzzled frown.

"My son. I want to take his place. With the boy he hurt."

Comprehension showed on Vai's face, "Sin'Odras!"

"Yes. Sin'Odras Daniel. Pallas Vaideh, I appeal to you as one parent to another, let me take his place."

We all recognized a formal plea, and Vai's spontaneous answer made me thank the fates for the fact that she, rather than Alexander, should be the first to hear it, "That would not be wise, little father, if you value his life, or his limbs."

The elder Sin'Odras furrowed his brow in a wordless question, and Vai elaborated without further bidding, "Pallas Kyet is a legate's son."

"Oh my God!"

"His Order didn't tell you, did they?"

The elder Sin'Odras snorted derisively, "Neither my clan, nor my son's other associates have been on speaking terms with me since the massacre."

My ears pricked up.

Covering his eyes with one hand, he started to shake his head and lamented quietly, "Fool! Overconfident, fog-brained, spoiled fool!"

Vai stepped forward and touched one arm very lightly, "Please, take your seat, little father." She pulled a chair next to his as he took her suggestion and let himself drop heavily. His hand still covering his eyes, he continued a little more steadily, "I had him late, after twenty years of traveling, and like all old fathers, I indulged him. He is my only child."

Before Vai could respond, a quiet hum interrupted us, and Alexander stepped into the room. She turned to him, "This is Sin'Odras' father. He came to implore us for his release. Sin'Odras, my husband, Pallas Alexander."

Alexander nodded a greeting.

The elder Sin'Odras dropped his hand from his eyes and threw a timid glance Alexander's way, but said nothing. I could tell from his expression that he was forcing himself to give up all hope.

Alexander coughed rather unnecessarily, then repeated the first half of Vai's answer word for word, "That would not be wise, little father."

The old man returned a dejected nod, and sighed, then his face set in a look of bitter determination exceedingly reminiscent of his son's usual demeanor.

"Since you have come all this way, I'll tell you this: I said in the beginning that your son tied his life to Kyet's. Well, Kyet lived. I won't lie to you: Had he not, there would be nothing left for us to speak about, but Kyet did live, and Daniel will be safe."

The elder Sin'Odras burst out, "The fog-brained fool lamed him! Threw himself into a permanent debt, and with a Mythran!"

"No," Alexander interjected, "Kyet is with Sufi, not Mythras."

The old man's next gaze lingered on Alexander. His visual perusal concluded with a sigh, "A dancer. Makes it worse, in a way."

Alexander's left eye-brow went up, then down again, "Mmm."

Sin'Odras lifted his basket in Vai's direction, "I brought you these."

To her initial "Thank you" she soon added a most delighted exclamation, "Manapris! Lemons! How absolutely marvelous! Where did you get these delicacies?"

"Grew 'em."

"You're a greenhouse man?"

"I am *the* greenhouse man of Sin-Odras Island. Nobody grows better than Sin'Odras Zhean!" Pride countered his downcast mood for a moment, then he deflated again and shrugged, "Of course now, with all my workers dead and gone . . ."

"Immigrants?" guessed Maskar behind me.

The old Islander nodded and infinite weariness spread over his face. Suddenly, he burst out, "Tomrys says we need to return to self-sufficiency. Self-sufficiency! You really think the proud Tomryn are going to come and help me pick fruit?"

I cleared my throat, broke into the conversation, "Is that why you fought?"

"Ever since I returned from traveling, I have been a greenhouse man, and for all my twenty-five years of growing, the people who worked with me were Heshtis! Then all of a sudden this madness comes over us. I can understand the Chanticos wanting justice after the attack, but you tell me how we achieve justice by killing people who never did us any harm!"

He stopped and none of us knew how to answer him. After a deep, calming breath, he continued a little less agitated, "Nineteen people worked with me, all but two Heshtis. Half had the good sense to leave after the Justiciar's visit. I hid five, tried to smuggle them out. Daniel found out before I could arrange final passage for the last two. Two men I had worked with for a decade. He killed them."

Vai shifted one manapris from one hand to the other, "And yet you came here to take Daniel's place?"

He turned to her, "Fool that he is, he's still my one child. The bastards made him a full Tomrys member as a reward for his butchery. I took the remains of my two workers to our people's pyre, gathered their ashes with my own hands. For their families. Had a terrible row with Daniel, of course."

We looked to each other not quite knowing what to do next until Alexander stepped forward. He offered his hand with something akin to a bow, "And now I . . .," the elder Sin'Odras looked up and took the offered hand, and Alexander tugged him to his feet, "will take you to your son, little father."

Alexander kept the old man's hand in his until the fear humming in him—harmonizing almost perfectly with his son's—lessened to the point of becoming imperceptible, even to me. Then, as I secretly marveled at Alexander's ability to soothe, he turned and guided the calmer elder out the door.

From then on until the end of winter, Kyet's immediate family received regular shipments of the rarest fruit, especially citrus fruit. The elder Sin'Odras even singled me out after a while, making sure each basket centered around a few soft, sweet, succulently ripe manapris. I never found out how he knew they were my favorite.

◆ EPISODE 25 ◆

Raymond and the Gang Return to Eden Hamlet

The weather turned nasty, especially in Zyss. On good days, a mild flurry would dump a foot of snow. Ice-storms blasted through the city on bad ones. I didn't need any lessons on the dangers of getting caught in an ice storm and pummeled by hail for a few hours. For the most part, we stayed indoors.

I soon realized I wasn't the only one going stir-crazy. The natives also longed for clear days, fairly rejoiced about tolerable ones. Apparently, a few centuries' worth of facilities and experiences couldn't cancel out Alnese winter-confinement completely. Weather reports gained a whole new meaning.

In our corner of the Pallas compound, we were counting the days. Both Vaideh and Leila awaited Doctor Peg's approval to take their children back to the more clement climate of Eden Hamlet. The good doctor initially held out until Kyet's rehab routine was worked out to her satisfaction. After that, she delayed our departure another fortnight because in her estimable opinion, no one in their right mind, least of all a patient of hers recovering from two rounds of back surgery, needed to get jostled about gliding through ice storms. Vaideh and Alexander did not put up much of a fight. Then, finally, arrived our long-awaited break in the weather.

We flew to Eden Hamlet through splendid blue skies. Since the good weather lasted, Kyet insisted on "getting out" two days after our arrival. His parents put me in charge of an outing that included Daniel, Goal, twins Odysseus and Iliad, and Lauran's son Justin, an eternally grave-looking nine-year old who had joined us shortly after his mother left with Leila's father, the ice mentor Vrezh. As usual, Kyet chose to forgo his hood in favor of an ear-band, and the rest of us followed suit. The sun sure made it look warmer than it was.

Goal and Justin immediately started to roll together a snow family. Daniel had bigger ideas. I kept stealing glances in his direction. After eight weeks, he was finally leaving some of his morose mood behind. His maroon and white Tomrys ear-band stood out against his black hair and dark visor, underscoring his resemblance to his father.

Over the next few hours, an impressive looking structure took form under his hands. As he put the finishing touches on a square of low walls, the twins and I climbed over one. We rounded two turrets inside the square, stuck our heads into an arc over the northeastern wall. We were ready to climb out again when a snowball flew by me straight at the architect. Daniel wasn't expecting it. He took a step back after it splattered against his shoulder, then dove behind his wall. I heard the next snow missile, maybe because it was aimed at me. The twins and I dropped to the ground. Three more snowballs whistled by. I rolled behind one wall as Daniel slid to a turret. Goal's ululation came as no surprise, but I didn't expect Justin's accompanying war cry. Twins Odysseus and Illiad started to squeal with pleasure.

For the next half hour, we defended our snow fortress valiantly. Trouble was, we couldn't really tell our adversaries' movements, whereas they had us pinned down. In the end, Kyet, Goal, and Justin came scrambling over our walls in a coordinated assault. Kyet threw himself on Daniel, Goal climbed right on top of me, and Justin took on the twins. One by one, visors, gloves, mufflers, earbands went flying into the snow. The twins and I gave up quickly. Daniel did not.

The rest of us settled around one wall as Kyet broke free from one of Daniel's locks and slipped behind the turret himself. They circled it. Kyet dove for Daniel's right arm, swung him closer to get a grip on him. The Tomrys warrior deliberately crashed into him and they both swayed onto the ground. They wrestled and rolled about in the snow, bumped into the wall where we loitered. For a while I couldn't tell which one of them would have the upper hand. Kyet was in no shape to be horsing around like that, but Daniel was holding back. Finally, Daniel's knees pressed against Kyet's chest, his hands secured both wrists, and Kyet stopped writhing about. His hair fanned out over the snow like auburn flames.

Daniel panted, "Yield?"

"Shit yes! Keep your fortress."

Daniel slid off Kyet.

Kyet smiled.

Suddenly Daniel swung about and slammed his fists into the snow behind him.

Kyet rolled up and leaned himself against our wall, catching his breath, "What?"

"Why d'you have to be so kind?"

Kyet shrugged, but Daniel wasn't looking. Kyet joked, "You want me to arrange for Goal, Justin, and the twins here to come and beat you up every morning?"

My Goal rose to the occasion, exclaiming with audible pleasure, "Yeah!"

Daniel's shoulders twitched for a second.

Kyet shot Goal a quick glance and said, "Goal, I need a moment with Daniel."

Nodding, Goal gathered up the other children and took them back to their collection of snow people. I threw Kyet a questioning glance. He shook his head, and I sat on the snow wall.

Kyet fished for his ear band and mitts as he directed towards Daniel, "I think you should just go home, but I know as well as you do that my father's people might come after you, no matter what I say. I presume you still prefer my kindness to a broken back?"

Keeping his back to us, Daniel nodded.

"Anyway, why these pangs of conscience over me? You've done worse."

Daniel put one forearm against the closest turret and leaned his forehead against it, "My father talked to you?"

"No. To my betrothed wife. Reshaped her sympathy for you, that's for sure."

"Wasn't the same thing."

"No? Why not? Because the two men you killed were Heshti? Or simply because you're not faced with them every morning?"

"My Order, my Clan, my wife, they all forced my hand. She's Chantico, for God's sake. She lost everyone in her immediate family."

"And the two workers you found were responsible for that? They slipped out between harvests to blow up Chantico House?"

Daniel put his other arm against the turret and his shoulders hunched defensively. Kyet slid next to him, leaned sideways against the turret. Daniel turned his head away.

"You found the two workers your dad was helping, Daniel. If you hadn't shot your mouth off, your Order, your Clan, your wife would never have known." Kyet paused, then ticked off each consequence mercilessly, "No killings. You'd still be a journeyman with Tomrys. No involvement with Akhmin Julia's little kidnapping project. No crash out there in the snow. No debts. Not with me, not with your father, not with your victims."

Daniel's shoulders shuddered. He wrapped his arms around his black hair and pressed his forehead into the snow wall of the turret.

Kyet relented, "On the other hand, another impulsive young warrior could just as easily have hurt me, or hurt Ray, or hurt my cousins."

Daniel slumped and let his arms drop. Kyet placed his back against the turret. Sweeping visually over our white domain, he waited for Daniel to regain his composure. With his back still to us, the Tomryn scooped up a handful of snow and rubbed it against his face. When he turned around, the last of the half-melted snow ran over one cheek. His voice barely rose above a whisper, "I have dreams about them, nightmares. I used to prune the Manapri-trees with them, and the vines. They taught me as much about growing as my dad."

Kyet's next move caught me by surprise. Angling his head towards me, he wondered, "You think my dad dreams about his victims?"

I had no answer, mumbled, "Uhh . . ."

"Not just the people he's killed. What's killing someone after you've scrambled their brains?" Keeping up his steady questioning gaze, he asked me, "Remember what you said after the boathouse?"

After the boathouse? Drawing a blank, I raised my shoulders and my hands.

Kyet got to his feet, explained, "After his first time interrogating you, you asked me why I was so careful around him and you said, 'You've seen things, haven't you?' Not seen, no. But I know about dad. I know what he does. Overheard him one day when he went after one of his own men." After a brief pause, he continued, "Now you've *seen* for yourself, with Minguard." He turned back to Daniel and gave him a hand. When they were face to face again, he asked him in a casual tone that didn't mask his intensity, "Did you see her interrogation?"

This time, Daniel didn't blink, "No. Fighting, I was hit. Delayed. I was . . . too late."

"Another debt."

Daniel sighed unhappily.

Kyet grabbed his head with both hands, "See, I can put on the screws. Are we a bit more even now?" He let go. Daniel backed away, looked at him as if he were a ghost.

Later, after we rejoined the children, I told Kyet, "You use the same moves as your father, you know."

He shook his head, "No, I didn't know."

I almost added, 'but you're not vicious.' Only I thought about the implications first and managed to swallow it.

◆ EPISODE 26 ◆

Raymond and Leila Work on Reconciliation

Leila and I had used great care with each other. One night, she had taken the first step and asked me for an Alnese massage, a slow, sensual exploration of the skin that stopped just short of fondling. I noticed that her back was as smooth as ever while her bottom had filled out. The next time I pressed her to me, I lingered over these fuller cheeks. I felt as if Socorro had reshaped them just for me, made them forever mine. A silly, yet strangely comforting possessiveness.

A little later, Leila started with, "So, fill me in on your re-awakening libido. Any morning hard-ons yet?"

Of course, the crazy, mixed-up San Antonio adolescent in me cut off my voice, as usual. Leila laughed and spent the next few nights discovering my irregular pattern for herself. "Is it me or your old mistress?" she asked on one of my off mornings, "If it's me, you might as well go back to Aria. I'll be jealous, but

I've learned not to force passion." My hands sought out her bottom again and I shook my head, "It's not you."

Then one lazy afternoon we slipped right into it, without preamble. One minute I was fondling my favorite ass, the next I was anticipating sweet surrender. Didn't take very long, but I wasn't trying to impress her. Her satisfied expression told me the old skill had not been expected. After that ice-breaker, we started to kiss again. Hers brought back memories, echoes of a time when even our looks would caress. Our familiarity made us comfortable with each other, made everything easy. When we made love the next time, our climax reminded me of our first months together.

In Eden Hamlet, her suite was much cozier and more personalized than in Zyss. Her desk, body chair and low settee were typical Alnese, but she had invested them with personal touches—a fountain pen I had given her for our second anniversary, monogrammed pillows in her favorite sky-blue.

We got together for a first real date the evening of my splendid outing with the kids. The warmth rising from the heated floor suffused the room. My tunic already on Leila's chair, I stripped off my jumpsuit and one layer of winter underwear. Slipping out of her robe, Leila settled on the sky-blue sheets, turned on her stomach. The sky color turned her skin into blue-hued alabaster. Deliberately, I started with her arms and shoulders. I wanted to reach her bottom last.

After I'd worked my way down both arms and started to knead her shoulders, she sighed appreciation and queried, "How much do you remember of the shell blast in the Islands when you and Dragon were helping Eden last year?"

An unexpected question.

"I wasn't there. Minguard Lauran was taking me around that particular island."

"Eden was called out of that hall right before the blast."

"M-hm. An urgent message from Zyss."

"A Tomrys message," she informed me. "A timed message."

I paused, "Timed?"

"To arrive when Kuan Kim was in position, ready to fire off her missile. To get him out of there. Lex told Eden that was the price."

I laid both hands between her shoulder-blades, "The price? For what?"

"Complicity."

I started little circles around each shoulder while I thought through Leila's revelation. By the time I was ready to voice my guesses, I was shifting to her legs, "An Arthmis mole conspired with Tomrys and Kuan Kim to get the Island Heshti leaders? Is that what you're saying?"

"Probably two or three. Not Lauran. Her break was above board."

"But why keep Eden safe?"

"Loyalty to the Order."

"Loyalty?" I paused again, "When they conspire with his enemies?"

"Remember: this preceded Chantico House. Beyond the usual rivalry, there was no enmity between Tomrys and Arthmis, and all my husband's people did was facilitate the flow of information to Tomrys. Eden never made a secret of his irritation with the Heshtis. That could easily have been interpreted as an opening."

I moved down to her left foot and caressed my way up, "And did Alexander find out who the mole was?"

"They knew to stay in the shadows, even when dealing with Tomrys. Lex said Arthmin make better conspirators than Tomryn. They know how to keep secrets."

I moved to her other leg. "Of course the ones to really watch out for are his own people."

"No Mythran in their right mind would ever go against their Order. Even if all they did was, say, direct some information, like Eden's people, the Order'd tie them up in bright ice until they'd go snow blind. Keep them warm and alive while they're losing their sight, too. Or make them walk a drift."

"Walk a drift?"

"They take away your snow clothes, your visor, your shoes, and take you to a glacier. A big one. If God sends clement weather and you make it across with only a bit of frostbite, your debt is paid. When my father was still with Mythras, he went against his Legate once. She liked him, so she waited for good weather. Still took him four days, and he was hallucinating when he got out."

I spread my fingers as my hands reached her rump. My appreciation must surely have come through. Leila continued as if to herself, "Of course Mythrans have the training to make it across a glacier, so just like my father's Legate, the Order varies which glacier and when, depending on what kind of chance they want to give you."

"What would they have done to Lauran?"

"Difficult to say. She shouldn't have turned against her Order, but the challenge was to Eden, and Eden did release her."

My hands still rounding her behind, I leaned forward and ran my tongue first up, then down her spinal column. Goose bumps appeared on my trail. Sitting up again, I asked, "So what does it all mean?"

"Mmm." She wiggled a little. I didn't move. "Oh, all right! It means there are two or three people in Eden's troupe that do not agree with his Heshti policy. Chantico House pushed them one way or the other. Back into the fold or towards a real betrayal."

"Dangerous?"

"Quite. Enough so Lex finally convinced Eden to let him widen his ever-vigilant net to our immediate family. Mythrans are damn good. You shouldn't notice them."

"I bet."

She rocked her hips slightly. I stretched alongside her, backed her into my embrace, caressed her waist, brushing down occasionally. She reached for my head and tugged me down for a kiss.

"Tell me, when did Eden discover he's gay?"

"Where does this question come from?"

"Just," I shrugged, "wondering."

"Are we comparing ourselves?" She was amused.

I shook my head.

"Alnos isn't Earth. Who you screw doesn't define who you are. But anyway, Eden always preferred men. I think when I set out to conquer him, he was flattered. And I was young and dumb at the time, and of course, for him, it was his chance to have a child, maybe his only chance. The sparks went all one way, though, and they stopped soon enough . . .

"Despite her implied lack of passion, her voice had turned dreamy. And yet, an unsettling satisfaction spread through me, belying my earlier denial. Why did I need to best Eden now when only a few months ago, I couldn't care less if I ever fucked again? As if to prick my vanity, Leila added slowly, "Lex is different. Brims with desire." She sounded a million miles away.

"You . . . have?"

"No." She twisted a little and reached for my hair, "Just . . . thinking aloud . . ."

I watched her wrap her fingers in my hair, then pulling them out again and rearranging the tuffs. I was going to have a fine time untangling it, but I let her keep playing. "I've only heard you and Lady Ciani call him that. Lex."

"He was her little brother and my big brother. My cousin-brother."

The fraternal ring of that description was even more satisfying than the fact that Eden hadn't measured up years ago. Now there was a rival I did not want.

"So he is your father's nephew? I mean, by blood?"

"Yes. Sister's child. My aunt Evlyn. She moved to Danyx after Ciani committed to becoming our leader. We call relatives outside our main clan our third circle. Family is the first, clan is the second, close blood-relatives in other clans are the third. Allied clans are a fourth."

She reached down to her sheets and pulled them over us, and we settled in interlaced, drifting off into our own daydreams. Going over the information she had relayed about the various intrigues surrounding us, I suddenly had an alarming thought. "Are our chaperones watching when we . . .," as usual, I couldn't speak the operative word.

She twisted her head to shoot me one of her looks, "Do you really want to know?"

I guess not.

But she was right about Mythrans. I certainly never knew they were shadowing us, and I didn't develop a sixth sense, either.

From The O'bonne Encyclopedia of Alnos

Settlement

The people who became the Alnese arrived in the Alnese star system after an extended period of space exploration. As Alnese lore tells it, a group of explorers from Orin started on a journey to the edge of their known universe about four millenia ago, and never turned back. Instead, these original voyagers created large space-faring habitats and just kept going. With no fixed destination, they apparently were never in a hurry. Still, during their space odyssey, the ancestors of the Alnese journeyed by most of the worlds in the Kobran Commonwealth, frequently picking up hitchhikers in the process, and this laid the foundation for their current population and their current culture.

In the year 5048 of the Kobran Era, after more than two millenia of meanderings, a spiritual leader named Pallas Yewa Fridjan convinced the wanderers that it was time to settle down on the fourth planet of a star system they were about to reach with their fleet of habitats. The planet was and still is in what we would consider an ice age. Its severity has been lessening since about the time of settlement, and Alnos's equatorial region has undergone significant changes in the past few centuries, transforming from a more tundra-dominated ecology to a fully forested one with something close to four seasons.

According to the Alnese, Pallas declared the planet a gift from God. Two of the clearest indications of this were that Alnos was the fourth planet of its star system and its solar year consisting of precisely 384 days. The fact that most of the planet was frozen solid and the habitable areas were limited to a narrow tropical zone was simply a form of protection. The place clearly had not elicited any interest from anybody else, and had no native populations. Yet it offered a breathable atmosphere and rich arctic ecologies that could be harnessed by a space-faring people used to devising solutions on the fly.

The Alnese say that Alnos may have a cold climate, but their home will never be as cold as space. They turned their habitats into satellites and moved to their new home over the course of their first century after arrival. They used the materials from their space habitats to start their first planetary outposts, gradually shifting material resources to the planet's surface and combining them with local materials to create both living quarters and their first greenhouses.

We estimate that the initial population numbered about 80,000. Once they started the settlement process, they reached out to their many relatives on other worlds, and quite a few of them decided to join them, doubling the early population within the first decade of their residency. Population growth has been slow but steady, around 2% per decade, and the current population is just short of eight million.

The Alnese Calendar

The Alnese calendar started the day the original Pallas and her followers landed on Alnos 1676 years before the start of *The Chronicler's Arrival.* An Alnese year lasts 384 days, divided into eight months of 48 days (six 8-day weeks each). The year starts with the month of Yanir, a month of transition from winter to spring. The spring month of Koreh follows, then the early summer month of Zhoni and the high summer month of Solstin. Ostyx, the "month of changes," is followed by winter months Loxi, Holdin, and Jotun, generally the nastiest month of the year.

Maps of Nyheim and Alnos

The Alnos Chronicles take place on Alnos, a planet that is undergoing climate change from a deep to a more moderate ice age. Most of the planet's population lives on the planet's sole equatorial continent, Nyheim. Nyheim enjoys a temperate climate with four seasons, though winter is still the longest. Alnos' capital, Zyss, and an area called 'The Lake Region', where the Pallas Clan maintains a summer vacation compound on Lake Limnos, are both in Nyheim. A third important setting is an archipelago called 'the Islands' that stretches from the southern arctic border to the southern edge of the planet's more temperate equatorial region.

Yvernon
Akurisa
Marsala
Zyss
Chaix
Patras
Ershal
Vik

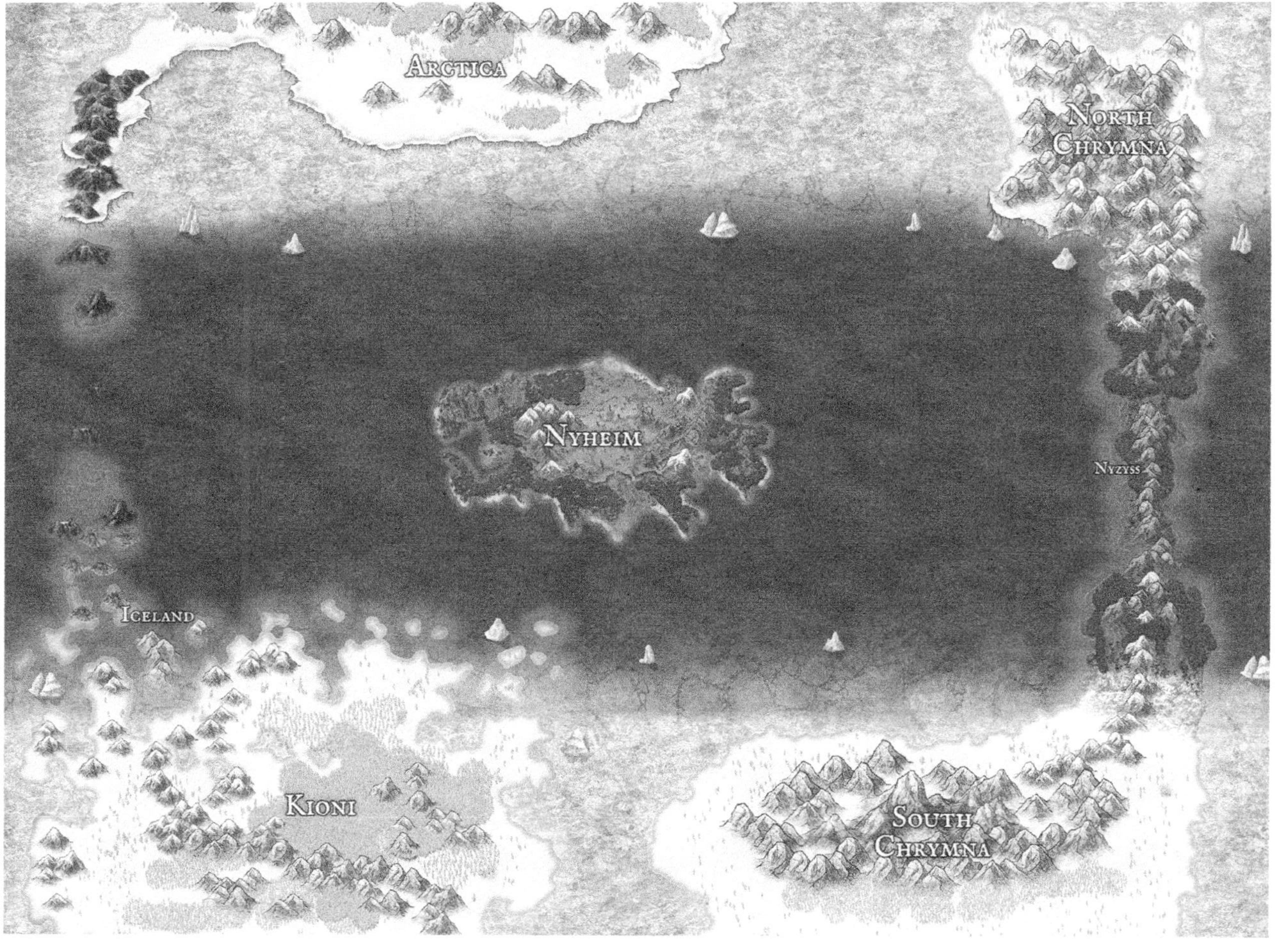
Arctica
North Chrymna
Nyheim
Nyzyss
Iceland
Kioni
South Chrymna

Made in the USA
Coppell, TX
03 March 2026

72754349R00236